Shadow Lands

By: L. A. Behm II

Three Ravens Publishing
Chickamauga, GA USA

Dedicated To Andre, and all the other Jarheads I spent time with, in the Land of Sun and Fun.

Prologue
Day 0, 2 April 2018

I grabbed the phone on the third ring. It had been a long six months, and Austin was down to two religious types for all the teams.

"Salazar."

"Dispatch. All hands alert. We need you to come in," the voice on the other end said.

"Roger that," I replied, while sitting up in bed. "Who's the team?"

"You're working with the Brute Squad tonight father," the voice replied. "APD has got a mess over on Red River they say is entirely ours."

"Right. Who's senior on shift tonight?"

"Michael," came the reply.

I started pulling on gear. Michael was Michelangelo, artist, vampire and vampire hunter. When he said jump, you jumped.

When Goodhart had taken over as Austin lead, he'd instituted a policy where there was a senior person on duty at all times to make the 'difficult' calls. Most of the time, 'senior' meant 'way too much time in the field, with the physical and or psychological scars to prove it'. Which meant occasionally the most senior member of QMG in existence short of Henry Keith got stuck running the night shift when things went to hell in a handbasket, which was the current description of the level of activity in Austin at this point. Michelangelo's been with the corporation since just after the Things incident in London, making him the second longest serving person on the payroll and the longest serving one in Austin so he got tapped, of course.

Downside to that was it meant we had a boss that never slept.

"Right," I said, running a hand through my hair. "I'll be in in half an hour."

"Negative. Michael says to report to the onsite command – the Brute Squad will be there by the time you get there."

"Roger that, anything else?"

"Have a nice evening," the dispatcher replied before hanging up.

So much for my sleep patterns. The undead have no respect for the living, I swear.

Twenty minutes later I was standing in the warm rain of a Texas spring evening, turnout bag slung over my shoulder, arguing with a rookie cop to get past him to the Mack Granite conversion (aka the Combat Winnebago) so I could go on the clock.

"Look officer, I appreciate your dedication to duty," I said as he scrutinized my ID for the fourth time, "but if you don't get the fuck out of my way so I can go to work, I'm going to see how far up your ass I can shove that god damned flashlight without lube."

"Threatening me is not going to get you through any faster," he replied.

My phone started ringing.

"What," I snapped, answering.

"Where are you, Jesse?" Jed, leader of the Brute Squad asked.

"Standing about fifty yards south of the Winnebago, with Barney fucking Fife inspecting my ID," I replied.

"Language Father," he replied with a chuckle. "I'll take care of it."

I watched the back door of the Granite open, someone dropped out and spoke to one of the figures standing by the rear of the truck. That person ran over to an APD command truck and returned with a third person. All three set out for where I was standing with my thumb firmly up my forth point of contact.

"Jennings, what the fuck are you doing?" a husky contralto growled.

"Mam?! I'm checking ID," the officer in front of me replied.

"You stupid time wasting fuck, let Father Salazar through," came the reply.

"Yes'm," Jennings replied, thrusting my ID back at me.

"Captain Brown, good to see you," I said, stepping past.

"Jesus, sorry Father. Fucking rookies on the perimeter. We've got a real mess for you," she said.

Brown had been with APD for ten years and had clawed her way to the top of the SWAT food chain. She was a rarity in Austin, a native. She knew the town was a festering cesspit of vampire and other supernatural activity, even telling me once over beers that she was glad to finally have someone here that thought the only good vampire was one that had been staked, decapitated, exposed to sunlight, and then the ash piles buried in separate locations. She'd thought Jed and the Brute Squad dragging one to death behind a Tahoe had been 'funny'.

"How bad?"

"Honestly? I don't know. We got a report of something going on in Eyelash, then nothing, except loud music and banging."

"Banging?"

"Yeah, like something was being dragged along the walls. Hard. So we called you guys when one of the kids in there came out screaming about these two 'really mean chicks who were beating the shit out of each other'," Brown said with a sardonic smile. "I figure two full grown women beating the crap out of each other who don't show up on thermal imagers are somebody else's problem."

"And QMG gets paid to handle SEP by the city fathers of Austin," I replied, dropping my bag and pulling out my body armor. "When they let us do our jobs."

"Something like that," she grinned back.

Jed's usual team priest, Terry Polk, aka Padre, stepped down from the Combat Winnebago. She was combat ineffective, because she'd managed to break an ankle and arm tap dancing with a pair of Akaname who'd decided that the rest rooms at the Barton Springs Pool were the perfect place for them to take up residence.

"Jesse."

"Padre. We got anything?"

"Yeah, before we got here, Michael sent in that new guy from London," Padre said.

Padre didn't look happy about that either.

We'd gotten the transfer from London a couple of weeks ago. Like Michelangelo, he was a 'Special'. In Group lingo that usually meant 'vampire'. It might occasionally mean 'werewolf' or 'bastard who should be dead but for some reason just won't die' like Henry Keith or Jed's great grandfather, but usually it meant 'vampire'.

"Okaaaaay,' I said, sliding my pistol into its holster.

"Yeah. He's been in there about a half hour – he reported that he was going to take an enthusiastic walk inside and see what was happening."

Great. A Group vampire with a sense of humor. Just what I wanted to deal with tonight on four hours of sleep.

"Anything after that?"

"Yeah, the volume of the crappy ass industrial-techno-goth-a-billy-ska that was playing went up," Padre replied. "And a couple of sheets of tin came off the building." "Oh, and one of the window AC units mounted by the door went flying into the parking lot across the street," Brown added helpfully.

"Peachy," I said, pulling my UMP out, inserting a magazine in the well and running a round up the spout.

"Whenever you want to go Boss," Padre said.

"Yeah, problem is the walls are a little thin for Capdepon's M240," I said.

Eyelash had started life as an industrial space, somewhere around the turn of the 19th into the 20th century. It had been a lot of things in its time, and the latest incarnation was an 'alternative' night club. Kinda place that things that go bump in the night can hang out in without having to disguise their nature. It had a brick façade along Red River, but the sides and rear were sheet metal with spray foam insulation. The .308 rounds from Capdepon's M240 would go through the brick like it wasn't there. The tin? We'd be pulling bullets out of cars blocks away. And shooting up the businesses along Red River drive would not be a mitzvah. Might even get me a warning from higher.

"Well, the Special is in there," Padre said.

"Apparently playing DJ for the fight," Jed said, stepping down from the Combat Winnebago. The rest of his team stepped up. "Joseph, you and Crash cover the door. Padre, stay outside. Jesse, you're with me. If you have to open up Capdepon, try to limit the damage to the back wall."

"Roger that, Boss," he said with a grin.

Have I ever mentioned I hate industrial music? The *dooka-dooka-dooka* always sounds like meth'd up ferrets dancing on a keyboard to me. That the volume inside Eyelash was louder than the last firefight I'd been in while deployed to Iraq probably didn't help either. Thank the gods for ear protection.

"How are you planning on handling this?" I asked Jed as he and I walked through the doors.

If anything the sound was worse on the inside. We both went live on our mikes as soon as the wall of sound hit us.

"Haven't got a clue," he said, keying his mike.

"Oh that's great, Gunny," I replied. Jed and I had been in the Corps together, and had even spent time in Sunny Iraq, breaking things for the US Government.

The combatants, for lack of a better term, were both resting – they'd taken up sides at the edges of the dance floor – to the left was a very butch looking blonde and her entourage, and to the right a petite, dark skinned Hispanic and hers. There were a few 'normals' huddled against the far wall, which showed signs of someone's face being run along it. And sure enough, the London 'Special' was in the DJ booth. He killed the sound as soon as he realized Jed and I were standing there.

"Ladies and gentlemen, may I introduce the final players in our little drama, the Reinhumation Specialists of the Quincy Morris Group!" the Special said into the mike.

"Fuck me running," I said.

"With a chainsaw," Jed finished.

The two groups of vampires turned and faced us.

"Remind me to kick Michael in his balls when we get back to the office," I said.

"You're going to have to get in line behind me," he replied.

"You can leave now, mortals," the blonde said with a slight German accent. She also had occult patterns tattooed around her eyes.

Which had to be a bitch, because she'd have had to have them redone every six months or so. Vampires heal.

"Yes, this doesn't involve you," the Hispanic said, accent pure San Fernando Valley.

"Jed, did I ever tell you how I feel about Valley Girls," I said, raising my voice.

"No. . ."

"Can't live with 'em, can't kill 'em", I replied, swinging my UMP up and cratering the Valley vampire's chest with three rounds, rapid into the fragile set of blood vessels above the heart. Sure, the pump still works, but there's nothing connected to it for what passes as blood in a vampire to spread. On top of that, company issue bullets are frangible silver, which vampires do not react well to.

And the dance was on. Damn Special at least had the good sense to put on Rammstein. *Mien Teil* came thundering out of the speakers as we started killing vampires. Gunny ran his M1897 Trench Gun dry in seven shots, dropped it to hang by a patrol sling, and switched to his ancient, family 1911. I ran my UMP dry on Valley Vamp's minions, then dropped the magazine and reloaded in time to dump the second one into the Butch Vampire as she leapt towards the ceiling to clear the tables between us and the dance floor. As soon as Butch went down, the other remaining vampires froze.

"Glamour," the Special called, stepping out of the booth. "I can control a lot of lesser vampires, but not until you got those two randy cunts thinking about how much they hurt."

"You fucking asshole," I said.

"Yes?" he replied.

I looked him over. He was wearing red – a red zoot suit complete with wide brimmed, pimp stylin' fedora, with the ubiquitous white peasant shirt. He even had on red tinted glacier glasses.

I felt his mind try to probe mine.

"Oh that hurt," he replied.

"Yeah, we don't work with Michelangelo for nothing," Jed replied.

I went through the messy business of staking and beheading, assisted by Capdepon. Crash and Jed sorted out the normal survivors, then started prepping the live lesser vampires for transport. Once all the work was done and the cleaners could move in, I stepped wearily to the Special.

"What's your name?" I asked.

"You can call me," he paused dramatically, "Tim."

I kicked him in the nuts with a steel toed boot. Even in the undead, it's a sensitive spot. He went to the floor, hard.

"Listen Tim, I don't give a shit how big a wonder you were in London. You pull shit like this again around any team in Austin I'm working with and I'll scrag you myself, and then file the god damned paperwork on why it was a necessary action, you read me?" I said.

He lay on the floor in a ball around his groin, but nodded, weakly. Finally he straightened out and stood up.

"What . . ." he coughed. "What kind of boots are you wearing?"

"No fucking clue," I replied. "Company issue, so there's probably a layer of silver in there, somewhere."

"Tim, allow me to introduce Father Jesse Salazar, formerly of the United States Marine Corps. He's a right bastard, and all we know for sure is he wreaks havoc on monsters," Capdepon said, grinning.

Jed turned to the head of the cleaners.

"Ya'll got this?" he asked.

She waved a thumbs up and we went back into the night.

"Jesse, debrief in the morning," Jed said as I walked to the Combat Winnebago.

"Right Gunny, see you in the office."

"Sure," he said with a tired smile.

Captain Brown was waiting when we got over to the Command Winnebago.

"I hate to do this to you," she said.

"Where?"

"Nah, I'm yanking your chain," Brown said. "Seriously, go home."

Chapter One
Day 1, 3 April 2018

Debrief over, Gunny had mentioned that Director Goodhart wanted to see me.

"Look Father Salazar, you've been pulling missions for the last six months straight," Goodhart said.

Things were never good when the boss mentioned my vocation. Usually it was just 'Salazar'. Occasionally if I'd done something exceptional, it'd be 'Jesse'. But 'Father Salazar'? That was Director Goodhart's version of your mother calling you by first, middle, and last name.

"Yeah, well if you'd get another priest down here," I replied.

"Polk is doing her share," he retorted.

"Yes, more than her share, actually, given her physical condition. But we need another six religious figures, minimum. At this point, I'd shake hands with a Priest of Eris if it meant we got more help down here. This town is going absolutely nuts. NVTS nuts!" I replied.

There was supposed to be a religious type for every team, plus backups. Problem was of the six in Austin, five were down for physical or mental reasons – including two cases of food poisoning. Never eat gas station sushi, especially not two hundred plus miles from the coast.

He looked at me for a minute like I'd grown a third eye. What can I say, I like Mel Brooks' films.

"Be that as it may, you assaulted a coworker on the scene last night," Goodhart said.

"He was an asshole, boss! Playing DJ while another two vampires beat the crap out of each other? Seriously? He's lucky I didn't shoot him," I said.

"And that's why you're on vacation as of now. I don't care what you do, but you're not doing it here. And get the hell out of Austin, because the tracking chip will show us if you're still here," he said, quietly.

Tracking/monitoring chips had become a mandatory thing a few years back when most of a team of hunters had 'gone over' – been drained – by some determined vampires to be used as guards. It took six months and a whole lot of help to clear that issue up, and the powers that be had decided that they needed to be sure of where we were at all times. The solution was a chip that could be pinged through any cell phone network. On top of that, the chips monitored heartbeat and respiration – and if those went to zero, and the person was still moving around, it was a pretty good bet they'd been subsumed.

"And before you ask, it wasn't my decision. The headshrinkers ordered it, in light of the report from last night."

That put it in a different light. The shrinks had the last word. If they said I was overworked and under rested, then it was time to take a vacation – or I'd be spending time wearing pajamas talking about how hunting monsters made me feel, and how that defined my relationship with my mother.

Not really how I wanted to spend a couple of months, if you got right down to it.

"Right. Do I need to file an itinerary, then?"

"No, just check in daily, huh? And take your kit. It might come in handy if I have to call you in, unexpectedly, ok?"

"Right." There was hope, after all.

I filed a partial itinerary anyway – Austin to San Antonio, San Antonio to Marfa, Marfa to Austin. I'd swing through Piccadilly on the way home and harass the Defender there, just because I could. And I took my kit – including the firearms and my Get Out of Jail Free card. Because you never knew when some official in Podunk was going to assert authority over someone travelling with enough weapons and ammunition to arm a rather large guerrilla band, even if they did have a US Marshalls badge.

I checked out a vehicle from the motor pool. We were so over equipped that I got one of the team Tahoe's, in the ever-popular matte black with Nightshade ™ tinted windows – the only windows tinted dark enough that we could move vampires during the day without worrying we were going to have to clean goo from the upholstery. Fuel economy was going to be horrible. But I could afford it – I hadn't had anything to spend money on since Mel died right before I went to work for QMG.

Most folks get the job after they see something weird. Unlike Jed, my old Gunny in Iraq, I'd turned down the first approach. But when Melissa had been killed in an 'auto' accident, I'd jumped at the chance to go to work for QMG.

I tossed my cases in the back of the Tahoe, locking them in place, then went by the safe house and grabbed my AWOL bag, and headed south on I-35.

Now, there's not really a good time to travel I-35 in Austin. Between the constant construction, the lack of a ring road, and Austin's very own special class of drivers, I'm convinced that that stretch is a very special kind of Hell. Dante would have included it in his book, if he'd known about it. I swear, the city fathers in Austin were recruiting the worst drivers they could find for years. It took about two hours to get out of Austin, and because traffic was moving so slowly, I'd had time to book a room in San Marcos, at a bed and breakfast off Hopkins. Thank the deity for slow week days.

I finally checked in around eight that evening, carried everything to my room (quaint two-story buildings built in the 1880's tend to lack elevators, so it was a couple of trips) and then wandered down to the Square to grab a bite to eat. And sitting in the 'College Café' ran into my old classmate, David Miller, now Father Miller, Society of Jesus.

"Jesse! Good to see you," he said over the rumble of students socializing.

"David? When did you join the Catholic Ecumenical Shock Troopers of Jesus?" I replied, grinning.

"Oh, ten years or so ago," he said. "Probably just before you went and became a heretical priest."

David and I had taken a bunch of anthropology classes together and drunk a lot of beer in late night BS sessions before I'd decided college wasn't for me, and dropped out to join the Corps.

He looked good, for someone in the Holy See's version of mufti – he was still dressed all in black, with the obligatory white tab collar. He had on a vest (his jacket was hanging from the back of his chair) and crossing his waist was a slender chain, like a watch fob, holding the crossed sword, key, and Petrine Cross emblem of the Knights of Saint Quintus.

I had on jeans, a t-shirt and a light jacket to hide the 1911 in a waist holster at the base of my spine. The jacket had a few goodies in it as well and was stiff enough to keep the pistol from printing though.

"Pull up a chair and make yourself comfortable," he said.

The greeter gave him a look, but I pulled up a chair.

"Not taking off your jacket?" he asked with a grin. I was pretty sure he knew who I worked for, based on who he was working for. It's a small world, after all.

"Not unless you want to explain to the local cops why I'm carrying concealed," I replied. "Being as we're both in the same line of work, after all."

"How's taking orders in a lesser church then going to work for The Man working for you?" he grinned.

"Yeah, get it out of your system," I replied, grinning back. "At least I can get married."

"Speaking of which, where's Mel?" he asked.

Back when he and I had been going to school in San Marcos, Mel had been a permanent fixture, and she had waited till I finished basic to pressure me into marrying her. Not that much pressure had been required.

I looked at him. "You want the official story? Or . . .?"

"Official story first," he said, patting his lips dry. "Then, if you're up to it, we can talk about what happened, unofficially."

"Car accident."

"Really?"

"Yeah," I said, rubbing my eyes. "That's the official story. And part of the unofficial one as well."

"I see," he said.

"Do you? Because unless we put this under the seal of confession, I can't tell you what happened," I said.

"Really?" Miller seemed taken aback for a moment.

"Really," I said pointing to the Knights of Saint Quintus fob he was wearing.

"Oh. Well, that puts a different light on things, doesn't it? Are you sure you want to discuss it here?" he said, gesturing to the room around us.

"Yeah, the noise should cover us. If someone is following me with a shotgun mike or spells, well, that's their lookout. Besides," I reached up and tapped the cross and medals under my T-shirt, "I'd know if they were listening magically."

He pulled a pocket missal out.

"Forgive me Father, for I have sinned. It's been …it's been a really long time since my last confession," I said with a wry grin.

"Go on," he replied.

I waited while the waiter topped off our glasses and swapped out the basket of chips and salsa.

"It really was a car wreck," I said. "Unfortunately for her, she ran into a trailer that was hauling a lich and his minions."

"Oh God …that's horrible," he said, crossing himself.

"Yeah, well, that's not really the worst part," I said. "I was six months out of training with QMG when we tracked her down. Because we'd been married, I was the one who had to drive the stake through her heart."

The waiter dropped our burgers. I picked mine up and started eating. Miller was staring at me like I'd grown a third arm.

"What's the matter, Father?" I asked.

"You're so, just so, I don't know, blasé about it," he replied.

"I've had a couple-few years to get used to it," I said. "Besides, she's free now."

"Is that how you got into this line of work?" he asked after crossing himself.

"More or less. They'd approached me after I came back from Iraq in '05. My company got tasked with covering a QMG insertion team that was looking for a ghoul farm that Saddam was running over there. Things did not go as planned and we had to pull the survivors out of the hole in the ground before the Air Force bombed the ghouls into a fine paste. My old Gunny runs a team out of Austin these days as well."

"I'm confused," Miller said. "When did you have time to take orders?"

"I did that after I got back. Used the GI Bill to go to seminary. Mel was making good money as a pharmaceutical rep. Until she, well, you know," I said between bites.

"Yes," he replied, picking up his burger. "So after the wreck?"

"QMG sent Gunny Thomas around to talk to me. He'd gotten the call when they found the car, and it stank of lich. I was filling in for his team priest when they found Mel, so I got to do the honors," I said. "Fries aren't up to what they were when we were going to school here, are they?"

"No," he replied. "Probably using just vegetable oil to fry them, rather than the same oil they fried everything in. Missing the flavor from the chicken fried steak, I think."

I looked him in the eye. "Dave, I'm sorry. The company shrink says I tend to have one of two reactions when talking about Mel – either I get angry, or I blow it off. Neither one of them, according to him, is, quote, healthy, end quote."

"Well, no, but you're not drinking as a coping mechanism," he replied.

"True. I have the best coping mechanism in the world. I get to kill the things that took her or their, what's the phrase? Close cognates," I said, finishing off my burger. "When did you go to work for the Knights?"

"They recruited me out of the seminary," he said. "I do research for them, mainly. I'm here to see a relic, actually."

"Oh?" I said, chasing catchup with a fry.

"It's, well, it's a bird bath, that's associated with visions of Saint Mark the Evangelist," he said, somewhat sheepishly.

I chuckled.

"Could be worse," I said. "Could have been a toilet seat."

Miller spewed tea across the table.

I buffed my fingernails on my jacket. "Timing is everything."

"You staying in town?" he asked once he could breathe again.

"Yeah, you?"

"Yeah," he said, sliding me his card across the table.

I slid him mine.

"Call you in the morning?"

"Make it afternoon," he said. "I've got to see the little old lady who owns the font in the morning."

"Font? I thought it was a bird bath?"

"Potato, po-tat-to," he replied, rising.

"I'll call you in the afternoon," I said. "I'm burning vacation at this point."

"Hey, on second thought, why don't we just meet at the Pearl at two or so?" he said, rising to put on his jacket.

The Pearl was a coffee shop on the north side of the Square. It had been our go to hang out when we were at Texas State.

"Works for me," I replied, taking his check while he had both arms in his jacket sleeves.

I waved a hand to forestall his complaints.

"My employer pays better," I said.

"True," he replied before going out the door.

I had one beer and nursed it, listening to the chatter around me. Nothing important, just the usual struggles of college life. The kind of thing we were trying to protect.

Chapter Two
Day 2, 4 April 2018

I woke up with my left knee killing me. It had been a harbinger of horrible weather ever since I'd landed on it falling out of a helicopter in Iraq. Problem was the forecast had been for 'partly cloudy, with a slight chance of rain', and my knee was saying 'buy all the gopher wood, hammers, nails, build a big boat and start rounding up the animals two by two'. I rolled over, grabbed the bottle of Marine Candy (ibuprofen) that was sitting on the nightstand and downed five of them. Over the years, I'd gotten used to the aches and pains of getting older – after all they indicated I was still above ground.

I gimped into the bathroom and took a hot shower, working my knee enough to get the limp down to a slight hitch in my giddy up. I looked out the windows, finally, and saw clear skies.

"Figures," I said to the world in general and got dressed.

After checking in – a quick text to a discrete number – I dressed. Combat boots, black tactical pants and a dark blue t-shirt. I swung a light blue short sleeved shirt on to cover the 1911 and headed out to find breakfast. And kill time before I met with Miller.

I figured I'd start at the Pearl. After all, they'd had pretty decent food and coffee when I'd last been in San Marcos. And ran full into the first 'change'. Because of a change in managers, they no longer had meat on the menu. They still had the baked goods, but no sandwiches. I'd really been looking forward to their Reuben.

The kid behind the counter, a tall, lanky blond with a bunch of tattoos, took pity on me.

"Used to come here, huh?" he said.

"Yeah," I replied, trying to decide if it was worth it to order coffee before going back out into the street.

He looked at the clock.

"Give it ten minutes, and the bar in back opens. When the new manager took over, she pissed off the cook, and he went to work back there. You can get the same food," he said with a wink.

"DAMNIT JOHN!" a voice shrilled from the office behind the counter. "Quit sending business back there!"

I gave John my best commiserating look and bought the coffee to go, giving the kid a ten dollar tip.

"Thanks," he said, pocketing the ten spot.

I took my time adjusting the coffee to sugar and cream ratio in my cup, then wandered down the hall to the bar, filled with dark panelling and dim light. I dawdled over breakfast, reading and generally trying to relax. It was forty-five minutes short of two when I finally paid the bill and rose, walking back to the front of the building.

First thing I noted on exiting the bar was that the light had gone flat. I walked all the way to the front of the Pearl and looked out the windows. There still wasn't a cloud in the sky, but the sunlight had taken on the same qualities as it did in the minutes before a thunderstorm – flat with a slight gray-green tinge. My knee was twinging as well. I had enough time to walk down to my B&B and put on my brace, so I did.

For some reason, I also changed shirts, and put on my 'work' shirt, with the clerical collar, and shrugged into a gray herringbone tweed jacket with silver woven into the threads. The silver had been blessed before being woven into the jacket.

I don't know why I changed. But I'd come to listen to the little voice in the noise at the back of my head a long time ago. It had kept me from dying more than once in Iraq, and again once I went to work for QMG. I looked at the cases on the wall – one had bottles of holy water and wafers, with a little sacramental wine. I glanced at the pair of Pelican 1660's I'd placed at the foot of the bed. One had body armor, load bearing equipment, and about a thousand rounds of ammunition. The other wheeled Pelican case held three sub guns – two H&K UMP .45's and a special order MP5 in .45 (hey, when you spend the kind of money on firearms that QMG does in a year, manufacturers will bend over backwards to do special orders – and that's just for the 'legal' bodyguard work the company does) in a hard shell briefcase, along with a few other party supplies. Ginsberg, the company armorer and resident mad-weapons-genius, had gotten a few of the original H&K 'operational' brief cases as a test, decided they were a joke, and designed his own. He'd started with a hard shell sample case that opened from the top, then added a carrying system for a very small MP5 and ten magazines. There was even a stock that could be added if you had time. His model wasn't set up to be fired through the case, but I could have the MP5 out and be firing it in under five seconds. If I had to, I could fire it through the case. Although, in that case, Ginsberg might be a bit miffed about what I'd done to his labor of love.

I hated the damn things. Short MP5's with just a pistol grip are hard to control. The shoulder stock helped some, but not a whole lot. I still took the case with me.

If the sky had been gray before, it now looked like dross on the surface of molten lead. There still wasn't a cloud in the sky, and the birds, who had been cheerily shouting when I awoke hours before, were huddled motionless, silent balls of feathers clinging to the power lines with a death grip.

I started to cross Guadalupe, jumping back to avoid being run over by an ancient Lincoln Town Car that was apparently seeking revenge on John Wilkes Booth. I could see a mound of blue hair peeking above the steering wheel, and a pair of skeletal hands gripping the wheel. The car roared through the intersection and disappeared down Guadalupe.

I looked at the guy crossing the street from the other direction. He shrugged. I shrugged back – it was the normal kind of thing that happened in San Marcos - and walked on to the Pearl, five minutes late. Miller had already gotten a table and was going over the menu – a couple of sheets of printer paper in a page protector. The same blond kid from earlier was behind the bar, watching a pair of obvious sorority girls try to decide how they wanted their coffee. I dropped the case next to the table Miller had picked and walked to the bar.

"Are you sure you don't have Diet Coke?" one of the sorority girls asked as I stepped up behind them.

"Yes," the barista said.

You could hear the exasperation in his voice.

"Well, can you look and be sure?" she whined.

I could see a vein throbbing in his temple. I think I caught the actual moment he snapped.

"I tell you what. I'll take a look in our vast cooler," he pointed to the glass-fronted case behind the bar, "if you can answer one question."

I watched the girl's reflection in the front of the case. Her eyes lit up.

"I'll try," she responded.

He struck a pose, one hip cocked, and one hand resting on that hip, the other on the bar.

"Why do sorority girls drink Diet Coke?"

She gave him a smile that clearly said she was in on the joke, and said, "I don't know. Why do sorority girls drink Diet Coke?"

"Because they think they're fat, and they're thirsty!" the barista said.

"I never!" the sorority girl shouted, flouncing off.

"I hope so," he responded to her back. He turned to me and saw my collar. "Um, sorry about that, Father. She comes in here about once a day, always asking for Diet Coke."

I grinned at him. "I imagine it would be a bit wearing. John, wasn't it?"

"Yes sir. What can I get you?"

"Coffee's fine. And when my friend over there figures out what he wants, put it on my check, ok?"

"Can do," John replied, handing me a cup.

I drew a cup of coffee from the pot, fixed to my liking and went and sat down with Miller.

"You get your holy Winston Churchill Garden Gnome?" I asked.

"Bird bath. And yes. The owner was quite reasonable, and I was able to document a vision of Saint Mark the Evangelist while we were talking."

"That's …that's not good," I replied.

"Well, from our point of view it is," he said.

"Really? Think about it. Did you ask her how frequently the visions were occurring?" I asked.

"Yesss," he replied, pulling out a notebook.

There was an irritating background whine, like a gnat or a mosquito buzzing my ear. Miller waved a hand at his head before flipping to the last page with something written on it.

"Once a year for ten years, then once a week for the last three months, and once a day until today, when she started seeing a vision every hour or so . . ." he trailed off.

The buzzing had gone from an irritant to something that was causing the filings in my teeth to vibrate.

"You hear that?" Miller asked.

"Hear it? I feel it," I said.

There was a crash behind the bar. We turned – John was gone. Miller and I stood and walked over.

John lay on the ground, twitching.

"Seizure?" Miller asked.

I looked at the kid.

"No medic alert tags, but that doesn't mean . . ."

The buzzing was actually causing the crockery to move on the shelves.

"Damn, grab his feet, huh?" I shouted, picking John up by the shoulders.

We moved him out to the hall, under a beam, just in case. The buzzing became physically punishing, and I slipped down the wall I was braced against. Miller crumpled to the floor.

"Earthquake?" he managed to gasp before he passed out.

I must have followed his example within a few seconds. When I came to, John was leaning over me. A thin stream of blood had leaked from one of his nostrils.

"Damn Father, you look like shit," he said.

"Well, you don't look so good yourself," I managed to croak.

"Your buddy's still out of it," John said, unconsciously wiping the blood from his lip with the back of his hand. "What the hell happened?"

"Good question," said, reaching for my cell phone.

The screen read 'No Signal'.

"Interesting," I said, as Miller started to moan.

"Dave, you OK?" I asked.

"Yeah, but what were we drinking last night? My mouth tastes like something used it as a litter box, and my head feels four sizes too small for my brain."

"I don't know about you, but I had water," I grinned. I stood then helped him to his feet.

"Damn," he said, crossing himself and looking out the windows.

The sky was flame-shot black over metallic gray-green.

"That's not normal," I said.

John had walked to the phone behind the counter.

"Weird, it's dead too," he said, before noticing the sky. "Fuck me."

"Sorry, you're not my type," I snarked, walking to my case.

I flipped it open and rooted around in it for a minute, before I found the sat-phone. I flipped it open, getting the same message as my cell – No Signal.

I snapped it closed and dropped it in the bag, then looked at the other two.

"This is not good," I said, pulling out the MP5 and adding the stock.

"What kind of priest are you?" John asked.

"Church Militant," David replied. "He's a priest of the Church Militant."

"Let's just say I work for folks who deal with this kind of thing on a regular basis," I said, snapping a sling into place and dropping the MP5 to hang over my shoulder.

"Dave, where's the font?" I asked.

"Back of my van in the parking lot," he replied.

"Font?" John asked.

"Relic," I replied, turning to Miller.

My hands were belting on, for lack of a better term, a utility belt, festooned with pouches. Once it was in place I started pulling the rest of the gear out of the hard case.

"You think?" Miller asked.

"Probably not," I replied as something struck the windows. I turned.

A red mud ball was slowly rolling down the window.

"Damn," I said. "Haven't seen it rain mud since Iraq."

"Guys, I don't think that's mud," John said, turning and dry heaving.

I turned and looked. Sure enough, there was an eyeball in the 'mud' sliding down the wall.

"Oh, that's not good at all," was all I said.

"Have you got a plan?" David asked.

"Yeah. I don't know that you're going to like it, though," I said. "First, we need to get my other cases from the hotel. Then, transfer the font to my vehicle, and move to consecrated ground."

"Why your vehicle?" Miller asked.

John was staring at us like we'd sprouted horns. Given what was going outside, that wouldn't have surprised me in the least.

"Is yours, well, blessed?"

"No, it's a rental," Miller said, chuckling.

Outside it began to pour rain. Dim shapes moved in the rain, seeking shelter, I hoped.

"Probably be shorter and drier to go through the bar," John said.

One of the sorority girls came flying through one of the windows, taking out the large clam with a pearl that was painted on the glass. Both eyes were missing and her skin, from the neck down, had been peeled in alternating strips. I heard a woman's shriek through the broken window and assumed it was the second sorority girl, in trouble.

I looked at Miller.

"So, do the Knights train archivists in firearms?" I asked.

"For self-defense," he replied. "Sometimes the places and things we're looking at can get a bit strange."

"This kind of strange?" John asked.

"This? This is nothing," I replied. "Wait till you've seen a ghoul nest or a vampire hang out," I said, handing Miller my 1911 and a couple of spare magazines. "It's got the old, military style sights."

"Right. I should be able to hit the wall with it," Miller said with a small grin.

"Wait here, I'll be right back," I said. "John, stay with Father Miller."

"I'm not going anywhere," he said.

The rain wasn't rain, I realized when I stepped outside. It was ectoplasm. It also evaporated just before touching me, retreating from my footsteps.

"Oh that is definitely not good," I murmured.

Something had pinned the other sorority girl to the back deck of a faded, metallic gold 1969 Chevy Impala, and was removing her clothes preparatory to defiling her and probably peeling her skin like her friend. Or worse. I could also see someone trying to get out of the car without attracting the attention of whatever it was with the girl.

"Hey, ASSHOLE," I shouted.

If I survived, I'd get Miller to assign penance. Right now, I was thinking like a Marine, not a priest. And wishing I'd pulled the suppressor out of the bag and attached it to the MP5. If nothing else, the weight of the can would have helped with keeping the barrel down, a bit.

The beast looked at me, and I saw the single horn on its forehead. It then averted its eyes and roared, leaping to the roof of the car. I put a three round burst into it, starting in the crotch – full auto tends to climb, even on controlled bursts, so starting low and letting the aim point rise will usually put you into the center of mass. Especially if the target moves to your right.

It was definitely male. Impressively, rampantly so. The silver cored bullets shredded its member, and it shrieked in agony before leaping again, this time towards me. I put the remainder of the clip into it, walking the burst along the torso. I stepped to the side, dropping the magazine and reloading as the beast squelched into the car behind me. It twitched as I put three more rounds into the base of its equine looking skull, just to be sure.

"DUDE, YOU OK?" a male voice called from the Impala.

"Yeah. You?"

"I'm fine," the voice replied. "I think the girl is ok too."

I walked over to the Impala. If anything popped out, I should be able to handle it with twenty two rounds of silver cored .45. If not, I still had eight more full magazines. If it took more than nine magazines to put down, I'd try negotiations at that point. Or, conversely I might be in a bit of trouble.

When I got to the car there was a male standing there, looking everywhere but at the back of the car. I could see the sorority girl's arms sticking up through a T-shirt she was pulling on.

"I'm John, John Davis," the guy said, offering me his hand. In the other he had a baseball bat wrapped in plaid duct tape.

"Nice to meet you John. We're starting a collection," I quipped back, shaking his hand quickly then going back to covering the area.

The rain of ectoplasm had stopped. The sky was still the dirty gray of a television tuned to a dead channel, and I couldn't see anyone else in the Square.

The girl joined us.

"I'm Dalma," she said. "What the fuck was that thing?"

"Daemon," I replied. "Type three, I think."

Something skittered in the corner of my eye. I turned and watched a pair of imps trying to remove the daemon's horn.

"Seriously?" Dalma replied. "Those things aren't real!"

I just grinned. "Welcome to the 'aren't real' world then. Because that thing sure looks real to me."

"Aw damnit," John said.

He'd moved to the trunk of the Impala. I walked to where he was standing and looked, giving a low whistle.

"Damn," I said, looking at the deep scratches in the metal. "Look, you got anything you need to grab from the trunk?"

"Yeah, my backpack – it's got my clean clothes in it," John replied.

"Grab it, and let's go," I said.

"Right," he replied, popping the trunk and reaching inside.

"Look, it's not like I'm not grateful," Dalma started.

I raised a hand to forestall her.

"Tell you what, Dalma. Let's get somewhere where we know we're not going to be jumped by vulgar unicorns, and we can talk, huh?" I said.

"Fine," she hissed, stomping towards the Pearl.

"You know, one of the problems with this town is all the damn sorority girls," John said, slamming the trunk lid.

"That hasn't changed in the last ten years," I replied with a grin. "After you."

He trotted across the Square, and I followed, my head swiveling from side to side to watch for anything trying to take advantage of us. I saw a couple more imps sneaking about, but nothing major.

"COMING IN!" I shouted out of habit before stepping through the broken window into the Pearl.

Father Miller and John (the first one) had drug the body out of the way, covering it with some table cloths.

I pointed to John (the second) and then to John (the first). "John, meet John."

"He's a regular," John (the first) answered. "You want anything, Davis?"

"Yes, Mr. Padgett, after my adventures out there, I need a cup of coffee," John Davis replied.

"You know where the cups are. On your tab?" John Padgett answered.

Davis looked at him, then at the leaden sky outside.

"Really?"

"Yeah, ok," Padgett said.

"Oh," Dalma said, looking at the body under the table cloth. "Is that . . ."

"Yes," Padgett said in an oddly soft tone. "You don't want to look at her now, ok?"

Dalma slumped into a chair, then started to cry. Davis brought his coffee over and sat down next to her. She wrapped her arms around him and started bawling. Padgett disappeared down the hall, and Miller and I looked at each other.

"Got room in the van?" I asked.

"Sorta. It's a cargo job, so there's only the front seats."

"Not a problem. Once Padgett gets back, we'll move. You have any ideas for consecrated ground?"

Miller scratched his head. "There's a number of churches here in town we could use that are close. They're not Catholic, but they should be on consecrated ground, as long as they believe in the Trinity. I've got to ask, though, have you ever heard of something like this happening?" he said.

"It reminds me of something but I'm not sure what. And we won't be able to do any research."

"About that," he replied. "I've got most of the collected works on matters arcane that are in the Church library on a hard drive with my computer in the van. If the computer and the drives still work. But even with the right search parameters, it's going to take a while to figure out where we are."

"That's the easy part," I said.

"How so?"

"Getting back's going to be the bitch," I replied.

He just shook his head. "Language, Father."

I replied with a feral look.

Padgett came back from wherever he'd gone, a six pack of Diet Coke in hand. He put it on the bar, then filled a glass with ice and brought them to where Dalma sat, drying her eyes.

"Thank ...thank you," she said.

"Sorry about earlier," he replied. "But every day?"

"Yeah, I just thought it was fun to aggravate you," Dalma replied before taking a sip.

Padgett rolled his eyes at Davis then came walking over to where we were standing.

"I didn't see anyone in the bar back there," he said. "But there was blood in the storage room."

"Great," Miller said.

"Bother," I replied.

They both looked at me.

"Look, I screwed up. I've been thinking short term, ok?"

"How so?" Miller asked.

"We get a place to hide out, then what?" I asked.

"We start doing research," Miller started.

"What are we going to eat?" Davis asked, walking over.

"Points for the new guy," I said.

"I ...I hadn't thought of that," Padgett said.

Miller looked contemplative.

"Newer plan. You guys," I pointed to Davis and Miller, "go bless your van. Padgett, you and Dalma start gathering all the canned goods and other things you can from the bar and in here."

"What are you going to do?" Dalma asked.

"I'm going for a walk," I said with a wicked grin. "A very enthusiastic walk."

I walked out the door and started west down Hopkins to my B&B. We needed those cases.

I didn't go inside when I got there, however. I walked to the Tahoe and hit the remote start. It farted to life with a diesel rumble.

"Is there anyone there?" someone called from the B&B.

"One moment," I shouted, crossing the street and going through the door of the B&B.

The voice had come from the second floor, and I went up the stairs two at a time. It wasn't hard to figure out which room the voice was calling from – there were half a dozen imps outside the door, trying to figure out how to get in. They looked up when I walked into the hallway and hissed before charging.

I snap shot the largest one as it bounded in my direction. It folded around the bullet, then vanished in a puff of smoke. The other ones stopped and looked at me, twisting their heads from side to side in a dog-like fashion. Their ears waggled, and one of them paused to pick its nose.

"Begone," I said.

They thought it over. The door behind them opened, and a stately woman in her mid-forties to early fifties, dressed somewhat archaically, stepped out. She struck the closest imp with the stick in her hand. It disappeared in a puff like the first one.

"You heard him, you little imps! Begone!" she shouted, lying about her with her stick.

The imps fled.

The woman paused, breathing lightly from her exertions.

"You are real?" she asked.

Her voice had the buzz of an accent. She spoke English, but as if she'd learned English from a Brit, but as a second or third language.

"Yes," I replied. "I'm Father Jesse Salazar, QMG," I replied.

She raised a questioning eyebrow, "QMG?"

"Quentin Morris Group. We specialize in - well strange things," I replied, lamely.

"Henry and Abraham's Great Project," I swear I could hear the capitals, "still in existence."

That's when I noticed the pistol in her other hand.

"Uh, ma'am? Do you mind pointing that another direction?" I asked, adjusting the aim of my submachine gun.

"Oh, sorry. I don't know why I brought it out with me, I ran out of ammunition for it years ago," She replied, slipping it into a slit in her outer dress. "I am Diindiisi."

"Ma'am. I've got to pick up a few things here, but if you've got your things together, you're welcome to join us," I said.

"There are others?" she replied.

"Yes'm," I said, sidling to my door. "I'll be a few minutes - I need to change clothes and grab some things."

I'd spent far too long living in tight spaces to be embarrassed if she saw me changing. I'd even woken up one morning in a transient tent in Iraq with an Air Force female staring at my really bad moto-tattoo. Most of what I was going to do involved putting things on, not taking them off, and swapping firearms.

"Ma'am, can I ask you a question?" I said, tossing my jacket and utility belt on the bed.

I grabbed a couple of rubber bands and bloused my trousers to the top of my boots. Thank God for fashionable tactical pants in black.

"Go ahead," she answered from the doorway.

"How long have you been here?" I asked.

"What year is it, out there?" she replied.

"2018."

She stepped around the corner as I started slinging on my body armor/load-bearing equipment from the case.

"Two thousand and eighteen?" she whispered.

"Yes'm," I replied, sealing the Velcro, then shrugging my shoulders to set the armor.

"Then I've been in the Shadow Lands for one hundred and five years. I look remarkable for a woman of one hundred and forty-six years, do I not?" she trilled, spinning lightly on her toes.

"One hundred and five years?" I asked, doing the math mentally. "So 1913 or so?"

"Yes. Henry had asked me to look into something in the archives that he and Abraham had established in the United States. I was on my way to Long Island when a strange storm appeared. I woke in the Shadow Lands," she said. "Today, I stepped through a door and was here." She shrugged. "Things operate differently in the Shadow Lands."

"Long Island? You're in Texas now," I said, checking one of the spare 1911's in my gun case, loading it and sliding it into the holster under my left arm.

"Ma'am? You said your pistol was out of ammunition. Could I see it?" I asked.

"Here," she said, handing it over.

It was a British Bulldog revolver, in .44 Russian. The gun itself was a work of art – arabesques on the barrel and cylinder, and silver inlay on the grip.

"Damn," I said. "I don't have any .44 Russian. Had you seen any other pistols before you were swept into the shadows?

"Henry had purchased some, what were they, semi-automatic pistols in January of 1912," she said. "Made by Colt, if I remember correctly."

I reached into the case and pulled out the final 1911 I had. Ginsberg, the company's resident mad-armorer, had bought an entire run of 1911's not 1911A1's from somewhere, as an experiment. For some reason most of them had ended up in Austin. I wasn't going to complain about the lack of a grip safety at this point, if it meant she could use it.

"Something like this?" I asked, locking the slide back and dropping the magazine before handing it over.

"Yes!"

It might be considered blasphemous, but I whispered a quick alleluia to the soul of John Moses Browning, unofficial patron saint of gunsmiths everywhere.

"Ma'am, I need to get these cases to my vehicle downstairs - " I said, handing her the loose magazine and a pouch with four more. "If you wouldn't mind covering my back, we can start moving them any time."

She took the pouch, and it disappeared under her skirt. The magazine went in the well, and she ran the slide forward before putting the pistol under her skirt. Diindiisi walked to the closed case and, after looking at it, shifted it up on its wheels.

"Do you need to take anything else?" she asked.

I handed her my jacket. "It's not much," I said, "but the jacket has silver woven into the cloth. It might help keep an imp or daemon off your back."

She took it and put it on. It was a little large on her, but not cumbersome. She transferred the pistol and ammunition pouch to the outer pockets of the jacket.

I turned and swept everything else in the room into my AWOL bag and tossed it into the other Pelican case, slamming the lid. I'd have to live with the hairs and skin cells I'd left behind being here, since there wasn't time to vacuum. And I'd swap the MP5 for a UMP when we got where the others were.

"I'll lead, ma'am," I said, dragging the case out into the hall and down the stairs.

"I need to get something," she said when we were in the hall.

I waited while she dodged back into the room she'd come out of. A few seconds later, she returned with a largish carpet bag, and a leather-wrapped bindle.

"After you, Father," she said, an urchin's grin on her face.

We thumped the cases downstairs and across the street to where the Tahoe waited. I checked the street, then hit the unlock button on the SUV's remote. Diindiisi watched the street while I swung the heavy cases up into the back of the SUV. I slammed the door, then walked down the driver's side. Diindiisi opened the passenger door, front, and climbed in.

"This is what automobiles have become in 2018?" she asked as I backed out.

I hadn't bothered with the seat belts. If I saw something, for now, my plan was to run, not ram.

"Yes'm. Well, this one has a few aftermarket goodies installed," I replied, putting it in drive and heading for the Square.

My five-minute paranoid walk was a minute or so ride. Davis, with his baseball bat, was waiting out front for us.

"Father Miller, Padgett, and Dalma are waiting out back," he said, stepping to my window.

"Hop in," I said.

Once he was seated, I introduced him to Diindiisi.

"Ma'am," was all he said.

I drove around back, where the others were waiting with the van.

"Took you long enough," Miller said when we got there.

Davis hopped out and walked to his car, which was parked next to the van.

"Figured we'd need another set of wheels," Padgett said. "Father Miller agreed."

Diindiisi and I stepped out of the SUV.

"Everyone, this is Diindiisi. I found her when I went to get my gear," I said.

Diindiisi curtseyed.

"Diindiisi, this is everyone. Dave, did you find a church close by?"

"Yes, but I don't know that it's going to work like we thought," he replied, pointing.

Sticking up about a block over, I could see a steeple. As I watched, smoke started pouring from it.

"That's been happening off and on since you left," Padgett said.

"Not good," I said. Before Padgett could ask the obvious question, I continued. "Yes, the ground will still be consecrated, unless some of the locals here are busy defiling it. We can still go by; it might be a signal. I'll lead, Davis, you follow, and Father Miller, bring up the rear."

Everyone got in their respective vehicles. This time, I took a minute to strap Diindiisi in before I climbed in. I started to go around to my side, then walked between the van and the Impala, motioning for them to roll down the windows.

"Look," I said. "If we get there and it's a no-go, I'm not stopping. If it's bad enough, I'll bull through and you can follow, ok?"

Davis swallowed and nodded.

"Right," was Miller's reply.

I climbed into the SUV and belted in myself.

Diindiisi was playing with the window controls, fascinated.

I drove down the alley and onto the street, turning towards the church. It was far worse than I had imagined. What had probably been a nice wooden late 19th early 20th century church now looked like the bastard step-child of Bosch and Escher. Daemons were forcing their way inside, coming out with bits of people. They watched us drive by, but didn't do anything else.

"Ok, so the other side can desecrate holy places," I said.

"That's normal here," Diindiisi said, nodding. "Sometimes things are far worse."

"Where is here?" I asked.

"The Shadow Lands," she replied, sadly. "I realized that after I'd been here for a while."

"You said that a couple of times before," I said. "The name rings a bell, but it's been a long time since I heard it."

"Yes, we're going to have to have a long talk at some point," Diindiisi said.

"True," I replied, taking my foot off the brake and driving down the road until I found a half-empty parking lot, pulling in.

"Any other suggestions, that are close?" I asked Miller when he pulled up next to me.

"One. But it's gonna be a bit weird," he replied.

"Lead on then," I said. "Davis follow Miller, huh?"

Miller drove up another block, then turned right. He passed the first building on the left, then turned into the second.

"Interesting," Diindiisi and I both said at the same time, reading the sign out front.

It read 'Monmouth Funeral Home'. Miller drove to the back of the building and parked. Davis followed. I pulled up across the open garage doors, breaking out one of the full-sized UMP's in my gearbox.

"Y'all wait here," I said, going into the garage. It took about ten minutes to sweep the building, but it was empty.

I came back outside to a spirited discussion between Miller and Padgett.

"Hey Father, are you sure about this place?" Padgett asked.

"Yes, why?" Father Miller answered.

"It's ...it's a funeral home," Padgett replied.

"Yes, but it's got a chapel," Miller responded.

"Kinda creepy though," Padgett said.

"The first church was blocked and desecrated. Ms. Diindiisi says that's her experience here with most major religious structures. Whatever controls the place desecrates them quickly. Whatever brought us here was thorough," Miller said, turning to me. "Building clear?"

"Yes."

"John, would you give me a hand with the font?"

I watched as Padgett moved over and helped Miller move the font into the building, while Dalma and Davis started moving the other supplies into the building. I took overwatch. Diindiisi watched the other side of the building, assisting as needed.

Once everything was staged in the garage, I backed the SUV into a parking space.

"We need a plan," Miller said, leaning against the hearse in the garage.

"You're Catholic, correct?" Diindiisi asked him.

"Yes, why?" Miller replied.

"That makes you the senior, religiously," she said.

"I'm an archivist," he replied. "I've never done the kind of field work that Jesse here has," Dave said.

"Not a problem," I replied. "I'll handle the Church Militant side of things while you're going through the hard drives. Besides, we're going to need to collect some more things."

"Such as?" Dalma asked.

"More food. Ammunition. Weapons. Body armor if we can find it. See if there are other survivors. Consecrated wafers and wine – the ones I've got in my tabernacle aren't going to last forever, and they're useful things," I said.

"I've got a few in my bag, but you're right," Davis said, before interjecting, "Salt. A whole lot of salt."

"Salt," Diindiisi said in agreement. "A way to project holy water onto the damned. A change of clothes would be nice."

She gestured to her outfit and Dalma's.

"That makes sense," Dalma said grudgingly.

"I'm pretty sure Hell was not where my boss meant me to go when he told me to take a vacation," I said. "There's two apartments up-stairs. Why don't y'all argue over who's sleeping where while Father Miller and I bless the building and the yard, just in case?"

Father Miller and I set the wards, then walked into the garage and up the stairs. Everyone was gathered in the far apartment, around the kitchen table.

"I think we need to discuss a few things," Diindiisi said.

"Shoot," I replied, leaning up against a wall.

Miller took the last chair at the table.

"I'm going to place a great deal of trust in you," she said. "We're in the Shadow Lands, neither Heaven or Hell, nor Limbo."

"Another plane?" Davis asked.

"Something like that, yes," Diindiisi asked, turning to face him. "What do you know about the planes?"

"Uh, just what I learned playing D&D," he replied.

"D&D?"

"It's a game," I said. "Players take on the roles of fighters, clerics, wizards, and such."

"Ah. You'll have to teach me this game, Mr. Davis," Diindiisi said.

"Sure," he replied, blushing.

Dalma was giving him a look that said 'NERD'. Padgett covered his snicker with his hand.

"In my experience, we will have to watch over each other," Diindiisi said. "I don't know how well you know one another, but working together gives us a better chance of surviving."

"How long have you been here?" Father Miller asked.

"One hundred and five years," she replied.

"Where did you enter the Shadow Lands?" Miller continued.

"I was on Long Island, working for Henry and Abraham," she said.

"Father? Is now the best time for this?" I asked, breaking Miller's chain of thought.

"I'm not sure," he replied. "However, Ms. Diindiisi, was it? Is there anything else we need to talk about right now?"

"Yes. We will be able to take and use things here," Diindiisi continued. "And if we are in one location for a long time, we'll be able to return to some of the same places and get more supplies, as they will restock. I think it has something to do with the way time passes here in the Shadow Lands compared with the real world, but I'm not sure."

I snapped my fingers.

"Of course – the missing sock theory," I said.

Diindiisi gave me a puzzled look.

"So, I'm not sure how far back the technology goes, but there's a theory about how you lose one sock out of a pair in the dryer. It slips through or is acquired by someone or something somewhere else," I said, gesturing. "Here, most likely. Kinda kills Hawking's black hole theory."

"I do not know what a dryer is," Diindiisi said, "but the rest of that sounds right. Things will appear here from time to time. As do people. People are more of a disruption to the way things work than objects, however, and if the ...the rift is big enough, we'll be pulled to wherever the people came into this realm."

"Why would something here need one sock?" Dalma asked.

"I don't know. Outside of hunger and sex as a motivation, I haven't had much chance to talk to the things that people the realm. From the look of things outside, right now they're thin on the ground here. That will change," Diindiisi said, her tone grim.

"How long do we have?" I asked.

"Depends. If there are more people than us here, the daemons will find us faster," she said.

I looked out the window, then glanced at my watch. If there had been a sun in the sky it should have been going down. Instead the sky was static gray

"Ok, everyone, it's been a long day. Think about what you need and or want. Write it down. Then get some rest," I said.

Chapter Three
Day 3, 5 April 2018

Dalma and Diindiisi took the apartment where we'd had the meeting – it was set up like a normal, two-bedroom apartment. The other one was broken into five rooms, not counting the kitchen, with three beds and two couches. I ended up on a couch in the room closest to the entrance, for no other reason than I was the most heavily armed.

I'd also spent a couple of hours making lists before going to sleep. Once I climbed out of a very rump-sprung couch, and read the note on the door, I adjourned to the other apartment, where Diindiisi was overseeing the production of breakfast.

"How do you like your eggs?" Padgett asked from the stove.

"Long as they're not green, I don't care," I replied.

I thumped into a chair, battle rattle pushing me back from the table.

"I forgot how much fun this crap is to wear all your waking hours," I said, grimly.

"Need a hand taking it off?" Diindiisi asked.

"No," I replied, rising and pulling the Velcro on the side loose. I ducked out of the armor and dropped it next to me. "Thank you though."

"Where's everyone else?" I asked as Padgett set a plate of bacon and eggs before me.

"They're downstairs taking stock of supplies here," Diindiisi replied, sitting with a cup of coffee. "I haven't had coffee this good in a while."

"Thank you, ma'am," Padgett said. "We're well stocked with coffee if nothing else."

"We should be able to keep supplied, at least," Diindiisi said. "Until we're pulled to the next intrusion."

"Is that how you got here?" I asked.

"Yes. Time passes very slowly here, until there's another event. Then you find yourself there, wherever there is, and starting all over. Events tend to be rare, however."

"How rare?" Padgett asked.

"Well, time is different in the Shadow Lands," Diindiisi replied.

"Obviously," I said.

"Yes, but beyond that. We're essentially going to be replaying the same day for a long time."

"Groundhog Day?" Padgett asked me.

"I don't think so. I think she means that the weather will be the same, and not a lot is going to change until the next event. Which makes it hard to keep track of time, right?" I asked Diindiisi.

"Yes," she replied. "If there is a long time between events we should be able to build up quite a supply of useful items. Although I'd suggest that bags or some sort of carrying equipment be high on our list of items. That way everyone can have a minimum amount of equipment on them at all times if there's another event."

"On my list," I said, turning and pulling my lists out.

"You've thought about this," she replied, looking at the lists.

"Yes'm," I replied around a mouthful of eggs.

There was the sound of feet on the stairwell from the garage, and Miller, Dalma, and Davis trooped in.

"Well, if nothing else, we've got proof that we're no longer in Kansas," Davis said.

"How so?" Padgett asked.

"There's a bird bath full of glowing water in the chapel," he replied.

"God provides," Miller said, handing me several small water bottles. The water had a, well, the only way to describe it is the bottles gave off a pure, calming radiance.

"You know, we could be rich with this stuff," I said.

"How?" Miller asked.

"We could win the Amazing Randi's challenge, for one thing," I said. "And real holy water? We'd put Peter Popov Ministries out of business."

"I did not become a priest to repeat the mistakes of the Middle Ages," Miller intoned.

"Oddly enough, I didn't either," I replied. "On to other things. Other than Father Miller and Diindiisi, can any of you use firearms?"

"I'm pretty good with a rifle," Dalma said. "Bagged my limit with deer."

"Scope or open sights?"

"Both," she replied. "Got a cousin who tried to prove he was a better shot, so he loaned me his No 4 Mk 1 Enfield. They're set up with battlefield sights, so it's either a 300 or 600 yard peep sight on the back."

She leaned on a wall, folded her arms and smirked.

"Got a twelve point buck with that gun," she said.

"John? Other John?"

Davis shook his head.

"I was raised around guns," Padgett said. "But I prefer to throw knives at people, why?"

"In this line of work, throwing knives doesn't help much. But we could be here for years, so everyone will get a chance to learn. Right now, though, that means Diindiisi, Dalma and I get to go shopping."

"Oh? Why those two?" Father Miller asked.

"Because Father," I adopted a bad movie cowboy accent, "You can per-tect the homestead while me an' tha wimmon folk get supplies from town."

"Bless you, my son, for you seem to have been possessed," Miller said, crossing himself, then me. "I'll need to go over the Rite of Exorcism."

I tried to smother a smile, but it broke out across my face anyway.

"But seriously, I need to go search the police station…"

"Problem?" Diindiisi asked, following my gaze out the window.

There was nothing there. My brain was firing on five of six cylinders, and I just needed to stare at nothing for a few minutes.

"Just with me," I said. "Hang on a minute."

I went into the other apartment and grabbed my phone. It showed eighty-five percent charge and 'No Signal'. I unlocked it, then went to the contacts page. Sure enough, under the 'Emergency, Work' listings was one for San Marcos. It was a street address and a six-digit number.

"YES!" I shouted, heading into the other apartment again. "One of our problems may have a solution. Well, weapons and body armor, at least."

"Really?" Miller said.

"Yeah. The guy I work for in Austin, well the vampire that advises him anyway, is paranoid as fu...frag," I temporized. "Michelangelo has insisted that we set up emergency caches in the cities where we don't have an office."

"Wait a minute," Davis said. "Michelangelo? As in the artist and sculptor?"

"Well, I'm not talking about the Ninja Turtle," I said.

"He's a vampire?" Davis asked again.

"Yeah, and he's looking for the vampire who turned him. But that doesn't bear on what's happening now," I said.

While I'd been talking to Davis, Diindiisi left the room and came back wearing blue jeans and my tweed jacket. Under the jacket, she had a wide leather belt, with a long Bowie knife on the left, balancing the 1911 I'd given her on the right.

"Working clothes?" I asked.

"Except for the boots, yes," she replied. "I haven't been able to find a decent pair of riding boots since I entered the Shadow Lands. And the heels on most of the boots I've found are ridiculous for anything other than walking at a sedate pace."

"Could we swing by my dorm room at some point?" Dalma asked. "I'd like to pick up some clothes and my hunting boots."

"Right," I replied. "Father, if you'd re-do the protective wards when we leave?"

"I'll keep the research going as well," he said.

We trooped downstairs to the SUV, with one stop. I swung by the font, filling a pitcher, then filled the CamelBak in my armor.

"You're going to drink holy water?" Miller asked, watching, aghast.

"If I have to, yes. But I might need to seal a door or two, and ready-made is better than having to find water on the fly. The little bottles you gave me might not be enough," I said.

"I hadn't thought of that," he replied, watching the font refill. "Give me a minute to fill the aspergillum, then I'll follow you out.

We loaded and left, Miller sprinkling the driveway with holy water and chanting as we drove away. The address from my phone turned out to be down the alley from the Pearl.

I looked at the plain steel door set in the brick wall. There wasn't a door knob.

"How do we get in?" Dalma asked.

"Magic," I replied, sliding up the steel cover over the keypad next to the door. I fed it the code, and there was a clunk as the lock disengaged. The door opened.

"Oh my god," Dalma said, stepping inside. "I've gone to heaven."

"No, but close," I said.

Michelangelo was paranoid, but being almost six hundred years old would do that to a fellow. He was also right when it came to arms and armament. More is better. The caches had been established so that any two teams could roll up, replace all their weapons, ammunition, body armor, and other assorted implements of destruction, then return to the fight. There were even uniform and boot replacements – because there's nothing like trying to fight the undead bare assed and barefoot to ruin an otherwise perfect day.

"How big are your employers that they can afford this?" Diindiisi asked.

"Worldwide, ma'am. Most of this is actually paid for by the 'legal' side of things. QMG runs professional bodyguard services, charging a pretty penny for it. Then there's Group – governments and individuals pay us to protect the innocent from the things that go bump in the night. Most of the major churches, and quite a few minor ones throw money our way as well."

"All of this. Henry would be proud of what he founded," she said.

"Ma'am, that's the second time you've mentioned Henry. Do you mean Henry Keith?"

"Yes," she replied. "Do you know of him?"

"Ma'am, I've met him."

"He stopped hiding his secret?" she asked.

"Ma'am that 'secret' is probably the worst kept thing in the company, other than the number of vampires and other 'exotics' employed. He hasn't had to 'hide' that for fifty years or more," I said.

"Oh. Has society become that open?" she asked, looking at the stack of boxed boots.

"No'm. He's just protected by the company. And we don't care," I said, unlocking the gun cage.

"Dalma, I'm not sure there's a long arm here that'll fit your frame," I said. There were a pair of very long cases racked flat under the gun rack.

I slid one out.

"Heyyy now," Dalma said, looking at the case.

Inside was a Barrett M82. The full-sized, thirty pounds empty, fifty-seven-inch long version. There was even a suppressor in the case. The rifle, without suppressor, was six inches shorter than Dalma herself. She was salivating over the big Murfreesboro Five-O.

I could picture the argument, but I knew when I was beat.

"Put them in the SUV," I said with a sigh.

We cleared the cache. I did one last thing before leaving. There was a whiteboard on one wall, showing the dates of inspection. At the bottom, I wrote 'Ninja Pigeon' before we left.

"What's a 'Ninja Pigeon'?" Dalma asked as we were closing up the SUV.

"It's a joke from my time in Iraq," I replied. "A way of marking where I'd been."

"Surely there's more to it than that," Diindiisi said.

"There is. So I'd screwed up at one point, and rather than going formal and writing me up for Non Judicial Punishment my Gunny started giving me every shitty job he could think of – more to get my headspace and timing right than anything else," I started, going around the SUV and climbing in. "Anyway, we're way the hell out in the middle of nowhere, looking for weapons caches that Hajji had been burying everywhere in the Anbar. One of the terps comes over. . ."

"Hajji? Terps?" Diindiisi asked.

I coughed.

"Hajji was a name we had for the insurgents over there – most of them claimed to be devout Muslims, fighting the 'evil Americans' so, they got stuck with Hajji, the term for one of the faithful who'd made the trip to Mecca," I said. "And terps is just shorthand for Interpreters. So this terp comes over and says it looks like someone had been digging under this pigeon coop. Gunny and I go over and look at the pile of fossilized pigeon crap under the coop – and the local who owned it, who looked older than Moses. Anyway, sure enough it looks like someone has been digging under the coop, so guess who gets to crawl up under it and see what he can find?"

I pointed at myself.

"I crawl under there with a bayonet and start probing the disturbed area. Older than Moses is freaking out, because we're disturbing his pigeons. Before you ask, yes, the ones in the coop were shitting all over me. Cheesy, the translator, is losing his shit he's laughing so hard. Finally, I come crawling back out, covered in pigeon crap, the dust from pigeon crap, and crapped on pigeon feathers. Gunny's got a grin on his face. I reach into my pocket to pull out my lighter and light a cigarette and the first thing I find is a piece of fossilized pigeon poop. I lose control of my mouth and shout 'HOW THE HELL DID I GET PIGEON SHIT IN MY POCKET!'"

"And?" Dalma asked from the back seat.

"Gunny looks at me and says 'Ninja Pigeon', before walking back to the Humvee. Since we were Marines, that became my nickname, and I'd put it on whiteboards anywhere I saw one. Kinda like Kilroy was here in WWII," I said, making sure everyone had their seat belts on.

"Kilroy?" Diindiisi asked.

"I'll explain that one later," I said. "Let's just say there's a lot we need to catch you up on, leaving it at that for now."

The SUV had settled considerably on its suspension – they'd beefed up the frame when the armor went on but we'd probably added close to fifteen hundred pounds of ammo and weapons. Dalma and Diindiisi both had put on body armor, and Dalma had taken an UMP .45, while Diindiisi was carrying an 870 shotgun.

I made sure Dalma knew where the selector was, and prayed she'd keep it on 'semi' until we had time for training. I also took a moment to show Diindiisi where where the safety on the 870 was. Just in case.

"Let's go offload," I said, starting the SUV and trundling back down the alley.

"Jesse," Diindiisi said.

"I see it," I replied. It had started to rain ectoplasm, again. "Hang on."

I hit the brakes, then put the SUV in reverse.

"Raining back here too," Dalma said.

I mentally flipped a coin, then put it back in drive. I eased forward at a walk, waiting for the other shoe to drop. The SUV started to glow.

"Oh, that's not good," I said. "Weapons on safe, because this could get nasty."

The first daemon appeared at the head of the alley. There wasn't much room to accelerate, but I put the pedal to the floor, and the big Cummings diesel roared. The daemon didn't make it – the bumper folded him in half. We were rolling faster than the ectoplasm was withdrawing from the blessings on the SUV, so we fishtailed on the ectoplasm at the alley entrance. I got the SUV under control, but not before I hit three parked cars.

"That's going to be fun to explain," I shouted.

We were straight again. Pointed in the wrong direction, admittedly, but straight. I goosed it. We clipped three more daemons as we accelerated out of the Square, east on Hopkins.

"They're following us," Dalma called from the back seat. "I can shoot at them if you want."

"DON'T!" I shouted. "The windows are armored. I knew we should have rigged the Golf, even if it meant you driving, Dalma."

Diindiisi sniffed.

"What's a Golf?" she asked.

"Machine gun," I replied. "Technically an M240G, and Golf is from the military alphabet."

"Ah. But why would Dalma have to drive?"

"Can you drive?" I asked.

"A team? Yes. An automobile? Honestly, no," she replied. "I'd give it a try, but I never learned. Although Amelia and Fred offered to teach me once. There weren't many cars on that island, and we couldn't find the keys for the ones that were there, though. And the few horses that have come through to the Shadow Lands are never quite right after the experience."

She sighed. "Poor animals."

"Wait, Amelia and Fred?" Dalma asked. "Earhart and Noonan?"

"Yes," Diindiisi said.

"How long have you..."

"HANG ON!" I shouted again. We'd run out of downtown and shot past the San Marcos Public library.

I slung a left-hand turn at sixty, rocking the SUV on its suspension, then barreled down Charles S. Austin Drive, foot firmly planted on the firewall.

"SLOW THE FUCK DOWN!" Dalma screamed. "THE RAILROAD TRACKS!"

"SHIT!" I shouted, remembering the tracks.

Coming from the other direction, the tracks were steep, but doable. From this side they were a ramp. At eighty and climbing, we caught air. It wasn't for long, probably only two Tahoe lengths, but it was still air. We hit and grounded the suspension before continuing down the road.

"Anything close by?" I asked, taking my foot out of the firewall.

"No, why?"

I slid the Tahoe to a stop.

"Cover me,' I said, stepping out and doing a quick walk around. Nothing was obviously leaking.

I opened the back door and grabbed the case with the M240. Inside, along with the gun was a clamp-on mount.

"Dalma, grab two boxes of seven six two belted from the back, huh?" I said, hitting the button on the door to open the sunroof.

It wasn't a real ring mount. But with some effort you could fire backward or forward, as needed.

"I'm driving?" Dalma asked, throwing the two cans on the seat.

"Yeah, you drive from here," I said, clamping the mount in place. I pulled the M240 out of the case, slapping it in place, then rigged a belt. "Since I'm going to be standing on the back seat and all. Try not to take my head off with a branch, huh?"

"Can't be worse than your driving," she replied.

"I also don't have a harness," I said. "So take it slow, huh?"

She stepped on the accelerator, revving the engine to redline. She followed that by driving off at a very sedate pace. She even used the turn signal to turn left on Aquarena Springs, waiting for the light.

"Did you see any traffic?" I asked, dumbfounded.

"No, but that doesn't mean things operate the same way here that they do in the real world. Besides, one of your coworkers could be coming from the other direction," she said, seriously.

I broke up laughing. "You win. Just get us there in one piece."

She took a roundabout route back to the funeral home. Along the way we could see evidence of other desecrations – two churches stood blackened, and one strip center was burned to the ground.

"That's a break in the pattern," Diindiisi said.

"How so?" I shouted.

"Normally there's a reason for the destruction. That looks random," Diindiisi said.

"Wonder if the daemons have something against coffee shops," Dalma said. "There was one in that building, along with a pie shop."

"Who knows what drives the minds of the creatures of the Shadow Lands," Diindiisi said.

"Jesse?" Dalma said.

"Yeah?"

"Can we stop by my dorm? We'll go past it on the way back, I swear."

"Yes. I'll stay down here and cover the vehicle while you and Diindiisi go in. Be quick about it, huh?"

"Yes," she replied, hitting the turn signal and turning left. We tooled around and up hills until we arrived at Smith Hall, where she and Diindiisi left the vehicle. I was trying to cover 360 degrees by myself when I heard a short, sharp burst of fire from the building they'd entered, followed by two shots from a shotgun.

I hadn't quite decided whether I was going to disconnect the Golf and enter the building when the emergency exit opened, and Dalma and Diindiisi came trotting down the stairs.

"What happened?" I asked as they both jumped in the front seat.

Dalma tossed a Hello Kitty backpack in the seat at my feet.

"Oh there were a couple of imps there," Diindiisi said. "Dalma wanted to check the sights on her gun, so...."

"And I wanted to see how bad it rose on full auto," Dalma said. "I've never shot one before."

"Next time warn me, huh?" I said, as we pulled out of the parking lot and headed to the funeral home. "I almost came inside."

"That might have been suboptimal," Dalma said.

"No, really?"

"Well, yeah," she replied.

I swear, I could hear her rolling her eyes at me.

"Jesse, I'm confused," Diindiisi said.

"How?"

"I thought you were a priest," she said.

"I am ordained, yes," I said.

"Yet, you swear," she replied.

"Yeah, that. I was a Marine before I became a priest. Sometimes in high stress situations, the Marine comes to the fore," I said. "My bishop sees it as a weakness of mine. My team lead thinks it's funny. And my boss doesn't care as long as I get the job done."

"That makes sense," Diindiisi said. "Your bishop sounds like a throwback to my time. The rest sound practical."

"Practical is what works in this business, unfortunately," I said as we turned into the funeral home parking lot. "Hold up a second."

Dalma stopped, and I hopped down, then reset the ward we'd broken by crossing it.

"Go ahead and pull up to the garage," I said. I'll look for leaks while you're driving."

Everyone helped unload, and I found a mechanic's creeper in the garage, and rolled under the SUV looking for damage.

Miller was waiting for me when I wheeled out from under the back axle.

"Find anything?" he asked.

"No. And it ran ok on the way back, but I wanted to be sure," I said.

"How well do you know Diindiisi?" he asked abruptly.

"Met her here. I vaguely remember her being mentioned during training. Other than that, not well, why?"

"She's mentioned in the archives I've got. Three times," he said.

"Ok, give."

"First time is for a work she co-authored about the Shadow Lands in," he checked a note, "1908. Rare piece."

"Ok, that would explain her knowledge. Well, that and spending over a hundred years here," I said, sitting up on the creeper.

"Her biography is very interesting. She shouldn't be what she is," he said somewhat sternly.

"How so?" I asked.

"Her people look down on women of power," Miller replied.

"Much like your church looks down on female priests, Father," Diindiisi said, walking from the garage, and handing me a glass of water.

"Yes, but…" Miller started.

"But what? Is there a test you'd like me to perform? Hot iron, perhaps? Or I know, I can drink from the font," Diindiisi said. "If I don't melt or fade away, would that prove I'm on the side of right to you, Father Miller?"

"No, no test is needed," Miller replied. "I …just wanted Jesse to be aware that you are mentioned in the Church Archives, relating to fighting evil."

"Did you tell him about the wendigo?" she asked, opening the back door on the Tahoe and sitting on the bumper.

I smacked my head with my hand.

"Wendigo, that's why your name is familiar," I said. "Jack the Ripper, right?"

"Yes," they both said.

"You've heard of it, then," Diindiisi said.

"Yes, they spend a couple of days on the case in training. As an illustration of why you shouldn't get locked into one kind of thinking when dealing with the monstrous," I said.

"Well, the two vampires running around London at that point didn't help things," she said.

"Two vampires?" Miller asked.

"Yes. Two. Doctor van Helsing and his companions chased the elder one to earth in Transylvania and permanently inhumed him, losing Quentin Morris in the process, and then told a slightly modified version of the story to an Irish author. Henry Keith and I tracked the second one down in 1891 and eliminated him as a threat," she replied.

"What do the vampires have to do with a wendigo?" Miller asked.

"The elder vampire? Nothing. The second? He was using the wendigo to cover his feeding habits. And hadn't realized that we'd killed the wendigo before returning to London and resuming his behavior."

"I see," Miller said. "That fills in some gaps in the archives as well. Why didn't the Quintus Society release all that data to the church then?"

"Given the animosity between the Catholic Church and the Anglican Church at the time? There was some discussion about giving your Church the information even back then, which ultimately went nowhere," she said. "Father Miller, I'm not a prostitute, nor am I a minion of Satan. I really just want to get back to the real world. If I can't do that, then working with you will suffice."

"I apologize for my mistrust," Miller said. "I just wasn't sure, and that makes me nervous."

"Understand completely," I said. "Now that we've worked that out, what's for lunch?"

***

After lunch, Padgett drove us to his house so he could pick up some clothes. And we ran into a problem.

"That's new," Padgett said, looking at the specter standing in front of the house. "Well, not really. It's just the first time I've actually seen him."

"Let me guess, the house is haunted," I snarked.

"Yeah, you could say that. Usually something that's throwing things around at three am, not standing there with a grim expression," he said. "Things were really bad for a while when the ghost found the litter box. He was literally flinging shit at us for a while. Then the cat protested, I guess, and that stopped."

"Yeah, cats can have that effect on ghosts, from time to time," I said.

"Let me try something," Diindiisi said. She reached into the leather bindle she'd brought along and took out some sage.

"Uh, last time someone tried smudging him out, he really got pissed off," Padgett said.

"Smudging?" Diindiisi asked.

"Yeah, lighting sage on fire and waving it about to 'clear the negative waves' or some other bullshit," Padgett replied.

"I wasn't going to light it," Diindiisi said with a chuckle.

She took a stem out of the bundle of sage, and stripped the leaves, crushing them before casting them to the winds. She then walked over near the specter, holding a low voiced conversation with him.

Padgett looked at me.

"You see a lot of this in your line of work, Father?" he asked.

"Nope. First time. Usually ghosts aren't worth the effort – sure we can exorcise them, but unless they're a major league poltergeist, most of them don't do damage. Most folks don't even see them, most of the time," I replied.

Diindiisi bowed to the ghost, who stepped aside. She waved Padgett over, then followed him inside. They came out a few minutes later with several bags. Padgett dumped the bags in the back seat then ran inside again. Diindiisi started shifting the load around in the back of the SUV.

"I've got to ask…"

"I talked to the spirit," she replied. "Asked his permission. He's actually quite the gentleman."

"So what was the sage for?"

"To clear my mind and help me focus. Honestly, the smoke sets my teeth on edge," she laughed.

I smiled back.

"Do me a favor?" I asked while we were waiting on Padgett to bring out the third and final load.

"Sure. What?"

"Step up to the driver's side, and turn the key to 'ACC', then look at the fuel gauge. It should be the one on the top left, above the one that looks like an oil lamp," I said.

I heard the ignition click.

"Just above a quarter tank," she said. "If I'm reading the markings correctly."

"What's up?" Padgett called from the porch.

"Gonna need to fuel up before we head back," I said. "Any place close to get diesel?"

"Yeah, couple places out by the highway. How're you going to pay for it?" he asked.

"We're not. We are going to swing by Farmall Supply, however, before we head back to the casa," I said.

"What the hell are we getting at Farmall Supply?" he asked.

"Pumps," I replied. "And then we're going to learn how to pump out a fuel tank without power."

"That sounds like work," he said.

"Oh, it is," I replied.

"I'm getting paid for this, right?" he asked.

"Oh, at some point, if we make it back to the real world, we'll talk fiduciary recompense," I said as he climbed into the front seat and started the Tahoe.

"That sounds frightening and downright sexy at the same time," he replied, dropping the SUV into gear and driving off. The specter had taken up a guarding position, again.

"When we make it back, the experts are going to want to pick your brain, and well, they'll pay a lot of money to talk with you," I replied. "That's not including if you find you want to go to work for QMG and Group." I waved to the ghost.

He waved back. It was that kind of day.

"What is Group?" Padgett and Diindiisi both asked over the wind roar.

"It's the unofficial name for those of us who kill monsters. Officially we're personal security specialists, just like every other body guard working for QMG. But back in the 1960's and 1970's, the company hired a bunch of former Special Forces Operators. I'm not sure there's a historical reference for SF," I said to answer Diindiisi's obvious question. "They're good at sneaking around and killing things, as well as talking with and teaching the locals how to do the same. Anyway, most of the guys they hired came from First Special Forces Group, which they'd just called Group while they were in the service, and the nickname stuck," I said.

"OK," Padgett shouted back. "Hang on."

Ahead, there was a short rain of fish.

"Well, great, Fortean Phenomenon," I said as Padgett slalomed around the fish flopping on the concrete.

"Stop a minute," I heard Diindiisi say.

Padgett slid the SUV to a stop, Diindiisi hopped out, and ran back to the fish pile. She grabbed three or four of the largest, then carried them back to the SUV, tossing them into the back.

"I haven't had salmon in years," she said. "Well, that didn't come out of a can. Nasty stuff, that."

"Dinner tonight I guess," I said as Padgett rolled back towards the funeral home.

Chapter Four
Day 4, 6 April 2018

I waited a day to raid Farmall Supply. We'd need a way to hold the pumps once they'd been dipped in fuel – I wasn't going to chance a fire in the vehicles because some daemon got lucky with a hunk of fuel soaked carpet. Besides, I'd been there, done that in Iraq.

And the ball for the Tahoe's trailer hitch was buried under all of Padgett's gear, and Diindiisi's fish.

So, on an electric gray Thursday morning (so far they'd all been electric gray, but who was counting) we started out on an all hands evolution to raid Farmall Supply.

Everyone was kitted out – Davis had refused a weapon other than his bat, so he was the designated hitter – seriously though, he was humping a huge pack of medical gear for Dalma, who in addition to her talents behind a rifle was a third year nursing student at Texas State.

While we were getting ready, I'd gone ahead and pulled the last bit of kit out of my case – my mace.

"Wait a minute, Father," Davis said, eyeing the footman's mace I tossed in the back of the Tahoe.

"Yes?"

"Why a mace? You've already got the honking great knife," he said, gesturing. "Besides, I thought you guys couldn't carry blade weapons."

"Ah, D&D again," I said.

I handed him the mace.

"There are a couple things Gygax got wrong. This weighs about the same as your bat," I said. "More than my bolo here. And does more damage than most swords. You take one of these to the knee and your walking days are probably over, let alone your adventuring days."

"So you should be using this instead of the blade, then," he said.

"Yeah, except you ever try to behead a staked vampire with a sledge hammer?"

"Well, no, and that doesn't sound like it'd work," he replied.

"Oh, it won't, trust me," I said. "But a mace to the face will slow down most rampaging monsters. Ruins their whole day, honestly. And it's less likely to stick. The bolo is for after we've got the monsters manageable."

"Oh. I see, I think," Davis said.

"You guys ready to roll?" Dalma asked. She was carrying an UMP, but insisted on tossing one of the cased Barrett's and a box of fifty cal in the back.

She was also driving the Tahoe so I could man the Golf, again. I really needed to find a better vehicle and bless it for travelling around town. I'd pulled the windows out last night in hopes of getting rid of the fish smell. It hadn't worked. It'd air out eventually, like the Humvee the terp had puked in, but for now there was a lingering pong of fish.

We'd lead, and Father Miller, along with Diindiisi and Padgett would follow in the van. If things went to hell, they were to run while we slowed the monsters down. It wasn't my best plan by far, but it was the closest we'd get to perfect, here and now.

I slammed the tailgate shut, then climbed into the back seat. Plan was we'd go out the south side of the parking lot, pause for Father Miller to reset the wards, then roll by the direct route to Farmall Supply. We hadn't seen any showers of ectoplasm this morning, so, so far, so good.

I put a set of noise cancelling earplugs in – I'd shown everyone how to work the built in radios last night, then decided to leave them all on 'open'. It meant a lot of noise, but it was better than someone forgetting to key the mike at the wrong moment.

"Go," I said.

We rolled. And stopped. And waited while Miller did the wards again. I will admit, his gestures were cleaner than mine. But I was used to using, to misquote George Carlin, the version of the wards you did as you were going under the bus. Miller waved and jumped back in the van. I nudged the front seat and off we went, signaling every turn.

It should have been a simple trip. Problem was the short route, which we were taking due to fuel status, cut through the square. Every time we'd been through the Square something had found us. And I wasn't sure that either Dalma or Padgett was up to combat driving. All the way to the Farmall Supply, I was nervous. Nothing. We pulled up in the parking lot, and dodged the cars there, finally stopping in front of the trailers lined along the fence.

Where they were chained, of course.

We dismounted, and Miller sprinkled holy water around the vehicles. I looked things over.

"Do you have a plan?" Miller asked when he was done.

"Yeah. We need two pumps, manual ones if they have them, and at least one trailer. I'd be ecstatic if they had a couple of fuel tanks we could put on the trailer, but at this point, I'm not going to hold out hope. A couple of sprayers would be nice, too," I said.

"Sprayers?"

"Yes, sprayers. Delivering holy water at a distance since the early days," I grinned. "Oh, and a universal key or three."

"What's a universal key?" Dalma asked.

"Set of bolt cutters. If he asks for a hot wrench, he's asking for a cutting torch," Miller replied. "Marine joke."

"Hey, now, gear adrift is a gift,' I said. "And if I can cut it loose or pry it up, it's adrift."

Miller sighed.

"It's for a good cause," I said.

"What good cause is that?" Miller asked.

"Me, not getting eaten by a slavering grue. I've got to admit, that's my favorite cause," I said.

"You're incorrigible," Miller replied, before walking towards the door.

"My bishop says the same thing," I replied. "And nothing personal, let me go first."

"After you," he said, holding the door.

Tools first. We had a list, grabbing a couple of bags.

There was noise from the back.

I held up a fist, then realized that no one could probably read the hand signals. Training on tactical hand signals, right after training on firearms.

"Y'all wait here," I said, slipping down the aisle towards the back.

There was something, hulking, at the back of the store. It was making slurping noises as it fed, probably on another person who'd fallen into the Shadow Lands. It stopped feeding, one arm raised and sniffed.

"Fuck," I whispered.

It spun and stood. It stood about eight feet tall, and covered in lank, red fur. The head was ball shaped, with an orange nose, with a mouth that took up the remainder of the head. In one of its arms it held a human leg, torn loose from the hip socket. The other arm hung loosely at its side. It sniffed again.

"Is that ...Elmo?" Dalma whispered from behind me.

"No. It's his daemon possessed cousin, though. And I thought I told you to stay up front," I hissed back.

"Diindiisi thought you might need help. I won the toss," Dalma replied.

The monster sniffed one last time and roared, shaking dust from the suspended ceiling.

Something outside answered.

"Well, hell," I said.

Dalma pulled the trigger. I'll give her this – her aim was good. She had the selector on "Full", however, and the burst climbed from the red thing's chest over its shoulder, and into the wall and ceiling beyond, before the bolt clattered and locked back.

"Bursts," I shouted, swinging my UMP up and firing short, three round bursts.

I started with Eat Me Messily Elmo's knees, being a follower of Shepherd Book. It crashed to the ground as Dalma fumbled the reload. It was by no means dead. It was, however, seriously pissed off at this point. The body started squirming as it reconstructed itself.

I dumped the rest of the magazine into its maw, then pulled out the bolo on my left hip.

Three hard chops and the head rolled free. Dalma got the magazine seated, ran the bolt home with a proper HK slap.

"You ok?" came across my earphones.

"Yeah," I replied as something crashed through the front of the building.

I looked at Dalma.

"Pull the trigger, count three, release, rinse, repeat, until the mag runs dry, then replace, got it?" I asked. OJT combat training sucks.

"Yes," she replied.

Diindiisi's shotgun boomed, followed by the pistols carried by Padgett and Miller.

"Follow me," I said, praying she'd keep the muzzle elevated and her booger flinger off the bullet switch.

I watched a cash register and counter go flying. Diindiisi's shotgun boomed again, and something spun off and squelched into a wall. There was a pause, and a screech.

"COMING THROUGH!" I shouted before joining the scrum up front.

This thing was covered in greasy green fur and stank of garbage.

"I do not want to kill characters from my childhood," Dalma shouted.

"Get to work!" I shouted back. "Remember short bursts!"

We joined the party. Finally we put enough silver into the thing that it stayed down long enough for me to remove its head.

"Anyone hit?" I asked.

No one was. But the front of the store was a mess — greasy green fur hung in hunks, and there was goo and bits of body and goo everywhere.

"Catch your breath, count your ammo, and take five. We've still got to load the van and trailer," I said.

The green monster started to deliquesce.

"Oh my God! I'm gonna be sick!" Miller said.

"Aim out and try not to puke on one of the aisles we've got to go down," I said.

Miller dashed off down an aisle of 'farm clothes'.

"That was somewhat cold," Diindiisi said.

"Yup. I'll be nice later," I said as Miller was noisily sick.

"Are we going to see a lot of that?" Padgett asked Diindiisi.

"A lot of what?" she replied.

"Monsters shaped like, well, characters from our childhood?"

"Yes," she replied. "With a few caveats. We'll probably see a lot of things that take on a twisted form of something popular in your time. I once watched a pair of Billikens take out a Kewpie shortly after I arrived here."

"Ma'am?" Davis asked. "What's a Billiken?"

She reached into a pocket and pulled out a pouch. From the pouch she shook out a one inch figure and handed it to Davis. He looked at it, then passed it around. The figure was a seated baby, with a pointed head. The face was minimal – slanted slashes for eyes and a bump of a nose over a toothless grin.

"That's kinda frightening, all by itself," Dalma said, handing the figure back to Diindiisi. "Why do you carry it?"

"It's lucky," Diindiisi said. "Sam Clemons gave it to me when I met him in 1909."

"Wait, you met Mark Twain?" Davis asked.

"Yes," Diindiisi replied. "He'd gotten a bit far afield when his daughters died, and Henry and I visited him to help him get over it."

"Not to change the subject, but things are going to get weird, then," I said.

"Yes. Very," Diindiisi replied.

"So, a QMG Tuesday," I said, sighing.

"I'm fine, thanks," Miller said, coming back from where he'd been painting the tiles.

I tossed him a bottle of water from a cooler that had somehow survived the destruction in the front of the store.

"Good. You hear the discussion?"

"Yeah. I knew that things like this could happen, I just wasn't prepared for the, the reality," he replied before cracking the bottle and rinsing his mouth out. "I think I am now."

"Right then, we've got work to do," I said.

I went and found a set of bolt cutters and went out the front door. It wasn't raining ectoplasm locally, but I could see an area where it was. We needed to get things done and get the hell out of here.

I chuckled at the thought, then went and cut the chain holding the largest trailer to a bollard.

Well, the lock, anyway. It would have taken a stronger pair of bolt cutters, and someone muscled like Hercules to cut the chain.

"Hey, Jesse, you know how to operate a forklift?" Davis asked, coming over where I was coiling the chain before tossing it onto the trailer.

"No, why?"

"Well, there's a couple of thousand gallon fuel 'cubes' in there. "But we need a forklift to load them on the trailer."

"We'd need a forklift to unload them on the other end as well," I said.

"Hadn't thought about that. Good news is there's a forklift in there," he said.

"Just the things we talked about for now, John, ok?" I said, walking over to the Tahoe.

I backed it into place and hooked on the trailer as they started bringing the first loads out – bags of tools and bins of various items. The bags and bins went into the van until it was loaded, then we started on the trailer. I went back inside to find some cargo straps to tie everything down.

"Father Salazar?" Dalma called from farther inside the store.

"What's up?" I asked, walking to the sound of her voice.

"Would this help?" she asked, when I finally got to where she was.

She'd found the 'Hunting Equipment' section of the store. There was a pallet of twelve gauge bird shot in the middle of the floor, separating it from the rest of the area.

"Man, if Diindiisi's right, there's going to be some very pissed people on the other side," I said. "Cause we're clearing this section out, best we can."

"There's a couple of reloading sets as well," Dalma said. "I found setups for everything except the fifty cal."

"Bless you my child," I said before heading back to the front of the store so we could change plans and work this bounty into our load out.

Chapter Five
Day 7, 6 April 2018

After breakfast, it was training time. No live fire, but how to scoot and shoot. How not to stack up in doorways. And what the damn hand signals meant.

"Um, isn't this why we've got radios?" Davis asked at one point, having missed the signal for him to hose the target (a coffin, hey it's a funeral home, ok?) down with 'holy water' again.

"Yes and no," I replied. "Look, everyone grab a seat."

I waited while they sat down on the ground. Father Miller was inside, running searches on his Codex. Everyone else was outside with me, running drills.

"So, let's talk about yesterday in the Farmall. If you were carrying the pump then and I pointed to you, followed by the shotgun signal, and then pointed where Eat You Messily Elmo was standing, what do you think I'd have meant?"

"Hose the monster?" he replied.

"Hose the monster," I said. "Which would have been a lot quieter than saying it, even over the radio. And a hell of a lot quieter than what ended up happening. We might not have had to fight the second daemon if the first hadn't made all that noise before we shot the damn thing to doll rags."

"Ok, that makes sense," Davis said.

"That's why we're going over it," I said. "Now, let's do it again."

Wash, rinse, repeat.

Lunch came, and we ate. Miller had some news. Neither good nor bad, just news.

"So, it looks like we're not the first people recorded as having disappeared," he said.

"Oh?" Diindiisi asked.

"Yes, the earliest disappearance recorded is that of Benjamin Bathurst, an English Envoy to Germany in 1809. There were probably other earlier examples, but Bathurst seems to have been the first one to make a splash, supernaturally. There are some records from both branches of the Quintus Society about the investigation, if you can read the early 19th century prose," Miller said.

"And Diindiisi told us about Earhart and Noonan the other day," Dalma said.

"Yes. Could we talk about them later?" Miller asked Diindiisi.

"If you'd like," she replied. "I don't know much about their actual disappearance, just what they told me."

"That'd be fine – I'd be able to update the Codex on their disappearance. There's been a lot of arguments about what happened to them. There was a report of strange phenomenon in the region from a Jesuit, but not a lot of support for it," Miller said.

"So, we know people have come through to this side," I said. "What about returning?"

"Yes, that," Miller said with a frown. "I haven't found any good sources on a return, actually. And the only source that records one was written by Diindiisi here."

She smiled.

"Yes, Boston Corbett, the poor man," she said. "Escaped from an insane asylum, then disappeared. We'd heard he might be alive in Minnesota and tracked him there. He confirmed to me that he'd spent two years or so in the Shadow Lands before returning."

"How did he do it?" Miller asked.

"He said his great purity led God to show him the way back," she replied, primly. "Honestly, he was a bit strange. The man castrated himself after an encounter with a pair of prostitutes, after all. Didn't even have sex with them, just talked to them on the street."

"CAS – sorry, castrated himself?" Padgett asked.

"Yes. With a pair of scissors. Even went to church and had a meal before seeking medical attention," Diindiisi said.

"That is totally hard corps," Dalma said.

"Totally loony corps, " I replied. "Were you able to get anything other than 'God' about his return?"

"No. The Great Hinckley Fire started shortly after we'd gotten him to talk to us about it, and he perished in the fire," she said. "Henry and I barely escaped the fire, ourselves."

I looked at her. There was a faraway look in her eyes.

"Besides, he didn't have a lot of useful information for us. His time in the asylum had strengthened his faith but it ground away at his sanity further. He thought his two years here had been a gift from God, and he hadn't seen any daemons or other creatures. Who knows? He might have been right, after all."

"Ah. I've got to ask, though, was the fire that bad?" I asked.

"Yes. Rail cars melted to the rails. Barrels of nails melted into a single mass. We barely escaped. If Henry hadn't survived the Great London Fire, I don't know that we'd have made it out. Before you ask, yes, it was an efreet that started the fire. Some rich idiot had brought one back from a trip to the Middle East, and it had escaped his control, and wasn't in a giving mood," she said. "Hopefully it got the idiot first, but the way that luck works, he probably survived without a clue of what he'd unleashed."

"That's one thing that hasn't changed," I said.

"What's that," she asked.

"Rich idiots buying things they can't understand," I replied.

"Dayum," Padgett said. "What else is real?"

"Oh, if you've seen it in a movie or read it in a book, it's probably out there," I said.

"Dracula?"

"Yes, killed by Van Helsing. He and his surviving companions founded the company that led to QMG," I said. "Although, when they told the story to Stoker, they, shall we say, embellished it a bit, and moved it in time to avoid the obvious connections to the Ripper case."

"Frankenstein's monster?"

"Yeah, he's a whiney, emo little bitch," Miller said, looking around. "What? I've met him. The Church keeps him locked up so he doesn't run amok. He spends most of his days whining about it and trying to convince his keepers he won't go on another killing rampage."

"Dragons?"

"Rare, but they exist," I said. "Mostly in places where they won't have a lot of human contact these days – tops of high mountains, and such. Mostly the Chinese type, too."

"Why's that?" Davis asked.

"Because knights in Europe followed the model of Saint George the Dragon Slayer, hunting the European dragons to near extinction."

"Oh. What about Elves?"

"Yeah, sorta. Most of the Fae are withdrawn into enclaves where they don't have to deal with humans. The ones you meet who aren't working for the company or the Church? They're about as trustworthy as a late night TV pitchman. As a matter of fact, some of those guys are part Fae at a minimum," I said.

"That explains a lot," Dalma said. "Anything else we need to look out for?"

"Yes," Diindiisi temporized. "What was that, DVD I think you called it, we watched the other night? The one in New York City where they fought the giant made of marshmallows?"

We were killing time watching DVDs and Blu-ray. Diindiisi had loved them and was catching up on over a century's worth of entertainment, along with some documentaries. I'd also introduced her to the term binge watching.

"*Ghostbusters?*"

"Yes, *Ghostbusters*. While some of the things we'll face here have a fixed form, like the daemon you killed when you arrived, some won't take form until you see them. They're going to pick a form you esteem, then twist it, to make you suffer more," Diindiisi said.

"Which explains Oscar the Homicidal Muppet and Eat Your Face Elmo," Dalma said, sighing.

"Yes. There are also going to be some manifestations that are, like the ghost at your residence, John Padgett, tied to the other world. If we had a listing of all the sites here," she started.

"Yeah, that's not going to happen," I said. "If I remember correctly, it's thought there have been people living here for 13000 years or so. There's no telling what was holy to who over that period."

"That could be a problem, yes," Diindiisi said with a slight smile.

"Not to change the subject," Davis said.

"But to change the subject," Dalma replied.

"Well, yeah. You said something about wanting to get some different vehicles last night, Jesse," he said, turning to me.

"Yeah, something that actually had a mount for the Golf would be nice," I said.

"What about the Guard Armory?" he asked.

"The what where?" I replied.

"The National Guard Armory," he replied. "It's down by the river, next to the Public Library. There's some sort of tank parked outside."

"Oh my," I said, with visions of avarice flashing before my eyes.

"Greed is a sin," Miller said, not even looking up from his book.

"Yes, yes it is," I replied. "And it's a shortcoming, I know. I'll talk to God about it in a bit. But, we need to check things out."

Miller sighed.

"Full court press?" he asked.

I thought. "Hmm, we'll take the Tacticool Tahoe and one spare driver for now, I think. If we find something, we'll bring it back, then go from there.

"Take two," he replied.

"Err?" I asked, raising an eyebrow at him.

"Take two spares. That way, if you run into something, you've got a shooter in both vehicles," he replied.

"You, know, Father Miller, for someone not of the Church Very Militant, you're coming along nicely," I said. "Who wants to go for a ride?"

"I can't drive, but I can shoot," Diindiisi said.

"You've got my bow," Padgett said with a grin.

No, we hadn't gotten to the *Fellowship of the Rings*, yet. So we'd probably be explaining the joke to Diindiisi, then watching the movie. Oh well. I could think of worse things to watch. The Bollywood version of *Superman* leapt to mind for some reason.

"I'm game," Dalma said. "Boring, sitting around here doing nothing."

"Right then, meet y'all downstairs in ten minutes," I said.

Ten minutes later we were rolling. We'd learned a few things, adapting a few things I'd learned doing patrols in Iraq to local conditions. While our approaches to the funeral home were limited by street layout (only two ways to get there), we had a whole lot of options for getting to and from it once we got off Comanche or Hutchinson. Today, it was north a short way on Comanche, then right on Pat Garrison, then straight on till morning. Or there about. Things were quiet.

Too quiet. There was an oppressive quality to the air, once we got away from the funeral home.

"Anyone else feel like something's going on?" Dalma asked over the radio.

"Yeah," Padgett replied.

"Keep your eyes open," I replied as we crossed the San Marcos River.

I realized Diindiisi was chanting under her breath as we turned into the Armory.

"Wait for it," I said when Padgett put the SUV in park.

He'd swung around the building and was pointed back towards the street. Escape parking, like emergency pants, was something we'd started practicing.

"There!" Dalma shouted, pointing to the river.

"You have got to be fucking kidding me," Padgett said, looking over his shoulder. "Is that a fucking koi?"

I turned around on the seat I was standing on, stepping on Dalma in the process.

"Sorry," I said in passing. Sure enough, I could see the head and fore body of a large white fish with a red patch on its head.

"Damn, that's big as a semi," Padgett said, putting the Tahoe back in gear.

The fish swam downstream and around the bend.

"Right," I said, unlocking the M240, and laying it on the roof behind me. I followed it out, then handed it to Diindiisi before jumping down. "Padgett, you and Dalma stay here. If the fish comes back, fire a warning shot, but get the hell outta here, then come back for Diindiisi and me, huh?"

I grabbed the 'entry kit' we'd put together, really wishing there had been some C4 in the cache.

"Right. Let y'all get eaten by the big nasty fish while we bravely run away," Dalma snarked, popping up through the sunroof.

"Something like that, yes," I grinned back.

The Armory had probably originally been built in the 1930's – it had the look of something built by the Civilian Construction Corps. But through the years, it had been updated, in part to probably 'soften' its look. I took a quick glance at the 'tank' parked outside. It was a self propelled artillery piece. I didn't even think about trying to take it.

Too heavy, and I'd never trained as a cannon cocker. So, I turned back to the doors. The main doors were tempered glass. I reached into the medium, bright red tool bag we'd assembled and pulled out a four pound cross peen hammer, smiled at Diindiisi, and threw the hammer into the glass of the door. The glass crazed and deformed around the hammer, the plastic inner layer keeping the hammer from penetrating. I picked up the hammer and swung it into the dimple caused by the first toss. The glass broke, and I hooked it with the hammer, pulling it out of the frame.

I turned and bowed to Diindiisi. She sniffed. The sniff said 'Men'. She then walked over, pulling the other door open, and avoiding the broken glass, entered the building.

"Shit," I said, following her into the building. "How'd you know the door was unlocked?"

"I didn't until I saw it bounce when the hammer hit it," she said.

"Why didn't you say anything?"

"You looked like you wanted to show off," she replied.

We followed the signs to the garage. Inside there were two squat, ugly, up armored Humvees.

"YES!" I shouted at the ceiling. They both had turrets.

"I take it these are what you were hoping for?" Diindiisi asked.

"All that and a bag of chips," I replied. I saw the look on her face. "I'll explain later."

"Do we need to find the keys?" she asked.

"No. These are Government Issue vehicles. No keys," I replied, swinging the driver's side door open.

The steering wheel was 'locked' with a chain run from a staple in the floor, up through the steering wheel, then back down to the staple. It took about ten seconds to pop the lock with a set of bolt cutters and toss the chain into the back of the Humvee. I twisted the starter, and it farted to life.

"Bingo!" I said.

I let the engine idle for a minute then cut it off, opened the back door and climbed into the turret.

"Wrong mount," I said, dropping out and going to the other Humvee.

"Mount?" Diindiisi asked.

"Yeah, it's what holds the gun," I said, climbing into the second Humvee. "Same problem here – they're both rigged for Ma Deuce. Wonder if they've got the other mounts in the vault."

I strode from the garage towards the weapons vault.

"What's a Ma Deuce?" Diindiisi asked.

"Browning heavy machine gun, model M2," I said, staring at the door to the weapons vault.

The door looked thick.

"We're going to have to go to plan B," I said.

"What's that?" she asked.

"Go back to the funeral home and get that cutting torch rig I picked up, because there is no way in hell I'm getting through that wall with what's in the bag," I replied resignedly.

Twenty minute round trip and we were back at work. Miller and Davis had come with us this go round, leaving in the second Humvee. Padgett and Dalma were back on over watch outside, and Diindiisi was looking for things to take with us when we left – we'd have room.

I'm not a dab hand with a cutting torch. It took about an hour to cut through the door. For comedic purposes, Diindiisi should have shown up with the keys about the time the door fell to the floor, but even in limbo God's sense of humor wasn't quite that bad. I wheeled the torch rig back out to the Tacticool Tahoe, and got Padgett to help me load it in the back, then went inside. The door had cooled enough that I could step inside the vault.

"Holy Saint John Moses Browning," I said, crossing myself.

There were two M2's in the vault. No ammo, but that didn't stop me from getting Padgett to help load the eighty three pound beasts in the back of the Humvee. We also loaded a few odds and ends, and both the Golf mounts. I swapped the mount out, dropping and locking the Golf in place on the turret.

"That's oddly beautiful," Padgett said, watching me finish up.

"Yeah. Who's driving?" I asked feeding a belt of silver core ammo into the Golf.

"Dalma. She won."

"Won?"

"Yeah, we did rock, paper, scissors for it. I threw scissors. She threw rock."

"Well, there's always tomorrow."

"Yeah," he replied. "Where are you going to get ammo for the big guns?"

"Ma Deuce? No idea. But I find them comforting, I guess," I replied.

He snapped his fingers.

"I must be losing my mind," he said.

"Occupational hazard when one deals with the strange and unusual," I said.

"No, there's this place out Ranch Road 12 towards Johnson City," he said. "Opened up oh, a couple years back. They have machine guns you can rent and fire."

Be still my beating heart, because there's always someone rich frat boy who wants to listen to Ma sing.

"That would be great," I said. "But we'll have to head that way tomorrow. With everybody."

"Right," he replied, grabbing a couple of bags of office supplies Diindiisi had brought out to the garage and heading towards the waiting SUV. "See you back at the casa."

Chapter Six
Day 8, 7 April 2018

We had a running brush with a pair of daemons once we left the funeral home. One of them was a giant pink starfish in bright green shorts, and the other was a square, bright yellow sponge in brown pants and a white shirt.

"I FUCKING HATE THIS PLACE!" Dalma shouted as she ran the sponge over. She was driving me again, having won the position from Padgett and Davis by the simple expedient of sleeping in the driver's seat.

No one said anything in response, although I will say that the 'sponge' crunched when we ran it over. Sponges ain't supposed to go crunch, man.

It took about ten minutes to get to the gun store/range combo on Old Ranch Road 12.

"Oh my god," I said.

The design had probably started as a throwback to an actual adobe frontier style dwelling. It had been enhanced. The ground floor looked like a bunker from the outside, and the upper floor looked very...defensible.

"Yeah," Padgett said over the radio. "Most folks refer to this place as 'Just Machine Guns and Rednecks.'"

"I can see why," I replied.

We dismounted, sweeping the surroundings for things that went bump in the night. Nothing. Dalma took over behind the Golf – not that she had any real experience, but she was probably the best bet to run it in a pinch, at least until she had a stoppage or a jam she couldn't clear.

Diindiisi backed her from the turret of the other Humvee, shotgun laid across the top of the turret.

I'd planned for door issues this time and brought the hot key (cutting torch). We torched the door off and waited.

Nothing. The sky was gun metal gray and clear. I went through the door. Sure enough, there were enough firearms to arm a medium sized putsch inside, including an M2, water cooled, on an anti-aircraft mount.

"Wonder where they keep the ammo?" Miller said.

"Based on this map, in a bunker out back," Davis said, pointing. He shifted the sprayer full of holy water on his back. "You want me to spray the area outside down?"

"Yeah, and see if you can knock some of the goo off the lead Humvee, huh?" Padgett said.

Davis gave him the finger and walked out.

"Ah, brotherly love," I said. "If we're here much longer, I swear being with y'all'll be just like being back in the Corps. Before we go to the bunker, let's see if we can find the office."

"Why?" Miller asked.

"Invoices, man, invoices," I replied.

"Huh?"

"Look, it's not going to do us a damn bit of good if all there is on hand is ten thousand rounds of .22 short, now is it?" I replied.

We found the office and the required storage documents, hard copy, one each, updated as of Saturday, 31 March. And I smiled. Miller smiled. Padgett was grinning like the Cheshire Cat.

"How much?"

"Fifteen hundred rounds of .50," I said. "Five thousand rounds of 7.62 NATO, and about the same in 5.56 NATO. God bless America."

"Thank God for machine gun shoots," Miller said. "You want to check out the bunker now?"

"Yes," I said, opening a key box. Sure enough, there was a key on the hook marked 'Ammo Storage Bunker'. I took it. "John, move the Humvee with the M2 around back, and we'll meet you out there, huh?"

"Right," he said, going out the door.

"Father," I said, gesturing Miller to the door.

"After you," he replied.

We went out of the office, found the door marked 'Range' and exited the building. Someone popped a round at us as we left the building. I became one with the Earth, while Miller froze. I jerked him down into a sprawling heap.

"WHO THE FUCK ARE YOU!" a voice shouted from a building marked 'Range Office'.

"HUMAN!" I shouted back. I'd managed to roll behind a large concrete planter.

"I CAN SEE THAT, YA DAMN FOOLS! WHO ARE YOU?"

"FATHER DAVID MILLER," Dave shouted, standing back up and taking off his armor.

"LIKE A PRIEST?"

"YES."

"COME AHEAD, BUT SLOW, I'VE GOT YA COVERED!"

I covered Miller as he advanced. He finally got to where whoever was in the building could see him. There was a much lower voiced conversation, which I couldn't hear, then Miller called for me to advance.

Padgett's voice crackled over the radio, "You guys need reinforcement?"

"Negative. Hold your position while we figure this out," I said, walking to where Miller was standing.

"Your buddy don't look much like a priest," the voice said when I got in range.

"He's a priest of the Church Militant," Miller replied.

"I can see that, but the way he's wearing his gear he looks like a damn Jarhead," the voice said. "I'm comin' out."

A tall man stepped onto the porch of the Range Office. He looked like he was in his early fifties, with thinning blonde hair, and was dressed in tactical gear, from his high speed boots to the cap turned backwards on his head. In his hands was a very serious looking AR based rifle.

"I'm Father Salazar," I said to him.

"Yeah, he told me," the figure said. "I'm John Johnson."

Sometimes my mouth overloads my brain. This was one of those times.

"You know, Father Miller, one more John, and we can be the first priests in a long time accused of running a house of ill repute."

Miller gave me the fish eye. Oddly enough Johnson thought it was a great joke. It broke the ice.

"Where the hell are we," Johnson asked when he had finished wheezing at my joke. "Hell?"

"No, not really hell," Miller replied. "More like Limbo, without all the fog and waiting."

"Or trying to go under bamboo poles to the sound of steel drums," I said.

Miller gave me the look again. I just smiled as angelically as I could. A scenic, all-expense paid, twelve week vacation to Marine Recruit Depot San Diego followed by multiple trips to the Land of Sun and Fun hadn't ground the smart ass out of me, and Father David Miller was hoeing a tough row.

"Ok. What can I do for ya'll?" Johnson asked.

"Well, we're collecting survivors. And ammunition," I snarked.

"Ah. Question is why?"

"Better chance of surviving in a group," I said.

"Makes sense," Johnson said. "Had a couple of tense nights out here, I'll admit. Y'all got room for one more?"

"We can always use another shooter," I said. "Mind if I have them bring the vehicles around?"

"Nah, go for it. Ya'll looking for any ammo. . . I think I know what you want," he said as the Humvee backed into place in front of the Ammo Storage Bunker.

"Ma up there is hungry," I admitted.

"Well, let's get her fed, huh? I hate to see a woman goin' hungry," Johnson said. appraising the vehicles with a critical eye.

It took about an hour to sort and load the Humvees. But I made sure that the M2 was locked and cocked, just in case. Johnson got out another fifty, and the vehicle mount from his arms locker and insisted we swap it for the Golf.

There was also a shit ton more .50 ammo in the bunker than on the invoices.

"Yeah, I got a deal on some Israeli production ammo about a year ago. Stuff sat in Houston for the last six months thanks to Customs Enforcement," he said around a mouthful of sandwich. "Showed up Monday. Hadn't had time to put it in the records yet. And when things went gray, I said fuck the government and its paperwork in the ass. Sorry ladies."

"No problem," Diindiisi said.

Dalma just smiled. "Say what you want, so long as there's more ammo to be had, I don't care.

"Anyway, been hanging out here wonderin' what I was gonna eat when the Twinkies in the snack machine ran out," he said. "Didn't want to wander too far, in case things went back to normal and I got lost where ever we are."

Johnson had a box truck, and it had a lift gate. He also had a pallet jack. Once we'd loaded the fifties, and put extra ammo for them in the Humvee's, it had taken little time to load what we were taking (.50 and 7.62 mainly, with all the .45 Raptor he had on site for Johnson's AR) in the back of the box truck, add the pallet jack and some assorted gear for Johnson and head back to the funeral home, after locking the bunker and putting a seal on the now open front door. We'd come back in a couple of weeks and make sure that nothing had disturbed the seals. Johnson even brought his own bed – an army cot with an inflatable mattress, but that would do until we could get him something better to sleep on.

We took the direct route home, and once we'd reset the wards, we unloaded everything. We had to move the hearse out of the garage to fit the ammo in, but I'd feel better with it undercover.

"I'da never thought of using a funeral home," Johnson said.

"Most of the churches we've seen have been burned out," I replied. He and I were going over the M2's in the turrets of the Humvees.

"Makes some sorta sense, I guess," he said.

"So, I've got to ask," I started.

"US Army, 19 Delta, Gulf War. Then I went and became an Eleven Bang Bang and lost three feet of small intestine in Mogadishu," he replied. "You?"

"Uncle Sam's Misguided Children, 0311. Iraq," I replied.

"Yeah, I thought you looked like a Jarhead," he said with a grin. "But how'd you become a priest?"

"Long story," I replied. "I saw somethings in Iraq that convinced me there was a higher power."

"Yeah, damn sun's hot enough over there that folks' brains melt and they start talkin' to God," he replied. "Although this place'd sure make an atheist believe."

"True that," I said, slipping down into the Humvee and out the rear door. "You married to that plate carrier you're wearing?"

"Yeah, why?" he asked.

It was a very high-speed, low drag piece of equipment, with no protection for his neck or upper arms. It was also considerably lighter and cooler than the models we'd pulled out of the supply cache.

"I've got some plates then," I said.

"What's the difference between yours and mine?" he asked.

"Mine were blessed by a bishop, and have holy silver worked into the ceramic. They repel some of the undead," I replied. "Might help here."

"Father, I'll take all the help I can get," he replied.

Chapter Seven
Day 9, 8 April 2018

With Johnson, we could actually do a bit more exploring. I didn't feel quite so bad about leaving Miller and Davis alone to research while I took the other shooters out to look for things or try to find clues on how to get out of here. Admittedly, the water-cooled fifty we'd brought back with us gave us at least one heavy weapon at our base – after Johnson and I had run the extremely short course on the care and feeding of the machine gun, fifty caliber, water-cooled. And with the Humvees, if four people wanted to go, we could do it, even if it was a bit cramped.

Thing is that most folks see a Humvee in the movies or on TV and think they're full of room. They aren't. Toss in personal weapons, food, ammo, and oh so important water, and there's barely room for folks inside.

At least the ACs worked.

"Where to?" Padgett asked as we pulled out of the funeral home parking lot.

"Surprise me," I replied.

This was going to be our first 'patrol' as such. We'd let the other team figure out where they were going tomorrow. Today, Padgett, Diindiisi, and I would drive around, burn fuel, and look for signs of daemons to kill. Because I wanted to see what Ma Deuce and several belts of fifty would do to a daemon, ok?

"Right," he said, turning south.

We went south for a while, then east, then north. We stopped and filled the tank with diesel and raided a stop and rob for snacks. We travelled north, and found a conundrum.

"Huh," I said, tapping Padgett to stop.

"What huh?" he asked. Diindiisi was scanning the area around us.

"By my calculations, and what I remember driving down here last week, we should be in Kyle," I said. "See anything?"

"Not much to Kyle," Padgett replied.

"Yeah, except for the honking big prison that was near northbound I-35," I said.

"Yeah, there is that," he replied.

The terrain around us looked like the gently rising terrain between Austin and San Marcos. Only all the structures were missing.

"So, not everything came into the Shadow Lands," Padgett said.

"In my experience, if we keep going north, we'll find ourselves on the south side of the city," Diindiisi said. "The Shadow Lands are a Mobius Strip."

"You know about Mobius?" Padgett asked.

She sighed.

"Yes. I read his and Listing's work in the original German, to pass the time when Henry was away. I even met his son when we were doing some research in Germany."

"I...I'm sorry. I assumed that, well, that, you know?" Padgett temporized.

"That because I was an Ojibwa woman, born in what William Warren called the Mississippi River Band in 1872, I had no formal learning?" she replied. "You'd be correct. By my people's traditions, I shouldn't have inherited my husband's powers, but I did. Henry took me away from that and gave me a larger world. Besides, he insisted I learn something, since I had an ear for languages, and was driving him absolutely crazy out of sheer boredom."

"I'm sorry," Padgett said. "Jesse, you want to keep going north?"

"No, turn around and head back. Let's go down Aquarena Springs to return to the house, ok?"

"Right," he replied, driving across the median and then down the center lane of the southbound side of I-35.

We rode in silence. I was thinking about the implications of the area being a Mobius strip. I don't know what the others were thinking, and didn't ask. We hadn't reached where Post Road splits off Aquarena Springs when we heard the first, thunderous squeal.

"Hey Jesse, should I paddle faster?" Padgett asked.

"Why, you hearing banjos?" I replied.

Another movie we'd have to watch and explain to Diindiisi.

"I've got visions of Ned Beatty and inbred hill folk dancing in my head," Padgett replied.

I saw something large, mottled pinkish, leap into the air by what was now known as the Meadows Center and come crashing back into Spring Lake. Water sheeted into the air.

"GO!" I shouted, after making sure the trigger block was on safe.

It's damn near impossible to break the tires loose on an up-armored Humvee. Not that Padgett didn't try to do it, of course.

He cut the angle and hopped the curb, crossing the sidewalk and tearing divots from the manicured grass of the golf course that surrounded the Meadows Center, then ran over a short bollard before swinging right on Laurel and running towards the area where, according to the signs, you could take glass bottom boat rides. The squealing got louder as we approached, and I watched the world's largest daemonic boar leap into the air again, and swine dive into the lake. Something human-shaped tumbled in the water thrown up this time.

"There are powers at work here!" Diindiisi shouted into the radio. "See how the water only falls in the lake?"

"Padgett, follow the pig," I said.

The daemon was jumping downstream in short hops. Padgett got ahead of it by turning down Spring Lake and thundering through a parking lot, dodging the cars there.

"Get down to the lake, if you can," I said.

"Right," Padgett replied, crossing the curb again, and angling towards the lake.

He pulled up just short of the bank in a small clearing. A person came swimming downstream, followed by el Puerco Grande. I flipped the trigger block to fire, pressing the butterfly trigger between the spade grips.

Ma started singing her song, at a stately seven hundred rounds a minute. Gouts of meat exploded from the daemon, and it turned towards us.

"Get ready to back the fuck up, fast," I said to Padgett over the radio.

"Right," he said back.

Two things happened at once. The belt fed the last three rounds through the gun, and the pig staggered ashore.

"GO!" I shouted, opening a box of ammo in the turret and pulling the belt out.

Dropping the belt into the box on the side of the gun, I waited until Padgett had backed onto the hardball before opening the feed tray cover on the M2 and feeding the belt in. It'd been a while since I'd reloaded an M2 in a moving Humvee (Iraq as a matter of fact, trying to keep from being eaten by ghouls) but that's what muscle memory is for. Feed cover down, locked. Padgett brushed the rear quarter panel of some imported compact, sending the econo-box spinning, and the daemon pig charged after us.

"Dude, I've got to turn around!" Padgett shouted over the radio.

"Not yet," I said, pulling the charging handle back, then running it forward.

Saying a quick prayer, I hit the triggers. This time, I could see the pig's head, sending fifty rounds smashing into it. It staggered and fell, about ten feet in front of the bumper. For good measure, I put a third box of ammo into the twitching corpse.

"Why does it smell like bar-b-que?" Padgett asked.

"Every fifth round's a tracer," I said, as Diindiisi handed up a couple of belts of ammo to replace the ones I'd fired. "Let's see if whoever this thing was chasing survived."

Padgett pulled down to the shore again. Sure enough, someone was clinging to the shore, unable to climb out of the water.

I got down, grabbed my UMP and unassed the Humvee. If there were any more daemon pigs in the area, we might be screwed but saving someone took priority.

"Hi," the guy floating in the lake said.

He was about fifty, with a short, white beard and light blue hair.

"Need a hand?" I asked.

"Oh, in a minute or so," he replied. "Gotta catch my breath first, I think."

Behind him, a pier stuck out into the water.

"Can you make the pier?" I asked.

"Yeah," he said, swimming towards it.

I trotted over, crouching down. He raised a hand, and I pulled him from the water. He sat down on the pier and started laughing.

"You alright?" I asked. I was a bit worried about his sanity.

"Yeah, I'm ok," he said, standing and offering me his hand. We shook. "I was just thinking. I was an extra in a really bad movie filmed here at Spring Lake oh, forty years ago, I guess. Got saved from the piranha in the movie because someone pulled me onto this pier. Thought I was going to be a big movie star at ten. Things didn't work out that way. I'm Jonathan, by the way."

I chuckled, thinking of the comment I'd made the other day. We'd found another John to save. Father Miller and I could now be said to be running a house of ill repute.

"Father Jesse Salazar. You can call me Jesse," I said.

Behind us there was, well, call it a floomp. The corpse of the daemon burst into flame.

"I guess we should go see what's going on up there," I said.

"Be nice to get somewhere I could get dry," Jonathan admitted.

"Got any gear?" I asked.

He gestured to the flaming pile of daemon.

"First thing he ate after washing me into the water with his first jump," Jonathan said.

We walked to the Humvee.

"What happened to the pig?" I asked. "This is," pause, "Jonathan. . ."

"Hiebert," he supplied.

Padgett grinned.

"Yeah, I know," I replied.

"Holy water," Diindiisi said, enigmatically.

"Huh?"

"The pig. Holy water," she replied. "Apparently, that particular daemon has an energetic endothermic reaction with holy water. Although I think calling the water we're getting from the Mystical Bird Bath of Saint Mark the Evangelist 'holy water' is a bit of a misnomer."

For a hundred and forty year old woman, she had a wicked sense of humor.

The daemon, all five or so thousand pounds of it, had become a fine ash, drifting on the wind.

"No shit. Mount up, everyone. Padgett, get us home, huh?"

"Right away, Jesse," he replied.

Once we were back at the funeral home, we went through the introductions again. Johnson grinned, and Dalma had a smile that said butter wouldn't melt in her mouth. Father Miller just sighed.

"You find anything else?" Miller asked.

Padgett led Hiebert into the 'male' apartment so he could shower, go through the tactical gear, and find something that was dry and didn't fit too badly.

"The water from the font has a, what Diindiisi call it. . ."

"Energetic and endothermic reaction," she supplied.

"What she said, with some of the local residents," I replied.

She and I talked Miller through what had happened before I told him that we'd also found that the region we were in was a Mobius strip.

"Sounds like a Klein bottle, but we're arguing semantics at that point," Miller said.

"Something like that, yeah," I replied. "Did you find anything?"

"Yes? Maybe?" he replied. "I need to do more research."

"Give," I replied.

"We might be able to get out of here and back to 2018," he said. "But I'm not sure how, yet."

It started raining outside.

"Crap," Miller said.

"Yeah," I replied. "GET YOUR GUNS!" I shouted.

Whatever was happening, we weren't going down without a fight.

Dalma came out of her room, a submachine gun slung, the big Murfreesboro Five-O carried across her body.

"Roof," I said. She went out the door and to the right, out the exterior door, and up onto the funeral home's flat roof.

Johnson came in, followed by Davis, Padgett, and Hiebert.

"Johnson, take the Golf, and go backstop Dalma on the roof. Davis grab a sprayer. Mr. Hiebert, are you familiar with guns?"

"No. But what's happening?"

"Probably nothing good," I said. "How do you feel about using a backpack water sprayer?"

"I can use one," Hiebert replied.

"Right. Davis?"

"Sprayer two," he replied, grabbing Hiebert by the arm. "Follow me."

"Miller, you and Padgett got the garage, with Mr. Hiebert and Davis for backstop. Diindiisi and I will go up on the roof to the front."

"Got it."

We dispersed. The ectoplasm was falling in sheets along the limits of the property line. You couldn't see the street, let alone across it, the goo was falling so thick.

"Ok, this isn't good," I said to Diindiisi. I keyed my mike. "Nobody fires unless you've got a clear target."

"Where do you want the sprayers?" Davis called.

"Backstop Father Miller for now," I replied.

The sheet of ectoplasm falling to the front of the funeral home thinned and a figure stepped up to the line.

"That's different," I said, stepping to the front of the roof.

"Mortals," the figure called.

"Nice, he speaks English," Diindiisi said.

"Would you prefer Akkadian?" the figure asked, morphing into a man wearing a wrapped skirt, with a long dark beard and a cone shaped hat.

"No, English is fine," I replied.

"I am Abzu, husband of Tiamat, Lord of this realm," he replied.

"Nice to meet you," I said.

"You have killed some of my children," Abzu replied.

"Several, by my count. In my defense, they were trying to kill me," I pointed out.

"Your mortal problems are not my concern," he replied.

I looked at Diindiisi. Abzu looked at her, then tried to take a step closer to the building. His foot burst into flame when it made contact with the grass. He stepped back.

"HOW HAVE YOU DONE THIS?" Abzu thundered.

"A true and certain faith in the resurrection of the dead," I replied.

He retreated into the falling ectoplasm, then returned once he had put his foot out. It still smoldered.

"Followers of that Judean upstart, I see," he sneered.

"Something like that, yeah," I replied. "Is there something we can do for you, or are we just going to stand here and yell at each other?"

"I wanted to see the beings that had defeated one of my ablest followers," Abzu admitted. "And tell you that your lives are forfeit if you leave the protection of your god."

"Good to know," I replied. I said a small prayer, then keyed the mike. "Dalma?"

"On the way," she replied.

The roof over the living quarters was about three feet higher than the rest of the funeral home. She was on the leading edge of that roof, behind us.

The Barrett barked. Abzu went down like he'd been poleaxed, then stood, looking at the smoking hole in his chest.

"Silver? You dare try to kill me with silver?" he laughed. "Your god protects you now, but know, I will be watching for an opportunity. He turned and stalked into the rain of ectoplasm.

"Stay frosty, people," I said, keying the mike again.

Something came flying through the ectoplasm.

"Sweet monkee of Jebus," Johnson muttered.

It was a griffin. It smashed against a barrier.

"Interesting," Diindiisi said.

"Jesse?" Johnson said.

"Light him up," I replied.

Dalma fired again. Her target was huge, but following a moving target through a scope isn't as easy as they make it out to be in the movies or video games. She fired a second round into the griffin, and Johnson came up to where Diindiisi and I stood, then opened up with the Golf from the hip, Rambo style.

The griffin went down in a welter of blood, goo, and feathers. The griffin's fall seemed to be a signal of some sort, and a horde of marauding, shambling things rushed the property.

"Go hot," I said before opening fire myself.

It was, to quote Willem Dafoe, a slaughter. Daemons and imps piled up along the barrier, the ones in front bursting into flame and being crushed down by the ones behind. The guns chewed into the mass, adding to the carnage.

"We're surrounded," Dalma reported.

"Good, then we're in a target-rich environment," I replied.

"Fucking Chesty Puller worshipping Jarheads," Johnson muttered into his mike.

I gave it ten minutes.

"Cease fire, cease fire. Davis and Hiebert to the front, please," I said over the radio, before running to the outside stairs and going to the ground.

Davis and Hiebert met me at the front of the building.

"Hose the edges of the property down," I said, looking at the mass of things that were still pressing against the barrier, trying to get in.

They did. And wherever the water touched daemons, they exploded. The mass pulled back, finally.

"Refill, and clear the rest of them off, ok?" I said, then keyed my mike. "Padgett, meet Davis and Hiebert in the chapel and escort them around to clear the sides and back. Break. Father Miller, Diindiisi, meet me on the roof."

Everyone acknowledged, and I went back up top.

Johnson was watching the cleaning crew, and Miller and Diindiisi stood nearby, waiting for me to say something.

"I've got an idea, I'd like to test," I said. "It's going to be a bit, well, damn actually, dangerous."

"What?" Miller asked.

"Well look, see how there are patches appearing in the ectoplasm?" I asked.

You could follow where Davis and Hiebert had cleared the daemons back from the property line – the ectoplasm avoided areas where the holy water had been sprayed.

"Yeah, so?" Miller asked.

"Well, we could enlarge the protected zone," I said.

He mulled it for a minute.

"Take a while with the backpack sprayers to do that, wouldn't it?"

I grinned like a shark.

"Yeah, but holy water purifies what it comes in contact with, right?"

"Yes," he said, voice full of exasperation.

"So, what happens when you pump it into a pressure washer through the soap valve?"

"You know," Miller said, "there is something very wrong with your brain that you thought of that."

"Blame D&D," I replied. "Purify food and water."

He signed. Diindiisi looked at both of us.

"What are you talking about?" she asked.

"There's a machine in the garage for washing cars," I said. "It shoots water at high pressure and can draw soap into the mix. I'm pretty sure we can use it to spray holy water at high pressure, long distances, to give us a wider 'safe zone'."

"And you need someone to help?" she asked.

"I need someone to cover my ass while I'm testing the theory, yes."

"If you go down, what're the rest of us supposed to do?" Miller asked.

"Listen to Diindiisi. She's been here longer than I have," I replied.

She smiled. "I'll cover your back," she said. "When do you want to try it out?"

"Now's as good a time as any," I replied. "We've got samples to test it on, after all."

We called Davis and Hiebert off of 'wash' duty, to help set up my latest mad scheme. It took about half an hour to do so. The tricky bit was getting the soap line to stay in the backpack sprayer – I ended up duct-taping it in place. Which would cause problems with switching tanks, but we'd burn that bridge when we got to it.

When everything was ready, I swung the sprayer up on my back. Hiebert started the pressure washer. It coughed, then settled to a roar. I started hosing down the daemons and imps that had once again collected right at the edge of the, for lack of a better term, safe zone. At first, they were simply irritated by the water. Then one of them realized there was soap in the stream, and they started taking a bath, as obscenely as possible. There's just something wrong about watching tiny lust imps mime having sex in a shower. They were clowning, blowing bubbles right up until the holy water replaced the soap in the tube.

Then they started exploding. I pushed them back, forming a square with the washer's spray. The daemons started scrabbling back from contact.

"Try bouncing the stream at them from the ground," Hiebert shouted over the pressure washer's roar. "It worked best with the backpack sprayers."

I tried it. If anything, it worked better than trying to just catch them in the spray. The water rebounding from the ground had a wider area of effect. I pushed the daemons across the street, into a parking lot, then turned and started working my way uphill. Diindiisi followed, staying in the cleared area. I hit the end of the fifty-foot-long-pressure line, then cut the nozzle and walked back to where the pressure washer sat.

"How's the water level in the tank?" I asked, taking a bottle of water from Miller.

"About half full. You could probably do the rest of the frontage here," he said. "That's interesting."

"What?" I asked.

"Seems the holy water is keeping its sanctity for a while," he replied, pointing downhill.

Sure enough, there were two channels in the rain of ectoplasm, following the curbs down the hill.

"Top me off, and I'll finish the street. Then we can clear the house next door," I said.

"Sure thing," Miller replied.

Chapter Eight
Day 10, 9 April 2018

"**I**'ve found someone else who made it back from the Shadow Realm to reality," Miller said the next morning at breakfast.

"Oh? Whom?" Diindiisi asked.

"The event was after you crossed over," Miller replied. "Did you run across a Lady Mallowan at any time?"

Diindiisi thought. "No. The name isn't familiar."

"There's a lot of crap in the archives, but this one appears real," Miller said, handing around a sheaf of papers.

"You have got to be kidding me," Dalma said. "Agatha Christie?"

"Explains why she wouldn't talk about the missing eleven days, doesn't it?" Davis said.

"Also explains why I felt like I was back in England before I ran into Amelia and Fred," Diindiisi said. "But if she was only there for eleven days, how did she get back?"

"Apparently, there was more to Conan-Doyle's medium than the press let on," Miller said. "She was able to contact Lady Mallowan from this side and then direct her to a rift in," he rifled through the pages, "Mother Shipton's Cave, about four miles from Harrogate."

"Any notes on how she got back?" I asked, trying to be practical.

"According to the records, they used 'Ye Grate Spelle' from Mother Shipton's notes. No, the spell isn't recorded. But, according to the notes, it has to be worked on both sides simultaneously, anyway," Miller said.

"So, no go," I said.

"It's more than we had last night," Miller replied.

"True but..." I started.

My phone started playing "Gallows Pole" by Robert Plant.

"Huh," I said, "I thought that thing was dead."

"I plugged them all in the other day," Padgett said. "Force of habit."

"Are you going to answer it?" Hiebert asked.

"Nah," I picked it up. "That's the message tone. Besides, the only folks I know who could spam my text message inbox like that are ...yup, my boss."

Technically, it was from another Jonathan, Jonathan Edward Thomas (aka Jed), my Gunnery Sergeant in Iraq. These days, Jed led the Brute Squad out of Austin, QMG's team of heavy hitters when it came to things supernatural.

I keyed in the password and opened the texts. When I opened it, I was looking at fifteen copies and climbing on the same message.

Ninja Pigeon your message received. Respond if you can here. If not, same location as original contact. Repeating, your message received, respond if you can.

. .

Message received. Verify?

Where did we meet Hotel Kilo?

I'll Take a Dump.

How're you doing?

I've had better days, Gunny.

The elf's idea about putting a repeater in the cache worked. More information to follow. How many in your party?

Eight. Suggest you research Mother Shipton's Ye Grate Spell.

Roger that. Keep your damn phone charged and with you, Jesse.

Roger that, Gunny. Ninja Pigeon out.

"We're saved?" Hiebert asked.

"Sort of. We're back in contact, at least," I replied. I thought for a minute. "Who else has a cell phone here? Give me the number."

I sent one more text, with all the numbers, and got a thumbs-up emoji from the other side.

"So, how long do you think it'll take them to figure things out?" Diindiisi asked.

She'd accepted the miracle of modern communications far better than some of my older relatives had, for example. But she also came from a time when technology was considered a savior, not the end of the world. One of my uncles, on the other hand, was convinced the Army had planted a chip in his brain to read his thoughts when he was outside the house, placing thick sheets of aluminum foil in every hat he owned to keep them from getting a signal.

"Jed'll probably put his team on it," I replied. "Michael will probably be involved as well. One good thing about working with a vampire, they don't have to sleep. Michael will probably see this as a challenge and work on it twenty-four-seven, if we're lucky."

"I still can't believe Michelangelo is a freakin' vampire," Padgett said.

"Eh, he's not that freaky," I replied. "Dresses pretty conservatively for a five-hundred-year-old guy. No tights or ruffled short pants, for example."

"That's not what I meant," Padgett said.

"I know. But if you only knew how many vampires we've caught because they thought wearing a leather banana hammock, leather straps and a gimp mask during a Blue Norther in Austin in January was a good fashion statement, you'd be amazed."

Diindiisi raised a hand.

"Yes?"

"What is a banana hammock?" she asked.

Miller spewed coffee across his papers and the table.

"Father Salazar, you get to answer that one all on your own," he said when he'd recovered from the coughing fit.

I thought for a second. "It's a garment, in this case of leather, made to enhance and display a man's genitals while covering them minimally."

"So, something like a codpiece or a koteka?" she replied.

"What's a koteka?" Dalma asked.

"A penis sheath," Diindiisi replied. "Worn by the tribesmen in the highlands of New Guinea as clothing."

"Oh, wait, I think we talked about them in one of my Anthropology Classes," Dalma replied. "I had to look up the reference."

I sighed. "Something like that, yes. Point is, if you see someone walking around in forty-degree weather wearing leatheroos and a bunch of leather straps, you glass them real quick to make sure their body temperature is above ambient," I said.

"You can tell their temperature now?" Diindiisi asked.

"Yes. With a thermal camera, we can tell their temperature from across the street," I replied.

"We also used cameras to detect a vampire," she replied. "If you took a photo of someone and they didn't show up in it, but everyone else did, it was a good bet they were a vampire."

"How'd that work?" Dalma asked, intrigued.

"Silver," I replied. "We don't know why, but vampires won't appear on silver film stock. Which means we couldn't film them until digital replaced analogue sources. But now? It's on like Donkey Kong."

"The Church's research indicates it has something to do with silver being a pure metal. Or the thirty pieces of silver Judas received for betraying Christ," Father Miller said.

"If that were the case, then why are there Roman accounts of werewolves being killed when struck by silver that predate Christ," Hiebert said.

Everyone looked at him.

"What? I saw it on *In Search of*...or was it *Arthur C. Clarke's Mysterious World?*" he said, with a shrug. "I've watched a lot of old TV shows."

"Either way, he's got a point," I replied. "And I know that both the Catholic Church and the Episcopal Church have records on killing vampires and werewolves prior to the birth of Christ. I've seen them. Well, copies and translations, anyway."

Miller pinched the bridge of his nose. "Yes, you're right. And we're going to have a talk about this, alone."

"Why? It's not like anyone here will be able to go back to being a mundane after having spent time in the Shadow Realm. I mean, if the USG doesn't keep an eye on them for 'their own good', your Church and Order will," I said.

"And yours won't?" Miller replied.

"My church? Perhaps. But my employer will probably offer them jobs," I said while looking at everyone and contemplating where they might end up.

"All of that depends on us getting out of here," Miller replied. "And that means I've got more work to do."

He rose and walked, into the other apartment.

"What is the USG?" Diindiisi asked.

"United States Government," I replied.

"There are so many abbreviations in modern life," she replied.

"Occupational hazard," I replied. "Started, oh, after World War II, and crept from government usage into everyday English after that. It probably doesn't help that I used to be a Marine, and now work for a somewhat secretive organization that, well, you know."

"True," she replied.

"So, what are we going to be doing on this fine, ectoplasm-less day?" Padgett asked.

"Day off. Smoke 'em if you got 'em," I replied. "I'm going to set up the reloading gear Dalma found. Y'all can do whatever you want, as long as you're not fire dancing anywhere near where I'm working."

"Sweet!"

The first thing I did was the dishes. I can't cook, unless you count dropping an MRE in a heater and adding water and Tabasco. But I can wash a mighty clean dish. Kinda like weapons maintenance. Cooking, on the other hand, involves chemistry and heat, and is, in my book, one step up from magic. Mel had laughed about that over the years we were together.

Dishes done, I checked my weapons, then pulled out a portable bench and started reading the manual for the reloading gear.

"Damn, I knew we forgot something," I said.

Hiebert was standing nearby.

"Oh?"

"Yeah, we forgot the tumbler for the brass," I replied.

"Hard to find one?" he asked.

"Not really, just wanted to see about doing some reloads today. Oh well, it'll wait," I said.

"Can I ask a question?" he said, watching me put the gear back in the garage.

"Shoot. On the more philosophical ones, I might have to ask Father Miller, but as long as we're not trying to see how many angels can dance on the head of the pin, I'm game," I replied.

"No, nothing like that," he said. "Do you really think we're going to get out of here?"

"I'd say the chances are pretty good," I replied. "We've got a good base here, and between Father Miller and the folks on the other side, I'm looking forward to sleeping in my own bed, eventually."

"Good," he said, sighing. "When I first realized things were different, I was scared I was in Hell, and the priests had been right about my lifestyle, honestly."

"Yeah," I looked around, "I can see how coming here would have that effect on someone."

The sky was still the dirty gray of an unused TV station. Ectoplasm was falling to the ground somewhere to the south of us. Just another day in the Shadow Realm.

"How did you, well, how did you get into this business, if you don't mind me asking, Father?" Hiebert said after a couple of minutes of silence.

"Iraq. My company got tasked with supporting a SEAL team that was looking for intelligence on a site that Saddam had run over there," I replied.

"I take it there was more to it?" he said.

"More to it is an understatement," I replied. "The SEALs weren't. Well, they had been SEALs before they'd gone to work for QMG. And the guy leading the team? Henry

Keith is a lot of things, including older than Michelangelo, and probably was with the teams at one point. Hell, he probably was there when they formed the Teams, for all I know, but I didn't know that at the time. What I saw was a bunch of SEALs that went down into a hole at Saddam's Primate Research Facility."

I took a breath and a sip of water.

"Not really sure what Saddam was using the chimps for – probably hunting stock, knowing that sick bastard. But it was the deep underground parts that the QMG team was interested in. Rumor had it they were looking into a secret WMD factory for either biological or nuclear weapons."

"I take it that was wrong?" he asked.

"Depends on how you define 'biological weapon'. Ever heard of a ghoul?"

"Arabic legendary creature that eats corpses?" he asked with a grin, as if proud of his knowledg. "*In Search of,* if I remember correctly."

"Something like that. Although, if they haven't been fed for a year, they're not that picky about how long their food has been dead," I said, shuddering. "Watched one pull the face off of a Marine in my squad and eat it with the kid standing there screaming."

"Oh."Hiebert blanched at the thought.

"Yeah. But that's not the worst part," I said.

"It's not?"

"Nah. We went in the hole to pull Henry and what was left of his SEAL team out, and found a ghoul queen in the hole," I said.

"Bad?" His forehead creased.

"Ugly bad. Fell out of the ugly tree and hit every branch on the way down bad, coupled with an insatiable hunger, and a desire to succor its young," I replied. "Basically, the Queen from Aliens with all the redeeming features removed."

"The Queen from Aliens didn't have any redeeming features, unless you count wanting to protect her brood from Ripley and the Marines."

"Exactly. Anyway, Gunny Thomas led us into that hole to pull what was left of the intel team out – we got Keith and two of his guys out of the twenty who'd gone down the hole. We brought back ten of our own."

"Damn."

"Yeah. Then we pulled back to the vehicles and filled the entrance to the facility with ghoul corpses until the Air Force got their collective thumbs out of their asses and vectored in the orbiting strike of F-15E's with GBU-28s in. I will say 630 pounds of high explosive wrapped in 3500 pounds of steel will put paid to even the strongest of ghoul queens. If you drop enough of them on her. And we did."

"And after that?"

"After that, I came home, hugged my wife and went to seminary. Got out, she got attacked by a lich, and I went to work killing the things that make humans fear the night," I said.

"You're shitting me, right? Did your wife die?" Heibert asked.

"Yeah," I nodded, feeling the raw emotions like it was fresh.

Hiebert studied me for a moment. He must have seen something in my face because he changed the subject. "I didn't get a chance to thank you yesterday," he said.

"Eh, it's what they pay me for," I replied.

"Really? You get paid to rescue people from giant pig daemons? Where do I sign up? More importantly, what's the insurance coverage like? Do you get dental, or just health care coverage? What about vision?"

I laughed, and it was infectious. We sat there laughing long enough that Diindiisi came out to check on us.

"You two ok?" she asked.

We were both red in the face, gasping for air.

"Yeah," I finally said, mastering my breathing. "Jonathan just asked the weirdest job interview question I've ever heard, is all."

"If you're sure you're ok?" she replied.

"Yes'm. Just fine. And I have to admit, it was a weird question," Hiebert said.

"And to answer the question, we get health, dental and vision coverage," I answered with a straight face. "Along with 'special' coverage in case of demonic possession or falling to a vampire or other undead."

Hiebert broke up laughing again. Diindiisi gave me a look that said I was an idiot, then went back inside. It was going to be one of those days.

Chapter Nine
Day 11, 10 April 2018

We ended up arguing about the tumbler that night. And I never got it. Johnson made the point that we could always raid his place for more ammo. Diindiisi argued that we could always send a textgram (her word, a portmanteau of text message and telegram) to QMG and ask for more silver ammo. Which should work, given the nature of the Shadow Realm.

Which in the end I did. And got the word that they were going to stock ammo and some special supplies and equipment, whatever that meant, and we should be able to pick them up on the 10th. So, we woke up and geared up for an all hands evolution, again. Only this time, it would be just like the old days of escorting convoys in Iraq. Of course, Humvee, box truck (I'd argued for the Tacticool Tahoe with trailer, but got voted down by the simple fact that the box truck could hold more weight, even if it had less armor and fewer wards), and Humvee would be the shortest convoy I'd ever ridden in,

But they pay me for this kind of crap, so off we went. In addition to weapons, water, ammo, more water, and food, we took four sprayers of holy water, just in case.

First step, we hosed down the building and a safe zone. Then we opened the door and started moving ammo and gear out to the vehicles, along with a sheaf of papers and the inevitable Pelican 1650 cases.

"Y'all want to hurry up in there?" Johnson called from where he was sitting in the turret of the lead Humvee. "It's starting to rain towards the Square."

I looked around the room. There were a couple more boxes of ammo, and two more of the large Pelican hard cases.

"Grab it and toss it in the back of the truck," I said, writing "Ninja Pigeon Was Here" on the whiteboard, as requested.

Jed had said they wanted proof it was us that took the gear, in the form of a mark inside the wards. I couldn't argue with the logic, so a mark went on the board.

It was pouring ectoplasm at the end of the alley towards the Square when I sealed the door.

"Can you drive the truck in reverse that far?" I asked Hiebert, who was driving the box truck. Dalma was literally riding shotgun for him.

"I think I can," he replied.

"Mount up," I called. "Hiebert, get the truck clear, and Davis, take the lead back to the funeral home. Padgett, we're back on tail end Charlie."

"Right," Padgett said, putting the Humvee in reverse and backing out of the alley.

He swung into the bar's parking lot, and we watched the box truck ease arthritically out of the alley, followed by Davis and Johnson's Humvee. Davis pulled ahead, and Hiebert followed him out towards the street. Padgett swung in behind the box truck, and I turned the turret to the rear, so I could cover the cloud of ectoplasm.

Something jumped up on the rooftop of the cache, and exploded in a rain of goo and meat.

"CONTACT!"

Something really large was forcing its way past the holy water barrier.

"Oh fuck, what the hell is that?" Padgett asked over the radio.

It looked like someone had stitched together a T-Rex and a stegosaurus and thrown in some bits from a velociraptor for good measure.

"DamnifIknow," I said, thumbing the butterfly trigger on the M2.

The monster roared.

"GO FASTER!" someone screamed over the radio.

I heard the other fifty start firing as well.

"Y'all got something out of Bob Bakker's nightmares back there, too?" Johnson asked.

"Yeah. Find an alternate route, Davis," I replied.

Diindiisi hopped out the side door of our Humvee and fired across the roof at something with a lever-action rifle, then slid back into the front seat.

There was a thump, followed by an explosion as something (hey, I didn't look that closely at it) fell into the safe zone we'd created.

"Reversing. Jonathan, follow us left," Davis said.

He then pulled off a bootlegger reverse in a Humvee. Not something I would have tried, but he didn't roll the vehicle, so if it's stupid and it works, it ain't stupid at the time.

"GO!" I shouted as we rolled out.

Davis put his foot into the Humvee's firewall, and Hiebert followed his example. Padgett did the same. Problem was, I was now blessed with a surfeit of large, angry monsters to shoot at.

"Fuck it," I shouted, shifting my fire between all of them.

The gun ran dry, and I dropped into the Humvee, and Diindiisi handed me one of the boxes of belted, silver core

.50 ammo that QMG had gifted us with. You ever tried to reload a machine gun in a small turret driving at high speed? It took an act of God and Congress to get the can open, the way Padgett was slaloming down the street. I bounced off everything in the turret. Thank God for body armor. I finally got the gun reloaded and aimed at the closest pursuing monster.

The first burst went wide, naturally. The second, however, walked right up the leading thing's chest, exploding its head. It tumbled to the ground in a heap, and the following monstrosity crashed into it with a sickening snap. The second struggled to rise before being swarmed from behind by a mob of imps and other, lesser daemons.

"Interesting," I said. *Were they eating each other, or just collecting parts like that first day in the square?*

"Turning north," Davis said.

I looked over my shoulder. We'd crossed the river again, slowing for the railroad crossing I'd jumped last week.

"Looks like we're clear this way," Miller called over the net.

"Take the short route home," I said. "I think I need to change my pants."

"Amen to that," Miller said.

"Shit Jesse, I haven't had this much fun since I lost three foot of small intestine in the Mog!" Johnson said in the silence.

"Roger that," I replied.

"CONTACT RIGHT!" he shouted as we passed the Theater Building.

"Damn, that is the biggest crawdad I've ever seen," Dalma said as the box truck slid past the monster.

It was rising from one of the old fish hatchery ponds around the Theater Building, followed by a horde of smaller imps that were a nightmare of imp and crawdad in form.

"DRIVE!" someone screamed over the radio.

I opened the dance. QMG silver .50 ammo is based on an 800-grain slug, with a silver core. The core is icing on the cake, because the slug removes chunks. Even daemon flesh wasn't withstanding the pounding, and the big mud bug was coming apart under the pounding.

"SHIT!" Dalma screamed over the radio. "They're on the roof!"

Several somethings had leaped on the roof of the box truck.

"Johnson?"

"Negative, we've got a target-rich environment up here," he replied.

"Right. Padgett bring us up alongside them, huh? Diindiisi, hand me the sprayer nozzle."

"Right."

The wand came up between my legs.

"Sorry," Diindiisi laughed.

"No worries," I replied, "Hand me the tank."

"I don't think that's going to fit, Jesse," she shouted over the windrush.

I hit the quick release on the harness holding me in the turret, boosting myself up to the top of the armor with a quick prayer.

Do not try this at home, viewers, the folks you're watching are idiots.

Diindiisi shoved the tank up, scraping it on the side of the guns receiver. I managed to grab one of the shoulder straps and slide back into the turret in what turned out to be one smooth maneuver. I'd like to say I'd practiced for just such an emergency, but we all know God watches over small children and idiots like me.

I propped the tank up in the turret, on the fifty ammo, while somebody, probably Diindiisi, got my harness snapped back in place. This next bit was going to be tricky. Fortunately, rather than being the pump action on the nozzle end, this sprayer was one of the 'pump up the tank' models.

"Everybody, try to drive straight for a minute," I said as we pulled up alongside the box truck.

Daemons looked down on me from the top. I hosed the closest one in the face with holy water. Not an easy thing to do, driving down the road. It exploded, knocking a second one off the top of the truck. Up ahead, I could hear the fifty on the lead Humvee go silent, followed by the sharp bark of Johnson's AR. Either he'd modified the weapon to fire burst, or he had a damn slick action on that gun. The final daemon jumped from the roof of the truck onto the hood of my Humvee.

"FUCK! FUCK! FUCK!" Padgett screamed over the radio, slamming on the brakes.

I bounced off the receiver of the fifty, again, and then the back of the turret. The only thing keeping me inside was the gunner's harness. The daemon sunk its three-toed feet into the hood of the Humvee, shattering the fiberglass. It also snatched the nozzle end of the sprayer out of my hands, clubbing me with the tank as it pulled the whole assembly out of the turret and tossed it to the ground.

"Now you are mine!" it gloated, reaching for me.

"Not yet," Diindiisi said.

Somehow, she'd managed to get the door open, her harness off, and was leaning out the door. She slammed her shotgun into contact with the daemon and pulled the trigger. She'd replaced the 870 pump gun with a ten gauge Ithaca Roadblocker from the cache. It meant one more type of ammunition for us to worry about, but damn, those ten gauge rounds punched above their weight class. Especially when the gun was close enough to the target that there wasn't room for the gas to dissipate – I muzzily watched the daemon's flesh expand from gas pressure before the silver buckshot caused it to go into convulsions. She fired a second round, and the daemon fell off the hood.

"Go!" she said, dropping back into her seat.

She let the acceleration close the door for her.

"Y'all alright?" Johnson asked over the radio.

"Yeah, just get back to base," I replied.

I took a minute to check the fifty, dropping some regular ammo in the box attached to the side of the gun. I added it to the short silver core belt stub hanging from the side of the receiver.

Man, I was going to be black and blue when today was done.

Chapter Ten
Day 12, 11 April 2018

The next morning, I looked like I'd gone ten rounds with someone armed with a baseball bat. I even had a beautiful set of marks from the gun impacting the chest plate of my armor, all over my upper torso.

"Free day," I groaned at breakfast. I'd be spending most of the day recovering, either soaking in a hot shower, or doing as little as possible. At least I hadn't broken any ribs.

"I could try something for your bruises," Diindiisi said. "I've got the stuff to make a poultice my husband taught me. Works pretty well on deep bruises. I even used it to set Fred Noonan's ribs."

"Ok," I replied. I hurt enough that I was willing to try anything, once.

And Marine Candy wasn't doing more than taking the edge off – although the look on everyone else's faces at the table when I'd popped sixteen two hundred milligram ibuprofen and washed them down with a coffee was priceless.

"Dude, is that even healthy?" Davis asked.

"Probably not," I replied. "But I'm less worried about my liver than being able to function at the moment."

"I've got research to do," Miller announced before trooping off into the other apartment.

"It's going to take me a while to make the poultice," Diindiisi said. "And you probably don't want to be here while I do. It can be a bit ...well, it stinks to high heaven, honestly."

"Oh joy," I groaned.

"I'm going to check that gun you beat up with your chest yesterday," Johnson announced, dropping his plate and cup in the sink.

"Need a hand?" Dalma asked.

"Yeah. Gonna be enough of a bitch dismounting it as is," he said.

"I'll help," Davis, Padgett and Hiebert all said at once.

"Did you plan this?" I asked Diindiisi as everyone else left.

"Do you mean did I talk to the others so I could get you alone?" she asked, lowering her eyes and giving me what was probably a sultry look for about 1910 or so.

"Yes."

"Honestly, no," she replied with an impish grin. "But since we're alone . . ."

"I'm a bit beat up at the moment for anything of that nature," I replied. "Besides, it's not that you're not a handsome woman, it's that you're . . ."

I was kind of proud of myself for remembering that handsome used to apply to women, not men. One of the benefits of reading a lot of 19th century literature while on stakeout.

"Old enough to be what, your great-great-great grandmother?" she purred.

"No. More like you're a colleague," I replied. "And I value that relationship."

She laughed suddenly.

"At least one thing hasn't changed," she said with a chuckle.

"What's that?"

"Men still do all their thinking with their groins," she replied. "I'm not a dollymop. But we need to talk about things here in the Shadow Lands."

"Ok, I'll bite. What's a dollymop?"

I got a look for asking.

"What about a soiled dove?" she continued.

"Never run across that one either," I said.

She peered over her shoulder to see if anyone was around. "They're both part time prostitutes."

"Ah. Some sort of quaint English slang?"

"Something like that, yes. Probably because one of the euphemisms for the male generative organ at the time was dolly," she said.

"Ah," I said, coughing. "What did you want to talk about?"

"There's something different this time," she said.

"How so?"

She rose and opened both the windows, then went into her room and brought back a deerskin pouch.

"My workings," she said, putting the pouch on the counter next to the stove. She pulled a deep cast iron frying pan out of the cabinet and placed it on the stove. "Iron works best for this one for some reasons. When my husband made it, he'd drop lumps of ocher in the mix."

"Diindiisi, what's different?" I asked, gently.

She started chopping something that had way too many legs for comfort.

"There's something drawing the daemons to us," she said. "I've been here for over a hundred years now, and I've never seen this kind of activity. Even when the things grabbed Fred and Amelia, there were only about half a dozen or so of them."

"What happened there?" I asked.

"I've been reading up on things so some of this may be mixed in with that," she said, turning to look at me over her shoulder. "I went to sleep in the cottage I'd appropriated in what I'm now sure was Kent, based on what Father Miller told us the other day. I woke up on an atoll somewhere, probably Nikumaroro Island, on the beach. My bag was with me, and I could smell smoke. So I got out my pistol and angled towards the fire. I'd learned that fire meant humans, not daemons, you see."

"Good to see that constant," I said.

"Something like that. Through the years the first thing most people try to do, if they don't just give up, is build a fire to stay warm or keep the things at bay, then gather food and supplies. I saw a rather plain woman tending a man who was stretched out on the sand. I could see the wreckage of what I first assumed was an unusual boat beyond the surf line, hung on the reef," she said. She turned back to the counter and did some things to the pot before continuing.

"Sorry, where was I?"

"On the beach, man and woman, and a weird boat hung up on the reef," I replied.

"Right," she said. "I approached their fire, introducing myself. They were pleasant, but I could tell the man was injured. The first thing I did was make this poultice for Fred."

She smiled at the memory.

"It helped. Amelia caught me up on how much things had changed since I entered the Shadow Lands. She really was a gentle soul," Diindiisi said wistfully. "We gathered what food there was, and I taught her to fish with a spear. I'm not sure how long we were there, honestly."

"What happened?"

"One day I'd gone to the north end of the atoll to see if I could find some palm fronds to make baskets from. While I was gone, it started raining ectoplasm between me and the campsite. This was the first time I'd seen anything like that, so I was cautious about approaching it – any changes here can be deadly," she said.

"Understandable," I replied.

"And by the time I got to the camp, the rain had stopped, and Fred was gone. The daemons had done things to Amelia."

I thought back to the dead coed.

"I've seen what they do to women," I replied.

"Yes, well, it wasn't quite as bad as what the wendigo did to poor Mary Kelly, but that beast was feeding. The daemons were playing with Amelia," she said. "And apparently Fred as well. I heard his screams for some time before they got tired of him."

She sat down with a sigh.

"I hid for days, then finally woke up in what I think was the south of France, near Marseilles," she finally said. "I'm not sure though, and I was only there briefly."

"Briefly?"

"Yes, I bounced around quite a bit for the next few, I guess months or years. There was a long period of time where I was in the United States, however. I met the most disagreeable man."

"Oh? Anyone I might have heard of?"

"He led some union," she replied, rising and turning off the stove. She set the pot on a trivet to cool.

"Was it the Teamsters?" I asked.

"Yes, that was it," she replied.

I'd just solved the disappearance of Jimmy Hoffa.

"You know, when we get back to the other side, they're going to want to debrief you," I said. "Probably solve a number of 'unsolved' disappearances."

"Too bad the only folks who'll know about them are Church and government researchers," Miller said, walking back into the kitchen. "What is that stench?"

"Medicine," I replied.

"Well, if its efficacy is a function of its stench, you should be healthy as an ox just breathing it in," he said.

"I hadn't noticed," I replied.

"And I have to smear it on him," Diindiisi said, lasciviously.

Miller had the decency to blush.

Diindiisi and I broke out laughing.

"Even a Catholic Priest is still a man," she said.

Chapter Eleven
Day 13, 12 April 2018

I don't know what was in Diindiisi's magic goo, but it worked. I wasn't even bruised when I got up in the morning. She'd also spread some on my knee, and it was now working like it had before I fell out of the helicopter.

"You know," I said around a mouthful of eggs, "when we get back, you should share that poultice with the medical team."

"I've tried," she said. "It can't be made ahead of time, and if you screw up one step, it causes excruciating pain rather than healing."

"That could be a problem," Johnson pointed out. "Nothing worse than clotting powder and shellfish allergies, but you know."

"Yeah," I said.

"What's the plan for today?" Hiebert asked.

"I'd planned on another day of rest, honestly," I said. "But since I'm feelin' pert as a ruttin' buck, hmm, Dave, do you have a list of possible sites here in San Marcos?"

"Ritual sites? I put the program to searching for them but I haven't checked the search lately. I can look and see what's come up," he said.

"Please do."

He went to the other apartment.

"Pert as a ruttin' buck?" Padgett asked.

"Sorry, I watched *The Outlaw Josey Wales* while I was laying there slathered in goo. Seemed appropriate," I said.

"We need some groceries," Dalma said.

"Got a list?"

"Not yet," she replied. "But give me some time. Oh, and I get to go with you."

"Sure thing," I said. "Two truck run? Johnson could use a bed."

"Eh, my cot's fine," he said. "Better than a leaky air mattress in a hole in the sand."

"True. But I think there's a BentonMart SuperCenter across the highway where we can get food and a bed and bedding," I said.

"Hadn't thought of that. You want to take the box truck?"

"Yeah, just for the size. We can back it up to the loading dock, clear the store and start loading with pallet jacks," I replied.

"Works for me."

"Sample is still running," Miller said. "But so far there's over a hundred possible sites in the area."

"Damn. What did you set as the search parameters?"

"Known archaeological sites, ritual sites, and cult activity," he replied.

"That last one is going to get every bored frat boy dressing up in cheap robes he bought off the internet to scare pledges," I said. "Like that giant cow thing up in Picadilly a while back."

"Don't get me started on that one. I've had to talk with the Defender there. William Thomas is a bit strange, even for someone with a geas laid on him," Miller said.

I looked around the room. Sure enough, Johnson had been to Picadilly, because he was wearing an 'I saw the Damned Cow' T-shirt. Odds were pretty good that, in this part of Texas at least, someone had been there after the possessed bovine had been shot. And Thomas was making bank off of it – had the head hung in the bar he owned, and for a while had sold the meat from it with an iron clad legal disclaimer about it coming from a possessed cow, and the eater taking all responsibility for any personal side effects cause by consuming the meat, etc. He'd even made a big deal about bringing in a priest to 'exorcise' the meat.

"Yeah, I've met him as well. Worked a couple of cases in that area. I wonder …no, we'd probably get Klein bottled back here before we got there," I said.

"Yeah, probably," Miller replied.

"What are you two talking about?" Diindiisi asked.

"Picadilly is this weird little town a couple hours north of here," I said. "That apparently sits on a Ley line nexus and is a sink for paranormal activity. It makes Marfa look calm on the scale of 'weird stuff happens here', among other things. Which might get us out of here, but you've said the zone is about twenty miles in any direction. So going there, saying Mother Shipton's Spell is a no go. But the really weird part is van Helsing's grand kids, or is it great grand kids, run a gas station there."

"And are probably the most redneck vampire hunters I've ever run across. Who names their kid Bubba?" Miller asked.

"Wait a minute," Johnson said. "Abraham 'Bubba' van Helsing IV? The guy who was on track to be one of the leading linebackers in the NFL before his knee injury? That Bubba van Helsing?"

"Yes," Miller replied.

"I'll be damned," Johnson said.

"Probably," I grinned. "But yeah, Bubba hunts monsters out of a truck stop over there. And yes, Diindiisi, he's related to your Abraham van Helsing."

"It would be nice to see what his descendants have become," she said.

"Bubba's about four hundred pounds of meat wrapped around some really bad anger management issues," I said. "And his brother Cletus is about the weaselliest little fuck I've ever run across. But that's not getting us anywhere. Who wants to go shopping?"

Davis and Father Miller stayed behind. Davis said he was going to pull maintenance on the safe zone with the pressure washer after we left, and Father Miller wanted to pare down his search parameters, along with setting up some of the goodies that we'd picked up at the cache. The rest of us loaded the box truck and one of the Humvees, Miller blessed us, Davis washed the vehicles down with holy water, and off we went.

Since Johnson was along, I rode in the back seat of the Humvee, across from Diindiisi, Padgett was driving, and Dalma was grumping along as shotgun.

"Why so dour?" I asked Dalma.

Padgett laughed. "She lost at rock, paper, scissors."

"You cheated!" Dalma said.

"Spock crushes scissors," he replied. "Your rules, not mine."

She grumped at him and went to staring out the window.

"Is this modern life?" Diindiisi asked me over the roar of the engine.

"Postmodern, but yeah, pretty much."

"I don't know that I want to go there," she said.

"It'll be fun."

"I'm not sure I understand that word as you are using it," Diindiisi said.

"Well, English is a language that confuses even native speakers," I replied.

We turned into the BentonMart parking lot, then went around back. It was clear, so we got out and started spraying holy water to form a protective zone. Once that was established, I tried the back door. It was locked, but one of the loading dock doors was up about a foot. Johnson carefully backed the box truck up to the bay door, and I climbed up onto the trucks loading gate, then squirmed under the door. And listened. Nothing. Someone stuck the nozzle of a sprayer through the gap, and I made another safe zone just in case, then took a hammer and chisel and knocked the lock off the bay door. I slipped the bolt out, running the door up.

"Diindiisi, Johnson, Dalma, start going through the stuff back here, and loading what you think we need. Hiebert, you stay with them, establish a perimeter around where they're working, but be sparing. Padgett, grab a sprayer, and let's go see what we can find in the store itself, shall we. And yes, ladies, we will get all the feminine hygiene products on the shelves," I said.

After chocolate, those were the number two item on the list. I was just glad things hadn't gotten messy, yet.

"Let's go up front and seal that door," I said.

I still had a bit of wafer left. I could consecrate wine and water all day long, and Father Miller and I had discussed using regular bread for a wafer replacement, but that meant a bit more work.

We sealed the door and grabbed a couple of shopping carts and loaded them up before pushing them to the back.

We were pushing the third set of carts to the back when I saw the chest freezers.

"We need those," I said to Padgett.

"Why so?"

"Load them full of meat, frozen veg, etc., and we're better able to hunker down. Only thing we need more would be a washer and dryer," I replied.

Washing clothes in a bathtub or sink full of water sucks, don't let anyone tell you anything different.

"Good point," he said, inspecting the freezers. "They're still on the pallets."

"Pallet jacks to the rescue, then," I said.

We pushed the baskets to the back, then looked at the loading process. They were doing pretty good – they'd managed to get three pallets of canned vegetables, assorted into the truck, along with...

"Oh dear god, an entire pallet of Spam?"

"Yeah, looks like they were having a sale," Dalma said.

"Christ save me, my sodium level is rising just looking at that stuff," I said, crossing myself.

"It's the low sodium version. I found some sticky rice too. If I could find some nori, I'd make spam musabi," she said.

"Oh dear God," I said, mock collapsing against a pallet of soft drinks. "I spent time with 3rd Marines at Marine Corps Base Hawaii. That stuff was everywhere."

"Do you have a better solution for storing meat?" Dalma asked.

"Well, there's three chest freezers in the store," I said.

She pushed the pallet of spam off to the side, and jerked the pallet jack out from under it.

"Well? What are we waiting for?" Dalma asked.

"What happened to finding some nori?" I replied.

"I can fake it up, but a case of Spam should be more than enough," she replied.

"I thought so," I replied, leading her out into the store.

We'd just about finished loading the truck when something slammed into the front of the store hard enough to move the building.

"Oh, that's not good," I said. "Time to do a Monty Python out of here."

"Monty Python?" Padgett said, pushing his basket to the rear of the store.

"Yeah, RUN AWAY!" I replied, picking up the pace behind my own basket.

The store shook again as we entered the storage area.

"What's happening? Earthquake?" Hiebert asked.

"Something has decided to face fuck the building, and Father Salazar suggested we run away," Padgett said.

"Sounds like a plan," Johnson said, tossing the two baskets on top of the load, then slamming the door on the box truck.

"Johnson, take shotgun with Hiebert," I said.

We, to quote a sergeant I had who really loved the movie *Full Metal Jacket,* unassed the building most ricky-tick. Vehicles were started while I climbed up into the turret. The building shook a third time, and I could see a mass of meat rising over the front.

"What is it?" Dalma shouted, pausing her climb into the Humvee.

"I've got no idea, but it's really big and royally pissed off," I replied. "Get in the damn truck."

"Where to?" Hiebert asked.

"Anywhere but here," I replied. "Away from that thing."

"Right," he said, turning right and running down the building. The lot tied into a road, and he turned left, with us following him.

"Well, that's a new one for Father Miller's report," I said as I finally got a decent view of the thing attacking the store front.

It was an amalgamation of all the daemons we'd killed so far. And damn it was ugly. The pig's head was front and center, with crawdad claws to either side. And it had way too many feet – a collection of hooves, claws, and other, stranger things. The pig's head came up just before it charged the building again and sniffed the air before bellowing a challenge.

"Drive faster," I said, slewing the turret to face the rear.

"Gonna take a minute," Hiebert replied over the radio. "This road is a bit rough."

The pile o'daemons started galumphing towards where we were running parallel to the Blanco River.

"Sharp turn," Hiebert said over the radio.

I still hadn't fired up the pile o' daemons, but it was getting close enough I was contemplating it. Padgett came off the accelerator long enough to turn right, then sharp left shortly afterwards. We went under a railroad bridge and sped along, the river colored a dirty gray by the sky.

For all its size and speed, the pile o'daemons wasn't all that agile. It made the first turn, slammed into the bridge, and fell in the river. Where it was promptly set upon by . . .

"Are those piranha?" I asked.

"Probably tilapia," Hiebert answered. "They stood in for the piranha in the movie I was in. They filmed scenes in the Blanco as well."

"How'd you know they'd be there?" Dalma broke in.

"I didn't. But I talked to Ms. Diindiisi, and she mentioned the daemons doing things like that, so I took a chance," he replied.

There must have been thousands of the tilapia, and they were busy reducing the pile o'daemons to a muddy swirl in the river.

"That's actually kind of scary," Johnson said. He was seated in the window of the box truck, looking back towards the fight in the river.

"Yeah, ain't it? Note to everyone. No swimming," I said.

"No shit," Padgett said. "I may never go swimming again."

"Yeah, you tend to lose little things like that over the years in this business," I said as we sped back towards the funeral home.

Chapter Twelve
Day 14, 13 April 2018

Miller was grinning the next morning. We'd plugged everything in, got the freezers loaded, and then collapsed from the effort.

"So, I was going through the boxes yesterday that we got from the cache," he said.

"You said you were going to," I replied.

"Yeah, well, there was a box marked for you," he said.

"Let's go take a look, I guess," I replied.

He and I trooped down to the garage where the gear was 'staged'. Well, we'd carefully piled it in separate piles, anyway. Miller and Davis had moved two of the Pelican cases over by the ammo pile, however.

"What's in them?" I asked.

"Oh, that's the surprise," Miller said. "The note specifically says not to tell you if anyone else opens them, let you see for yourself."

Oh great. Gunny was up to something.

I opened the Pelican case. Inside were several heavy duty bags. I grabbed one and opened the snap closures.

"Oh my," I said, taking the first M-PIMS out of the bag.

"What's that?" Miller asked.

"Mini-Multi-Purpose Infantry Munition," I replied. "M-PIMS for short."

"Ok, what's it do in its spare time?" Miller asked.

"You know what a claymore is, right?"

"The mine, not the sword, I'm guessing," he snarked back.

"Yeah. The mine. This is its modern, updated offspring. Although, I'm wondering where they came from. QMG doesn't do a lot of ambushes or positional defenses," I said. Then I saw the envelope.

I took it from the top of the case and opened it -

Jesse — had to call in a couple favors for these. Put them to good use.
      Gunny

"That's special," I said.

"How so?"

"We're going to plant these all over the place and watch daemons turn to goo," I replied. "Think of them as an early warning system that's really loud."

"More fun for you, I guess," Miller said.

"Something like that, yeah. How'd the sorting go yesterday?"

"I narrowed it down to five major sites, I think. Problem is one of them is under Spring Lake, and two of them are underground."

"And the other two?" I asked.

"One of them is where they built part of the Meadows Center," he said.

"Yeah, home of the giant swimming daemon pig," I replied.

"And the other one is under Jowers Center. It might be usable, but something tells me that it's probably under tons of concrete, if nothing else," he replied   .

"Yeah, structural concrete reinforced with steel can make trying to work magic interesting," I replied.

"So what are you going to do today?" Miller asked.

"Rig explosives, of course," I replied.

It wasn't that easy. Johnson helped — he'd had the same 'how to rig 'claymores and not blow yourself up' course I'd gone through, only about twenty years earlier. We talked about what had changed and what hadn't, while we rigged mines everywhere.

"These things are going to work on daemons?" he asked while we were daisy chaining the mines into a giant circle of boom.

"Should. According to the paperwork, these are a special order run QMG got from the manufacturer, they coated the normal steel shrapnel in the mine with silver. Should prove an interesting field test, if nothing else," I replied.

"And the cameras?"

Every fifth mine had a Picatinny rail, and one of the options was a small, wireless camera.

"Well, if it's another survivor wandering into the blast zone, we might want to see him before we blow him into goo," I replied.

"Good point," Johnson said. "How're we going to get in and out?"

"I wasn't planning on leaving for a while – the fridge is full, as are the freezers, we've got ammunition for days, and enough movies to binge watch for months," I said.

"So no more patrolling or searching for survivors?"

"I figured on a couple of down days, then we'd go looking. I'm not sure we're going to find anyone, but you never know," I said.

"Really?"

"Yeah, I've been looking over the data about disappearances. One or two individuals has been a 'mass' event since the Church has been keeping track of such things."

"What about things like Roanoke Colony?"

We'd all been doing some reading through Millers archives. The more eyes on the subject, the better the chance we'd find something.

"Probably killed by or subsumed into the Croatoan tribe, whoever they were. There were a number of blue eyed children born to local tribes after the colony went missing. *USS Cyclops* probably just sank, and we haven't found her yet. As for the Bermuda Triangle?" I wobbled a hand at him. "Again, if any of that lot had come through here, Diindiisi would have stories about being wet for a very long time."

He laughed.

"Good point," he said, shaking the sprayer on his back. "Speaking of wet, this thing's almost dry."

"No problems, we're done here," I said. "Now I've got to figure out how to configure the cameras to feed the laptop they sent along. Thank God for manuals."

"I thought Marines never read the fucking manual," Johnson said with a grin.

"Like crayon eating, it's a myth we spread so folks won't be awe struck by our perfection," I replied.

"Yeah, sure. Whatever you have to tell yourself to sleep at night, Jarhead," he said, slapping me on the back.

I looked at him and started back towards the garage, singing.

"Yippie-ti-yi-yah, get along little doggie, it's your misfortune and none of my own."

He gave me a look.

"Yippie-ti-yi-yah, get along little doggie, you know that Fort Hood will be your new home,"

"That's hittin' below the belt," Johnson said. "Although, yeah, Fort Hood sucks. Not as bad as Fort Lost in the Woods or Grafenwoer, but damn."

We walked to the garage and offloaded gear. Everyone else was busy, so I went upstairs and connected the cameras to the laptop. Things worked great – except for having six views on the screen at once.

After all that was done, I figured it was nap time.

Naturally, twenty minutes after I laid down, the alert on the laptop went off. It's my fault, I didn't check what it was set to, or how loud it was set. Have you ever seen one of those WWII submarine movies where they hit the dive klaxon? Imagine that, going off at 100 percent about six inches from your ear.

I nearly shot a hole in the ceiling.

I checked the computer. The program was set up so that it would key in on movement and expand that specific camera. More RTFM for the win. There was a goat man reaching for the camera on top of the M-MPIMS when the camera went blank, followed by an explosion.

"What's up?" Miller asked.

"Abzu's minions are testing the defenses," I replied.

"What was the sound before the boom?" he asked.

"Gunny's idea of a joke."

Everyone was standing in the hallway between the two apartments.

"Right, same positions, as last time, everyone. Keep an eye out for movement. And damn, next time we mount the camera's separate from the mines, I guess," I said.

I followed them out onto the roof, where we waited. And waited. And waited some more.

"Are you sure they're attacking?" Hiebert asked.

"Not really. Could have been what passes for a messenger that got blown up," I replied.

We waited some more.

After about an hour of nothing, I called it.

"Head inside. I'm going to go replace the mine and move the cameras off the mines," I said.

"Want some cover?" Johnson asked. He was toting the Golf.

"Sure, tag along if you want," I replied.

We stopped in the garage, grabbed a replacement mine and camera and headed to where the mine had blown.

"Are you going to wire it back into the chain?" Johnson asked as we rounded the house on the north side of the funeral home to replace the mine.

"Damn thing's tough, I'll give it that," Johnson said, looking at the remains of the goat man.

"Not tonight," I said.

"Good my master will make use of that," a voice rasped.

It was laying there, gasping for breath. It mostly looked like 180 pounds of ground round after the close encounter with 317 silver coated steel spheres driven by two pounds of explosives. A second daemon stood nearby. This one was whole and looked like a proboscis monkey on steroids crossed with a gorilla.

"How so?" I asked, rigging the mine.

"It will be a weak spot in your defenses," the daemon replied.

"Weak like your buddy found out," I said, setting the anti-tamper trigger before placing the mine. "Are you willing to sacrifice your power for that of Abzu?"

"You know not what the great one has promised us, mortal, for your body for him to torture, do you?"

It started making a rasping, ragged, guttural noise, which I realized was its version of laughter.

"Let me guess, promotion to the mortal realm to do his bidding there?"

"That is only the first gift!"

"Johnson?"

"Right, boss," Johnson said, before cutting it in half with the M240.

"Gonna need to beef up the defenses if you want to stay here," Johnson said as we watched the two daemons die.

"I fucking hate filling sandbags and stringing wire," I replied.

"Not high on my list of things either, boss," Johnson said. "But it's got to be done."

Chapter Thirteen
Day 18, 17 April 2018

Four days. Four days of dodging roving patrols of daemons and less savory things (I'd fought a ghoul queen, but ambulatory goo piles moving at about twenty miles an hour down the road freak me right out), to loot every building supply, contractor, Farmall, and garden supply center in town of every last bag of sand, concrete mix, plaster mix or anything else we could think of. We also grabbed sandbags – not that I'd insist we fill them unless we had to. Although a wall of various construction materials did look a bit odd – and no two bags were the same size or color.

"First time I ever built a sandbag wall that I covered with plastic drop cloths," Johnson said when we were done stacking bags.

"Yeah, well, I figure if it stays dry it'll be better protection. Besides, we're still washing down the street to keep the perimeter wider," I replied.

"And you don't want the concrete to set up?"

"Or the plaster, yeah," I said, stretching. "I'm going to go take a shower."

He waved.

"I'm already filthy. Figured I'd pull the fifty on Thing Two and check the mount. It's a little loose," he replied.

"More hot water for me," I chuckled, going upstairs.

I was in the 'repeat' phase of 'wash, rinse, repeat' when the house next door exploded, raining building fragments everywhere.

There are times when a man's gotta do what a man's got to do. Doesn't mean I like going into combat wearing nothing but Load Bearing Equipment, combat boots and a smile.

I came out of the bathroom and down the hall to the small porch at the top of the outside flight of stairs.

"How in the fuck did that get there?" Padgett shouted.

That was one of the piles of ambulatory goo where the house had been. Funny part was it hadn't leaked past where the walls had stood.

"Not sure," I said.

"Underground?" Davis offered. Followed by, "Dude, where are your pants?"

"I was in the shower ...shit. Grab a sprayer and follow me," I said.

Inside. Down the stairs, into what had been the embalming room – we were using it as a storage space, but sure enough, in the center of the floor was drain that was starting to ooze pink worms.

"Hose it down," I said.

Davis hit the oozing pink fingers with holy water from the sprayer. There was an ear-shattering shriek, and whatever it was withdrew into the floor drain.

"Keep pumping," I said. "Force it back."

"What the hell is going on?" Father Miller asked. "And Father Salazar? Pants?"

"Yeah, I'll get them," I said. "Something tried coming up through the sewer pipes."

"Crap," Miller replied.

"Yeah, we're going to have to start pouring holy water down them as well," I replied.

"But how? I mean I guess the pipes could be plastic, but this place is old enough and they should be cast iron. And the cold iron should be anathema to the daemonic," Miller said, handing me a sheet to drape myself with.

I was in the process of doing that when Diindiisi walked in. She quirked an eyebrow at me and a slight smile crossed her features.

"You said they used this room to embalm bodies," she said. "How does that process work?"

"You take a trocar," I found one in a drawer and showed it to her, "and you put it in a femoral artery in the leg and attach a hose. Then you take another trocar and put it in the subclavian artery in the neck and attach it to a pump full of formaldehyde, which is attached to a sink."

I pointed to the gear.

"Turn on the sink and turn on the pump. The pump pushes embalming fluid into the body, and the blood out through the leg. That's if the circulatory system is complete," I said.

"There's your answer then," she said, turning to Miller. "Blood goes down the drain. Even if the pipes are cold iron, the blood would protect the daemon long enough to get inside."

Johnson stepped out of the garage.

"Nice toga there, Bluto," he said. "You want us to light that thing up?"

"Yeah. Do it. Then flush whatever sewer pipes are left with holy water. Something else to add to the list of daily tasks."

"Well, at least here we can use the pump," Miller said.

"And the sewer clean out next door. Oh, and once that thing is down, we're going to need to find the water cut off, because I'm pretty sure it probably broke water pipes on the way out."

Johnson wasn't fooling around. I heard the compressor on the pressure washer kick in.

"Ya'll got this?" I asked.

"Why?" Miller replied.

"I'd like to go wash the soap off and put on pants, since everyone seems to be so concerned about my state of dress," I replied.

"Well, most folks do wear pants to fight evil," Miller replied as I stumped back upstairs.

I stopped next to my 'bed' long enough to grab two bottles of holy water, then poured them down the sink and shower in the bathroom, just to be sure. I finished my shower, rinsed off my LBE and boots, got dressed and went outside.

They'd forced the daemon back into the pipes and away – it had actually surfaced through a manhole cover a couple of hundred feet uphill from where we were, and was sitting there, brooding and licking its wounds. The skin was mottled, probably from contact with the iron and holy water.

"Notice anything?" Miller asked.

"Yeah, we're losing the arms race," I replied.

"How so?"

"When we first got here, silver killed them," I said, pointing to the pile of goo. "Dilute holy water would cause them to explode. Now?"

"Oh."

"Other thing is, you notice something missing?" I asked, gesturing broadly.

"No ectoplasm," Miller replied.

"Yeah. They're not warning us they're coming anymore," I said.

Miller looked like he'd really like to swear, but his vows were keeping him from it.

"That's great. Although, knowing you, you've got a plan of some sort. What do you want to try?"

"JOHNSON!" I shouted over the roar of the pressure washer.

He shut it down.

"Yeah?"

"Thing One and Thing Two. They both operable?"

"Yeah, I hadn't gotten the mount pulled on Thing Two. Take five-ten minutes to get the gun back in place," he replied. "Silver?"

"No. Those belts of tracer still around?"

"Damn, that's evil," he replied.

He'd made up some 'special purpose' belts for a night shoot – instead of the regular one in five tracer to regular ammo, these were nothing but tracer. They'd gotten mixed into the ammo we'd brought from his shop.

"Yeah, you want just the fifty ammo?"

"No, we've got a spare barrel or three for the Golf," I replied.

At night, nothing but tracer was flashy as hell. I was kind of hoping that if we fired them from close enough we'd set the damn thing on fire as well.

"How do you want to do this?" Johnson asked. He'd be running one of the machine guns.

"Thing One, fifty cal tracer," I replied. "I'll take the Golf and the thirty tracer in Thing Two. And just to be on the safe side, I'll have silver in the fifty on Thing Two."

"It'll take a couple minutes to pull the fifty and swap mounts on Thing Two," Johnson said.

"I'll Rambo it, standing in the turret," I said.

It took a few minutes to get everything set up. Goo-monster was still sitting there, watching us when we parked the two Humvees facing it in the street. Miller blessed everything, then took cover behind the Humvees.

Honestly, it felt like a day on the range.

"All ready on the right," I said. "All ready on the left. COMMENCE FIRE!"

Both guns opened up within seconds of each other. Johnson had an advantage over me – he had the gun mount to keep his fifty on target, while I was standing in the turret braced to fire.

It just meant I had to fire shorter bursts, that is all.

The pile of goo tried to run away. But even at its fastest (and it had taken a while for the other ones to build up to twenty miles an hour) it wasn't going to get out of the impact zone fast enough. It decided to try coming downhill and mashing us.

And ran right into the barrier provided by the magic bird bath of Saint Mark the Evangelist. Where it got stuck, finally catching fire.

"CEASE FIRE! CEASE FIRE!"

I'd burned through about five hundred rounds by this point, and even with firing short bursts, the Golf was hot. I set it down carefully and climbed up out of the turret.

"I'm dry," Johnson said. "You?"

"Ran about five hundred rounds through it. It worked, finally, but damn that thing stinks."

The goo pile was trying to run back uphill, but slipping on the fluids leaking from the blazing holes in its body.

And yeah, it stank. I've smelled burn pits that were more refreshing.

"I'm going to try to finish it off," I said, climbing back into Thing Two.

The Golf had cooled enough that I felt comfortable dropping it into the Humvee wouldn't melt the seats or burn flesh, so I dropped it into the vehicle, then set the M2 to single shot, and fired. It sounded like God's own typewriter backspacing.

Backspace. Backspace. Backspace. After the fourth round, the pile of goo went stiff (well, as stiff as a self-ambulatory non-Newtonian fluid can go) and started deliquescing into the street.

Oddly enough none of the goop flowed past the barrier either.

"That tell you anything?" Miller asked as I put the M2 on safe and climbed back down.

"Yeah. We can burn them, with tracers, if we have to," I replied. "Which makes me wonder if we've got any glass jars handy."

"I'm afraid to ask," Miller replied.

"Even I know that one," Dalma said, from where she was sitting in the driver's seat of Thing Two. "Molotov cocktail."

Miller shook his head at me.

"What? Don't we have grenades?"

I wasn't about to debate the proper use of white phosphorus marking grenades with the good Father. He was already saying more prayers daily than I was, after all. Although, I'd have given my left testicle for a Mark 19 40mm grenade launcher and a whole mess of Willie Pete. I had something in reserve, but I really didn't want to talk to

Father Miller about it, probably because he'd give me a
stern look and talking too.

Chapter Fourteen
Day 19, 18 April 2018

There's things you learn in combat. One of those is to never complain about it being quiet. Murphy, the patron saint of screwing everyone over, hears those complaints and goes to work.

We'd retrieved gasoline, Mason Jars, a bolt of cloth, and Styrofoam insulation, done a quick tour of the town, and come back to the funeral home, when Padgett decided to tempt fate.

"Man," he said, stepping back from the aluminum pot where he was stirring gasoline and Styrofoam, "it sure is quiet."

I crossed myself, and Johnson started swearing.

"What? It is quiet," Padgett said.

"Yeah, you never say that though," I replied. I'd swapped the barrel on the Golf while we were discussing the right mixture for the Molotovs

"That's just bad writing," Padgett said. "Every bad movie I've ever seen has the obligatory 'it's too quiet' scene, followed by someone dying."

"Yeah, why do you think that is?" Johnson asked. "My driver said that right before I lost three feet of my small intestine."

"Hold on," Padgett said. "You told me you got shot as part of the ground convoy in Mogadishu."

"Yeah, I did. But what do you think my driver said just before I got shot?" Johnson replied.

Padgett scoffed. I pointed over the retaining wall, where something was flying high in the sky.

"Well, we're being watched," I said.

"That's not good," Padgett said, carefully moving his bucket of sticky, flammable goop next to the retaining wall. "I'll go let everyone know something's up."

Johnson watched him disappear.

"You think something's up?" he asked.

"Not really. Whatever is up there has been there since we came out. Probably Abzu's equivalent of a drone. We know he threatened to keep an eye on us, and since we put up the walls, it's probably been harder to do," I replied.

"Hell, killing more than a few of his minions probably hasn't hurt, either."

"Roger that," I said, stirring the goop in the pot. "Give me a hand and we'll get these jars filled, huh?"

He looked at me.

"I thought you thought nothin' was going on," he said.

"Yeah, but that doesn't mean I want to stand out here with gasoline evaporating all over the place," I replied.

"Roger that," he said, taking a deep breath of that gasoline smell of victory.

We finished the Molotovs. Nothing disturbed us for the rest of the day, even though we obsessively checked the cameras and scanned the skies. Whatever it was (probably another griffin or worse) hung against the dirty static of the sky, sculling about lazily. If it hadn't been the size of a bus things might have been interesting.

We finally stood down around what should have been sunset – if there were a sun or if it set here. I checked the sensors one last time and went to bed. I'd get up in a couple or three hours and check on things, then swap out with Johnson, doing the same thing.

The buzzing started shortly afterwards.

We'd discussed this – it was the same noise we'd all heard when we'd transitioned to the Shadow Lands – and we had a plan. And as much as it pained Father Miller, the immediate plan didn't involve grabbing his magical bird bath and tossing it in the back of the Tacticool Tahoe.

It did, however, involve all of us getting in the Tacticool Tahoe, along with as many weapons and as much gear as we could fit inside.

The buzz got louder. I did a head count. We were all here. It increased in volume. Hiebert and Diindiisi swayed under the pressure. It started making my fillings itch. There was a bright flash of light, and we were still in the garage.

"That's never happened before," Diindiisi said.

"What?" I asked.

"When the noise starts, you transition. You're somewhere else. We went nowhere," she said.

There was a shriek, like the world's largest band saw trying to cut through concrete.

"Yeah, something tells me someone's not happy," Miller said.

"Positions, people," I replied.

We got out of the Tacticool Tahoe and spread around the building. It started raining ectoplasm, and shortly thereafter, we heard the M-MPIMs exploding.

"Oh, I think we have made something very, very angry," I said.

The ectoplasm rebounded from the barrier we'd established with the holy water. Things moved in the falling goo.

"MORTALS! HOW DARE YOU!" Abzu thundered.

"As if on cue," I said.

The ectoplasm parted, and he stood there, in all his fifth century before Common Era Akkadian finery.

"I cannot draw new mortals to my realm," he said. "What have you done?"

I looked at him. "Not a damn thing," I replied. "Might be the 'upstart' at work, though."

"Yes, you have his touch all over you," Abzu replied. "That will not stop me from collecting your souls, however."

Something enormously, stupidly big impacted, landed or crashed in the ectoplasm behind him. It was hard to tell which from all the noise it made, honestly.

"I can admit when I am out of my league, however," Abzu said. "It has been a while since I last had congress with my lady wife, after that vile idiot Marduk created the heavens and earth from her, but I found her spirit and was able to clothe it properly."

A head appeared out of the ectoplasm. Its mouth was big enough to swallow the Tacticool Tahoe whole.

"His wife?" Johnson asked.

"TIAMAT!" Abzu screamed.

"Chaos," Diindiisi replied, stepping forward. "You shall not pass."

"Yeah, fuck that, I saw that movie, and I don't think you're an angel disguised as a wizard," I said. "Light her up."

Tiamat raised one claw and gripped the barrier.

"Oh that's not good at all," I said. I keyed my mike. "Bring Thing One around as soon as possible."

Diindiisi was chanting. Johnson was lighting Tiamat up with the Golf. Dalma was somewhere banging away with the Barrett, and I went down the stairs. Tiamat climbed higher on the barrier. It was weird to see her front legs gripping the nothingness. Thing Two stopped at the base of the stairs and Miller hopped out. He had pulled out a thobe and a stole and went up the stairs. I went through the door and into the turret like I was still a twenty-four-year-old Marine, not a battered thirty-eight-year-old priest.

"Where?" Hiebert asked.

"Under that," I replied.

He pulled forward to the edge of the driveway and stopped.

"Set the brake and get the hell out," I said. "Man a sprayer."

"Right."

I checked that all the lids were off the ammo boxes in the turret. This would be a good death. I aimed at ...Tiamat's udder. Ancient gods of Chaos don't always follow the rules of evolution or good taste. I said a quick prayer.

At least I'll get to see Mel again. but I'll be leaving Diindiisi behind.

I shook my head once to clear those thoughts and slammed my thumbs against the butterfly trigger.

Something screamed when the first rounds hit it, and hot rain began to fall. The monster climbed higher, getting a third leg on the barrier. The belt ran out. I switched belts mechanically, and revised my aim point, going for the ankle on the lower leg. Tiamat toppled from the barrier as I cut her leg out from under her, destroying the buildings and parking lot across the street. She seemed to shrink in upon herself, her final form being that of a woman. She raised a hand to Abzu. He lifted her to her feet and healed the missing foot.

"You have the upper hand, for now," Abzu said before disappearing.

The ectoplasm stopped falling, and I passed out.

Really.

Chapter Fifteen
Day 24, 23 April 2018

"How long," I gasped. I was in bed, and didn't remember getting there. My left arm was strapped to a table, and an IV had been started.

"Five days," Diindiisi said, rising from a recliner in the corner. She came over and placed a hand on my forehead.

"Huh. Cause?"

She put a plastic straw between my lips and I drank tepid, room-temperature water.

"Apparently, other than being the foundation of the earth and heaven, it's her blood they're talking about when the myths say she filled the first dragons with 'poison rather than blood'."

"Ah," I replied. I sniffed. "More poultices?"

"Yes. Drew the poison right out," she said. "Although the paint job on Thing Two is, how did Johnson put it ...yes, 'right fucked'."

"I imagine," I said.

"Awake, finally, I see," Dalma said. She was wearing scrubs.

Dalma walked over and did the standard checks. BP, temp, etc. While she was doing that I noticed I was naked under the sheet. She notated everything on a chart, then walked out.

"Clothes?" I asked Diindiisi.

She grinned lasciviously at me.

"We had to cut them off of you," she said. "It's not like you've got anything I haven't seen before, when you were running around in boots and nothing else."

"True," I replied.

"Or me," Dalma said, returning. "Nursing school and all that."

"Ok, but y'all told me the other day I needed pants to fight evil," I replied.

"We're not fighting evil at the moment," Dalma replied. She cut the flow to the IV bag, and replaced it, then opened the valve again. "And unless something really breaks, you won't be up and moving for at least another day. Doctor's orders."

I thought about that for a couple of minutes.

"You're not a doctor," I replied, somewhat muzzily.

"No, but the doctor on the other end of your phone is," Miller said, entering the room. "And your password? Mel? Really?"

"Yeah. Well ...you were able to guess it," I said. I felt foggy. "Did you give me something?"

"Yes. Again, doctor's orders," Dalma replied. "It should help you sleep."

"I..."

I drifted off again.

Eight or so hours later, I woke again, with a raging need to take a leak. At least they hadn't cathed me. Diindiisi was sleeping in the chair in the corner.

"Diindiisi."

"Yes?"

"I need to..." trying to come up with 19th century euphemisms for urination when you're stoned out of your gourd isn't easy. I gestured at my crotch.

"Ah," she said, slipping a urinal under the sheets and into place.

I made use of it.

"Thanks," I said.

"No problem. I've nursed injured men before, you know," she said.

"I didn't know that."

"So much gets left out of books about one," she said.

"Tell me about your husband," I said.

Drugs. I swear it was the drugs.

"He was an older man," she said. "And a powerful wielder of magic. I was eleven when he and my father negotiated our marriage. He was much older."

"Eleven?"

"Yes, eleven. I was a woman by the standards of my people, having had my first menses," she said. "I know, from talking to Dalma and the others, your generation thinks that marrying that young is an abomination, but it was a different time. I was his third wife, the first two having died in childbirth."

"Did you have children?"

"No. While we were married when I was young, he waited until I was thirteen to consummate the marriage. 'Magic' was what he said to explain why. He'd had a vision that he and I were to be married, and we would wait for consummation."

"Ahh. How did he die?"

"Henry was on the Plains at the time visiting our band," she said. "Hunting and looking into 'local folklore' for the Quintus Society, along with another man, Randall, from Virginia."

She paused to drink from a cold mug of coffee.

"There was a disturbance, and Henry, Randall, and my husband fought a giant," she said. "The giant killed my husband, and his powers transferred to me, which was not a pleasant experience. Henry and Randall killed the giant, then returned my husband's body to us."

"Ah."

"Yes, ah," she said. "I later found out that my husband had foreseen all this in a vision, somehow calling Henry to us in our time of need. I was not ready to become a Woman Covered All Over at fourteen."

"Woman Covered All Over?" I said, feeling like the wrong half of a Socratic Dialogue.

"The term my people use for a female who gains the powers of her husband at his death. Henry had also promised to take me with him when he returned to England," she said. "Which is how I ended up fighting a wendigo there in 1888."

"You were what, sixteen at the time?"

"Yes," she said. "You have been paying attention. According to Henry, I was an imp as well. Although, after years here, I know what a real imp is like, and he was wrong. I was impish, but never an imp."

"You'll be able to tell him that soon," I replied.

"Yes, I will," she said wistfully. "Do you think we'll get out of here?"

"Something has changed," I replied. "Abzu has lost some power, obviously. I don't know if it's us, or the Holy Catholic Bird Bath, or his power lessening, but we've changed the rules."

She came over and sat on the edge of the bed.

"I have to tell you something," she said, looking down.

"Ok," I said.

"I didn't find you by chance," she replied. "I was, I was, I don't know where I was, honestly, but I had a vision of you behind a door. I gathered my things and stepped through, and there you were."

I'd heard stranger things in the last few years.

"How detailed was this vision?"

She looked me in the eye and smiled.

"Very. Bordering on the explicit," she replied.

"Oh."

"Yes, oh," she said. "If you're asking if I saw you getting injured, no. I saw that we would be together, however. If we make it out of here. I think I'm being told, not so subtly, that it is time for me to return to a more traditional role, according to my people's ways."

"And if we don't make it out of here?"

She looked down again. "Torment, pain, and death."

The words hung in the air between us. I reached over and took her hand in mine. Something clicked. Cliché, I know, but it was there. Had I been sent to the Shadow Lands like some paladin of old to rescue the princess fair? I shook my head internally at the image of me in shining armor and Diindiisi in a hennin, leaning from the window of a tower, guarded by a dragon. Although, with Tiamat around, we did have the dragon, if nothing else.

"Then I guess we have to get out of this place," I replied.

"That would be best," she said.

I moved over on the bed, and she slipped in next to me, on top of the covers.

"Tell me about your marriage traditions, Jesse," she said.

"Well, generally men no longer negotiate with women's fathers," I said.

"Dalma told me that," she replied.

"Good, because the only spiritualist I know charges an arm and a leg to contact specific persons. He's good, but damn, he's expensive," I said.

"My father would have liked you," she said. "Although I agree, after more than a hundred years in the spirit realm he might be a bit troubled to be negotiating about a daughter he thought he was rid of well before he died."

"We'll need a priest, eventually," I said.

"Yes, the vision was specific," she replied. "We have to wait. Do you think Father Miller would be willing to officiate?"

"Officiate what?" Miller asked. He took a moment to take in the image we presented. "Oh. Yes. Even if the heretic won't convert to the proper church, I'll officiate."

Miller was grinning like the Cheshire Cat.

"I see your mind is still in the gutter," I said.

"Occasionally, yes," he replied. "I'm celibate, not perfect. I'll confess my sins when we get out of here."

He tossed my phone on the bed.

"Your boss is texting again," he said before turning to leave. "I figured if you were awake you could go over everything with him."

"Dave?" I called to his back. He stopped and came back. "Yeah?"

"Thanks, man."

"No worries, Jesse."

Chapter Sixteen
Day 25, 24 April 2018

I ended up having to connect my phone to power to message Gunny. He had a huge info dump for me, which was a bitch until I connected the phone to a laptop via Bluetooth. The biggest part of the dump was 'Ye Grate Spelle', in both 16th and 21st century English. And the list of components we'd need.

"You're kidding me," I said, looking at the ingredients.

"They said they're going to push through the ingredients from their side," Miller said.

"I get that, I mean ammo and what-not works on this side when we steal it," I said.

Miller winced at steal. *That's why I used it, honestly.*

"But, this is magic," I said, looking at the list of ingredients. "Things that don't work if you use the wrong phrasing, let alone the wrong fenny snake. It's worse than cooking, and cooking is one step away from chemistry."

I failed chemistry. Twice. The second time with Mel and three tutors helping me all the way to an F. Which, honestly, was better than the unknown I'd received when I failed the first time. It was why I'd dropped out and joined the Corps.

Diindiisi was looking over the list.

"I've got most of this, except for the wool of bat and howlet's wing," she said.

"Could I see that?" Dalma asked. "Eye of newt, toe of frog ...why is this familiar?"

"Shakespeare," I replied.

"Henry said he'd spoken to Shakespeare about his research. Apparently some of his formulas were correct," Diindiisi said.

"So. our getting out of here depends on the writings of William fucking Shakespeare? English Lit is going to be the death of me," Davis moaned.

"Eh, I've read worse," was all Johnson would say. "We have a source for the missing ingredients, just in case?"

"Wool of bat should be easy," Padgett replied. "San Marcos has a lot of damn bats, and there should be hair from one somewhere, but what the hell is a howlet's wing?"

"Owl," I replied almost casually. "Diindiisi, why do you have the tongue of a dog?"

"Professional secret," she replied, a smile tugging at the corners of her mouth.

"Your life is going to be so much fun once we get out of here," Miller said.

I glared at him. He raised his eyebrows, spasmodically.

"Is a howlet a specific kind of owl?" Dalma asked.

"No. Unless Shakespeare meant the arm of a dirty, nosy person," Diindiisi replied.

"Uh ...there's the bone collection in the anthro department for that," Dalma said, seriously. "I don't know how we'd know the arm in question was from a dirty, nosy person though."

"Oh, Dalma, I was teasing you. It's an owl's wing. And that may be the sticking point – tracking down an owl's nest here won't be easy, and finding a dead owl will be worse."

"Would taxidermy work?" Hiebert asked.

"It should, why?"

"Well, the tobacco shop on the Square has a collection of strange things on the walls. I think one of them is an owl," he replied.

"We're also going to need a bloody great cauldron," Miller said.

"Define 'bloody great'," I replied.

"Big enough for 'bubble, bubble, toil, and trouble'," Miller replied.

"It doesn't have to be that big, just big enough for the components to drop in," Diindiisi said. "We will need water from a flowing spring and wood from a living tree to kindle the fire."

"Spring Lake is spring-fed," I said.

"And the place they want to try to open the rift is on the shores of Spring Lake," Padgett pointed out. "Several trees there."

"We've got a day to gather things, and then a day to prepare. How soon before the ritual do we draw the water?" I asked.

"Kindle the fire, draw the water with the cauldron, don't put out the fire, and start the incantation," Diindiisi said. "If things go right, once we complete the spell on this side, and they complete it on the other, the rift opens and we go home."

She looked like she was questioning this, however.

Finally she threw up her arms, saying, "It's not like I've done anything like this before. Spells take finesse and skill. Like the healing balm I made the other day, not just anyone can make it."

"Right. Looks like we're going out for a few things, then," I said. "Diindiisi, I need you to come along as you're the resident expert on things magical."

"Yes," she said.

"Who else?"

For once, everyone raised their hands. The wards were holding, and we'd performed the ritual flushing of the sewer pipes this morning, in both locations, along with dumping a few hundred gallons of blessed water down the manhole El Blobby had risen from as well.

"What about the Font?" Miller asked.

"They want us to try to bring it along," I said. "Which means making something so we can carry it. Hopefully, the rift will be big enough that it'll pass through."

"If not?"

"We either break it down so it will, or we leave it behind," I said. "Sorry, man, I know your church wanted it, but, if it's human lives or the Holy Betamax, the Betamax stays."

"Yeah, that's what I figured," he replied before going to the other side to get his gear.

Diindiisi had insisted that I move into the room with her. It was very 1950s sitcom – separate beds, and no hint of impropriety. But we weren't sleeping alone, and we were getting to know each other, slowly. We went to our room and grabbed gear.

"So, what's wrong?" I said, helping her swing her body armor on.

"It's too easy," she said.

"Err?" I asked, tilting my head to the side.

"The spell. Exactly like Shakespeare worded it. Missing ingredients we should be able to find, or that the other side will supply. I've been here a long time, and this just doesn't seem right," she said.

I hugged her, which was kind of hard to do, both of us being covered in armor and pouches and what-not.

"It'll work," I said. "You've got most of what you need in your bag, right?"

"Yes, but..."

"It'll work," I said. "You can work the spell from this side, and I'm pretty sure I know the voodoo priest who'll be working it on the other. To be on the safe side, we'll douse the funeral home down seriously before we pack the Font into the van, then triple ward everything. We'll also load a bunch of supplies into the box truck and set up a camp on the site."

"Voodoo priest?" she asked. She put a finger under her nose like a bone through the septum.

I laughed. "No, Obediah doesn't have a bone through his nose. Although his ears are gauged," I said.

"What is gauged?" she asked.

"A plug in the ear, sort of like a piercing," I said.

"I'll have to see one, I guess. Although you seem to have come up with a plan, in a very short time," she replied.

"Yeah, well, it's not that hard to figure out what we're going to need to do, contingency planning and what-not," I said.

"You make it sound so easy," she said.

"Eh, it's probably going to be a giant shit storm," I replied.

"Language, Father," she said, then kissed me on the tip of my nose.

"Wanton woman," I laughed. "We've got work to do."

The skies were their usual dull, gunmetal gray. And Abzu's aerial reconnaissance was in place – Tiamat, sculling about above us, probably just out of range.

"I can try," Dalma said, tapping the Barrett she'd laid on the roof of the Humvee.

"Not worth it," I said. "Besides, we'd never know if you hit it or not. One round doesn't seem to bother her, and the M2's don't have enough up angle to try from here. If she lands, however, all bets are off."

Dalma grinned. "Her head would make one hell of a trophy, no?"

"Oh yeah. If you could get it to the other side, and if it didn't become human when she died. That'd take a lot of explaining," Padgett said.

"I hadn't thought about that," Dalma replied, putting the Barrett in the rear of the Humvee, then climbing in.

We eased out of the parking lot, Miller did his thing, and the two Humvees headed south. We circled town for a while to throw off any followers, then pulled up under an overpass on I35.

"Phew, that doesn't half stink," Davis said.

"Bats, man, bats. This is," Padgett paused dramatically, "bat country."

"Dude, that movie sucked," Davis answered. "And that doesn't tell me why it fucking stinks around here."

"Several hundred to several thousand bats hanging out under the bridge all day, doing what bats do. And always lightening the load upon take off, coupled with baking shit in the Texas heat and you get a hell of a pong," Padgett said.

"That makes sense," Davis replied. "Still stinks though."

"That's the smell of money, man," Padgett replied. "High nitrate fertilizer, if nothing else."

Something moved in the dark, high up, under the bridge.

"CONTACT!"

"Fuck me with a chainsaw, running," Padgett said as the something resolved its self into a misshapen twisted man-bat-thing.

It dropped from the bridge overhead, landing on its feet, hissing at us.

Hiebert ran over and grabbed a handful of the dense fur that covered its chest, then, ducking a swing of the man-bat-thing's wing, ran back.

It screeched in fury.

"HOSE IT!"

Four UMPs – Father Miller was packing a submachine gun today. An M240. Diindiisi's Roadblocker, and the two sprayers all hit the thing at once. It howled and exploded, covering everyone with a fine red mist.

"That was fucking disgusting," Padgett said.

"Hiebert, what the hell, over?" I asked, scraping goo off my face.

"I figured 'wool of bat', right?" he replied, grinning, showing the handful of fur he'd torn from its chest.

The grin was disconcerting – bright white teeth in a face dripping with daemon bits.

"Next time warn us, ok? I seriously thought you'd lost your damned mind," I said.

"Roger that," he said.

"Let's scrape as much of this off as we can, and go get the howlet's wing," I said.

Diindiisi came over while I was still rinsing the lenses on my goggles. I hadn't had them on, but I wanted to be able to see through them going forward.

"Coincidence?" she asked.

"Probably," I replied. "There was something here. We needed something from a bat, so everyone was broadcasting 'bat' loudly, and the daemon took on the form it thought would freak us out the most."

"If you say so," she replied.

"I do," I replied. "Besides, how would Abzu get inside our communications network?"

"I don't know. I just don't trust coincidences," she replied.

"Me either," I replied. "I'll keep it in mind, though."

We still searched under the bridge and pulled out some hair. And just to be on the safe side, a small container of bat guano. All the collection was done wearing bright yellow, one-size-fits-nobody, Tyvek suits we'd looted from Farmall, with matching black rubber gloves and gas masks.

"What do you want to do with the suits?" Davis asked, stripping his off. He'd done the collection, with Dalma and Padgett on close watch, while the rest of us had watched from below.

"Bag 'em," I replied. "Damn things are probably full of all kinds of things the daemons could use to track you."

"I… I hadn't thought of that," Davis said.

"Bodies drop all kinds of things," Diindiisi said.

"*Dune*," Johnson said from the turret of Thing Two.

"Huh?" Diindiisi asked, while I held the garbage bag open for Davis.

"Sorry," Johnson said. "Series of books, set in the future. Anyway, in one of them, there's this bunch of folks who specialize in cloning."

He held up a hand to forestall the coming question. "Making copies of people from their cells," he said. "These folks, the Tleilax, they collect skin cells dropped by folks in rooms and what-not, using them to make copies of the people."

"I didn't know you'd read Herbert," I said, tying the bag shut.

He shrugged. "Man, you've been to Iraq. You know how fucking boring the desert can be. Northern Saud," he pronounced it Sa-ood, "is nothing but fucking sand for fucking miles. There was this guy in my platoon who'd schlepped the entire *Dune* series to that point over. We all ended up reading it."

"Y'all ready to roll?" Father Miller called over the radio.

He was up top on the bridge, watching for bad guys.

"Roger that," I replied. "Anything we need to know about?"

"Looks like it's raining north of here," he replied. "Hold on, I'm coming down."

He slid down the embankment. He'd tucked the ends of his stole under the armor he was wearing, but on the slide down, one of the ends worked loose.

"How bad does it look?" I asked.

He held up a hand, caught his breath, then tucked his stole back in.

"Pretty nasty, like that storm the first day we came here," he finally panted.

"Any sign of our overwatch?"

"Yeah, she was circling. Just like normal," he replied, climbing into Thing Two.

"Right, everyone mount up, and Padgett, take the lead. Drive…casual," I said.

"Drive casual? How do I do that?" he asked, grinning.

"I don't know. Just kinda drive, thataway," I said, waving a hand at the center of town before climbing up into the turret.

"Drive casual he says," Padgett snarked as I snapped the gunner's harness on.

We eased down the access road back towards town. I caught glimpses of Tiamat, sculling along above us, and once glanced back to see the horror that was the skies to the north. For once, the sky wasn't the color of a TV tuned to a dead channel. It was black, shot through with brief, throbbing flashes of light.

"Oh, that's ugly," Johnson said over the radio. "If we were back home, I'd say it was time to head for the tornado shelter."

"Long as it's not raining mud, blood, or body parts, we're fine," I replied.

"Contact left," Padgett called as we turned down Aquarena Springs.

There was a gaggle of imps standing in the parking lot of the hotel across the street, and another group trying to break into one of the lower-floor rooms.

"Go!" I said.

The OJT thing was working with Padgett, and he was learning fast.

Padgett turned left. The Humvee lurched over the concrete divider. Imps flowed across the parking lot towards us – until I opened up with the fifty, and then they scattered like a covey of quail taking wing. Padgett stopped near the room they were trying to get in, and I undid my harness and dropped into the Humvee.

"Keep the motor running," I said, slapping Padgett on the shoulder as Diindiisi and I exited the vehicle on the right.

The other two vehicles in our little convoy pulled into the lot – Davis got out of Thing Two, carrying his sprayer, and took up a position behind Thing One.

"Ready?" I asked.

"Yes."

I rounded the front fender of Thing One and led the way towards the room. The imps had managed to break in the door. One came stumbling out, gnawing on a human hand. I put three rounds into it, center mass, then stepped over the body into the room. I burned through a magazine, dropped it, and reloaded. I could hear Diindiisi's Roadblocker roaring as well.

Davis hung up in the door. I don't blame him, either. The room looked like someone had taken an abattoir, raised it to ceiling height, and dropped it, then spray-painted the walls with about a thousand gallons of blood and viscera. There were bits of bodies everywhere.

"Clear," I said over the radio. "Miller, come get Davis."

"Roger," was the only response.

Davis was on his knees and had puked until he had dry heaves, but couldn't move from the door. I stood, blocking as much of the Bosch nightmare in the room from view as I could. Miller looked at me as he helped Davis to stand. I shook my head.

"I'll take care of it," I said. "We're going to be here for a bit, though, so…"

"Right. I'll get everyone fed," Miller said, leading Davis away.

"Jesse? Do you need anything from the Humvee?" Diindiisi called from the room.

"No, I've got the things I need in my pouch," I said, tapping a pouch under my left arm. "Although we need a count, and to see if we can find any ID."

"I understand," she said. "I don't suppose there's time to bury them?"

"Not as such, no," I said. "But I'll make sure the imps don't get to feed when we're done, I assure you of that."

It probably took about an hour to collect and count the bodies. In the end, I figured there were twelve individuals in the room when the imps had hit it. In part because we had twenty-three hands, including the one from the doorway. Diindiisi had searched the blood-soaked clothing and bags, and come up with nine IDs – six female, three male. We'd done our best, but we were covered in blood when we were done – if nothing else, it had dripped from the ceiling onto us while we were gathering body parts. Fortunately, there was a hose attached to the wall, and we used it to wash off the worst of the goo when we were done.

"We are going to have to take so many shots," I said, watching Diindiisi wash off her gear.

"Starting now," Dalma said helpfully behind me. "I went over the kit, and there's some things I figure you need to take right off."

She also had several sets of syringes, loaded, waiting for us.

"Oh great, just like being back in the Corps," I muttered, pulling off my body armor and shirt.

Diindiisi finished, saw what I was doing, and did the same.

"How are you going to keep the imps off the bodies?" she asked, watching as Dalma gave me the first shot.

I waited until Dalma finished, then opened the grenade pouch attached to the other side of my armor. Inside were two white phosphorus grenades. I swung my shirt back on, then my armor. I waited until she'd done the same, then handed her the grenades.

"Hold those," I said. "Don't fuck with them, because they'll burn you to the point Jesus couldn't save you."

She nodded, holding the grenades gingerly. I walked to the back of Thing Two, where we'd put a case of Molotov's. Just in case. I grabbed the entire case, walking back to the room.

"You need a light?" Johnson called from Thing Two's turret.

"Negative. But I need everyone but Diindiisi to mount up, and the vehicles to pull back across the street," I replied.

I stood in the doorway and lobbed unlit Molotovs all over the room, making sure to splash the beds where we'd arranged what was left of the bodies well. When I was finished, I tossed the box in as well, then walked to where Diindiisi was standing, holding a grenade in each hand.

I took the first one, pulled my multi-tool out, and straightened the legs of the cotter pin holding the spoon in place, setting it on the steps behind me. I did the same to the second grenade, then looked at Diindiisi.

"Now for the tricky bit," I said, picking up a grenade in both hands, wrapping my fingers around the spoon on each.

"What do you want me to do?" Diindiisi asked.

"Grab the loops and pull them straight out, then run like hell and go stand by the vehicles, hon," I said.

She pulled both pins smoothly, spun like a dancer, and ran over to where the vehicles waited. I lobbed the grenade in my left hand, and before I heard the spoon release lobbed the second, then ran away, going down the parking lot rather than across the street. I made it about fifty feet when the first Willie Pete went off with a FOOMP! A billowing cloud of white smoke star-fished from the door behind me.

I'd overdone it with the Molotovs, apparently. I'd created a small fuel-rich and oh so contained atmosphere, and when the Willie Pete went off, the fumes exploded, just like a fuel-air explosive.

If this had been a movie, the blast would have ruffled my hair at the worst. Since it was reality, I was blown ass over tea kettle. I don't know that I heard the second grenade go off. But I smashed into the wooden fence that separated the no-tell motel from a fried chicken joint.

I watched the no-tell motel go up in flames from where I sat, leaning up against the fence, sucking on my CamelBak. At least my armor had kept any glass from shredding its bladder. I could feel the heat on my face from where I sat.

"You ok?" Diindiisi called from the other side of the parking lot.

"Nothing hurt but my pride," I said, rising, and climbing over the fence.

"And your face," she said from the turret of the Humvee.

I dropped onto the Humvee's roof, then to the ground. She came out the side door, first aid kit in hand.

"This is going to hurt, probably a lot," she said with a wry smile. "And Dalma will probably want to give you more shots as well."

"It's going to be one of those days, isn't it?" I replied as she started pulling splinters from my face.

At least the goggles had protected my eyes.

Chapter Seventeen
Day 26, 25 April 2018

We got the howlet's wing. And a text that it was raining on the other side, so the attempt today was no go. I say 'rain'. That really doesn't describe the weather on the other side. Gunny texted that the storm started like a cow pissing on a flat rock and went downhill from there. They pulled off the site when the river started rising. There were also overtones to the storm that had the religious side of the team there busting their asses to keep things under control.

On our side, it was the same old gray day. Again.

"Abzu is trying something," Diindiisi said. "On the other side, but he's working on keeping us here for some reason."

"It's good to be wanted," I said to the room at large. "We kicked him in the balls a couple of times. Old school gods tend to be, well, vengeful."

"Yeah," Davis said. "It's not like Yahweh didn't go through a phase for a while, that whole fire and brimstone thing."

"True. And the flood. But, to quote Monty Python, he got better," Miller replied.

"Took him a while, though," I said.

Dalma threw popcorn at me.

My phone burbled *Gallows Pole*. I grabbed it and read the message.

"Bad news, folks. They've declared a disaster on the other side. Officially, a tornado struck the Meadows Center for Water Studies," I said.

Diindiisi giggled. "What is it with the modern era and naming things for people?"

"Eh, give enough money, and you'll be immortalized," I replied. "It strokes some folk's vanity."

"Unofficially?" Hiebert asked.

"Same. A tornado. Which was being controlled by an air elemental,' I replied.

"They sure it wasn't a djinn?" Diindiisi asked. "Abzu's influence and all that."

"Gunny says 'air elemental', so I'm going with that. Besides, djinn are a little later than Abzu, and under the control of a different god or gods," I replied.

"That makes a difference?" she asked.

"Yes. All of them are, well, to an extent, conservative about their power. Loaning out elements of power to other groups tends to lessen one's own power, unless the being in question cuts a deal for power sharing. It's all very legalistic, honestly. Sometimes I think the whole reason some of the accounting software was created was so divine beings could keep track of what they'd loaned to whom," I said.

Johnson started laughing.

"That gives a whole new meaning to 'Death by PowerPoint', don't it?" he finally asked.

"Oh dear God," Miller said, crossing himself quickly. "The concept of spending eternity watching PowerPoint slides . . ."

"That one is definitely in the Light Bringer's bailiwick," I replied.

"Anything else in the text message?" Dalma asked.

"Yeah, we're to stand by to stand by," I replied. "They've got to assess the site and see if and when they can perform the ritual. Apparently, the rain is the worst since the flooding of 2015, so they've got to wait until it's finished."

"Then what are we going to do until they say 'go'?" she asked.

"Good question," I replied. "We can sit around here, fat, dumb, and happy, standing by to stand by, or...."

"Or?" Miller asked, raising his left eyebrow at me.

"Or, we can go do a sweep through town and see if there's anyone else here," I replied.

"Are you nuts?" he replied. "What evidence is there that there is anyone else alive?"

I pointed to the folder on the table between us. In the folder rested the IDs we'd pulled out of the hotel room before my understandable act of arson. We'd texted the info to the guys on the other side, but I was going to carry those IDs through the gate, so the families could have closure, if nothing else.

"We failed those folks, Dave, and you know it."

"We don't know how long they were here," he replied.

"Really? Those IDs are all current issue, either from the state or the university," I replied. "If I were a betting man, I'd bet they came through with us."

"One percent," Davis said, enigmatically.

"Huh?"

"In one of my classes, one of the professors said about one percent of the population disappears worldwide in a given year. Between Texas State and the city, that's about," he did the math, "eight hundred people who could be here. We've found eight out of eight hundred?"

"Nineteen, but yeah," I replied.

Davis was still broken up over not being able to do anything when we'd found the room full of bodies. I'd talked with him about it last night, but it still bugged him.

"Yeah, but some of those are found," Dalma

"One percent of one percent, worldwide," Davis replied. "If the theory holds, then Abzu's been feeding his minions for a very long time here."

"That's if they all ended up here over the years," Miller retorted.

"Where else would they go?" Davis replied.

"If we go out, what happens if we fail?" Johnson asked.

Timing is everything. We were watching *Heavy Metal* to kill time.

"If you refuse, you die, she dies, everybody dies!" Ard said from the screen.

"Yeah, what he said," I replied.

"Well, it ain't like I haven't been shot to shit for less," Johnson replied.

The others were nodding. Miller, on the other hand, looked aghast.

"Are you all mad?" he asked.

"No, just thinking about other folks who might spend a hundred years here like Ms. Diindiisi there," Johnson replied. "Or longer."

"But..."

"Father, you can stay behind," I said, gently.

I get it. Not everyone is constitutionally capable of looking Death in the face and spitting in his eye, day after day.

"It's not that," he temporized. "We've got a chance to get out, is all."

"What about the others?" Diindiisi asked, her words hanging in the air.

"We…we don't know that there are others," Miller said.

"And we don't know that there aren't," Diindiisi replied, calmly.

"If we find anyone else, where are we going to put them?" Miller asked. "It's not like we've got the house next door anymore."

"True. But we have got the building on the other side," I replied calmly. "It's a day care center. If nothing else, there should be mats for them to sleep on."

"Fine!" Miller said, throwing his hands up. "But I want to send a text to your people on the other side to let them know what you're doing. And so they have my phone number, just in case."

"No problems, Father," I replied. "We won't take everybody. Two per vehicle – driver and gunner on one of the Things, and driver and shotgun on the Tacticool Tahoe, for now."

"When do you want to start?" Davis asked.

I looked at my watch. "Now's as good a time as any."

Dalma Spocked Davis and Padgett to drive Thing Two, and Hiebert and Johnson were sitting in the Tacticool Tahoe when we got downstairs.

"Where to?" Dalma said.

"Let's go check the campus," I replied.

"Right," she said, turning uphill.

"You want to go towards the Quad or what?"

"Start with Tower Hall and head east on Woods," I replied.

She pulled up next to Tower Hall. We waited. I fired three shots in the air – if they came to Earth in an imp, I'd be fine with it.

Half an hour later, nothing.

"East on Woods it is," Dalma said, putting the Humvee in gear.

"Hiebert, lay on the horn," I said over the radio.

"Won't that attract, well, things?"

"It might. But if you'd heard a car horn when you were first here, what would you have done?"

"Makes sense," he said, leaning into the Tahoe's horn.

The horn cut through the stillness as we drove down Woods to North LBJ.

"You want to turn here?" Dalma asked as we hit North LBJ.

"Why? You want to ram the gates or something?" I laughed.

"Yeah, kinda," she replied. "Not often you get to do damage without repercussions."

"Damn girl, you'd have made a hell of a Marine," I replied.

We swung down Woods towards J. C. Kellum, then across that industrial ugly buildings parking lot and past it. The Humvee was edging onto Sessom Drive when we heard the first shots – three, then three, and three.

"SOS?" Dalma asked.

"Yeah," I replied, swiveling in the turret, trying to place the sound. "Hiebert, lay off the horn for a minute."

The mournful blare died.

This time, the shots weren't as well spaced – it was more the sound of frantic firing than a signal.

"Damn echoes," I said, then it hit me. "The QUAD! GO!"

I keep telling myself it's impossible to break the tires loose on a Humvee, especially one with the up-armor package, and the kids driving keep trying to prove me wrong. From the way the big Detroit Diesel under the hood was thundering, Dalma was trying to push her foot through the firewall and out the other side. Even the Tacticool Tahoe was having issues trying to keep up – Hiebert's driving style was a bit less aggressive than Dalma's. Probably due to the thirty odd year difference in their ages.

Old Main flew past, and we approached the Pleasant Street Parking Garage at a breakneck pace. Dalma actually managed to rock the Humvee on its suspension, making the turn onto the stub of North LBJ that came out of campus, then hopped the curb neatly between the bollards that were supposed to keep unauthorized vehicles out of the Quad.

There was a horrid, screeching roar as we started past the History Building and onto the Quad proper. Out of the corner of my eye, I watched as a brownish-green something missed the rear bumper of the Humvee and slid across the concrete covering the Quad.

The something resolved itself into the bronze statue of a bobcat that the student government had paid for and installed to remind the students they were attending a real school, damnit, not a, as our most famous graduate had referred to it, no-nothing little cow college.

"On it," Johnson said calmly from the Tacticool Tahoe, opening up with the M240, hammering the bronze statue. It roared in pain and leapt towards the Tahoe as we went around the corner into the Quad.

I could hear the Tahoe's engine roaring over the sound of the M240 and the Bobcat.

Towards the west end of the Quad there was a nightmare – well, unless you think anatomically correct bronze statues of stallions with naked riders fighting are a mitzvah. The horses had glowing green eyes and were busily stomping something into a fine red paste. I didn't even have to think about it, just held the butterfly trigger on the M2 down and started blowing chunks of glowing green bronze into the air. I could no longer hear the Golf over the heavy thud of Ma singing her song.

"RAMING SPEEED!" Dalma shouted joyfully into her radio.

"FUCK!" I replied, frantically cranking the turret around to keep the gun from spearing into whichever statue she was going to ram.

I had just ducked below the level of the turret when we struck. There was, I swear, the world's largest KABONG when we hit the statue. I earned a new set of bruises, on my back this time, as I bounced off the rear of the turret ring. The Humvee was still running, but the statue was down – swept off its legs, two of which had sheared from the impact. The leg holes were leaking a brownish green ectoplasm, and both the horse and the rider were keening in a nails-on-a-chalkboard manner. There was no sign of the other horse and rider.

"Backing up," Dalma said calmly.

I watched the bobcat statue, all 1500 pounds of bronze, stagger into the open space and collapse, leaking goo as well. The Tacticool Tahoe came around the corner, missing its front bumper, then backed towards Thing One.

"There's one other statue around here somewhere," I said over the radio, cranking the turret back forward.

"Yeah, it was behind the one I punched with the Humvee," Dalma replied. "It kinda bounced and then hit the stairs behind it, crumbling into dust."

"That explains the kabong," I said. "How's Thing One looking?"

"Gauges are good. You want to dismount and check the grill and the pile o'goo out there?" she replied.

She'd been reading again. Not a bad thing overall, but OJT was driving me nuts. I'd be glad when I could turn these ad hoc trainees over to the taskmasters up in Dallas, getting back to just dodging the things that go bump in the night for a living.

Not that I wouldn't warn them about the fun and games in Dallas if they chose to go that route. Overall, they were good kids, and hell, Johnson knew the score – he'd gone through Army basic back in the day. He and Hiebert were a little long in the tooth for actual door kickers, but they'd make hellish support guys – they'd have seen the elephant up close and personal, to put it in 19th century American.

"Dismounting," I said.

There were two clicks on the radio from the Tacticool Tahoe, indicating they'd heard and were acknowledging. I hit the quick release and dropped from the turret, then went out the side door, tossing the sling of a UMP over my shoulder as I stepped out.

The horses were Dead, Entirely Dead, which was a good thing. The light had faded from the bronze, and the goo had stopped flowing. They'd managed, however, to kick another survivor to death. The face was gone, but there was a wallet in the pants, which I grabbed.

"Hello?" someone called from the Liberal Arts Building.

"Contact," I said gently, followed by "Here."

"I'm coming out," came the response.

A small woman (seriously five foot nothing, with purple hair) stepped out of one of the side doors of the liberal arts building, followed by three kids.

"Damn," I said sotto voce. I now knew why Abzu had such a hard on for keeping us here. Kids. The potential uses for kids were endless – if Abzu could get his hands on them, if nothing else, he could raise them as followers and then set them loose back in 'reality' to spread the good word of obscure Babylonian Gods. Worst case, he could replace them with minions, controlling them if he chose to reinsert them into reality.

"I'm Stephanie," the woman said, carefully avoiding looking at the greasy red spot on the concrete.

I led them over closer to the Humvee. The three kids were at that age where they all looked similar, dressed in somewhat matching outfits – khaki shorts and t-shirts. Although the t-shirts were different colors – one was red, one was green, and one was blue.

"Father Jesse Salazar," I said, offering her my hand.

"Are you here to rescue us?" Stephanie asked.

"Something like that," I temporized. "And you are?"

I turned to the three kids.

"I'm Huey," the one in red said, "this is my brother Dewey," blue, "and my sister Louise," green. "We're trip-lets."

Great. Kids whose parents were fans of *Duck Tales*. Some days it doesn't pay to get up in the morning.

"Y'all can call me Jesse," I said, before turning back to Stephanie. "I take it you were with the body?"

"His name was Dave, Dave Jones," she replied. "I worked for the child development center here on campus, and Dave found us there. He's kept us alive since then."

I felt a tug at my pants leg. Louise was standing there, one of her hands wrapped in the thick fabric.

"Mister? We need to get our bags from the building," she said.

I heard Stephanie sniff. She was about two steps away from a major breakdown. Which, in this situation, was understandable.

"CONTACT!" Johnson shouted, opening up with his machine gun.

"Right now, y'all need to pile into the Humvee here," I said, opening the door and pointing. "Once we know for sure what's happening, we can go back for your things."

"Where are we supposed to sit?" one of the kids asked. "There's no kid seats."

"That's ok," Stephanie replied. "For now, you're going to be adults. Can you do that?"

Three little tow heads bobbed yes as one, then they climbed into the rear of Thing One. I waited until she'd gotten two of the boys strapped in under one seat belt, to the accompanying giggles, then climbed into the turret, buckling in and cranking the fifty around to the rear.

Stephanie buckled the last of the trio in, closed the door, and climbed in front next to Dalma.

"Kids," Dalma said. "I'm Dalma. Things are going to be loud, so put your hands over your ears."

I didn't see if they'd complied. Instead, I was watching two more statues lurch towards us – the first was LBJ, the only US President to graduate from a Texas School. And I couldn't help but think, *Take that, UT!*

The second was a vaquero – and he was twirling a lariat. I had a clear shot at him, so I hit the triggers and started knocking chunks off the statue.

"You got room to get past?" Hiebert called over the radio.

"If not, I'll make it," Dalma said, K-turning Thing One in the available space.

I managed to keep the gun on target, barely. She scraped past the Tahoe and hung a right on what would be North LBJ if the university hadn't blocked the street with a honking big gate.

"Kids," she shouted into the cacophony, "the ride is about to get rough. Hang on!"

She put the hammer down. We were still accelerating when we went through the gates, smashing them back.

"Uh oh," Dalma said as we turned right on Woods, headed back towards the funeral home.

"That doesn't sound good," I replied.

"I think I punched a hole in the radiator," she said. "Heat's rising on this side."

"Keep it together, it's not that far," I replied.

"Our stuff!" one of the kids wailed.

I could hear Stephanie trying to calm an upset six-year-old over the sounds of the engine and the fire from the Tahoe.

"I tell you what," Dalma shouted. "When we get where we're going, you tell me and Jesse where your stuff is and we'll go get it for you. Is that ok?"

I heard snuffles of assent.

"Clear," Johnson's voice said over the radio as the Tahoe turned to follow. "Y'all are leaving a trail, by the way."

"Punched the radiator, we think," I replied.

"Good thing it's a short trip."

"Roger that," I replied as we turned down Comanche to run back to the funeral home. "We're going to swap out for Thing Two and head back."

"Why for?"

"Kids left their supplies."

I could hear the pause in his train of thought. We'd ignore that request from an adult, who'd be able to handle it. Kids? They'd never understand why we couldn't go back for a beloved comrade who happened to be made of cloth.

"Roger that. We'll check out Thing One on return, then," Johnson said.

"Yeah, and we're going loaded for bear," I replied.

Because sure as God made little green apples, Abzu and his minions would be waiting for us, this time.

We pulled in, and I climbed out the top while Stephanie and Dalma pulled the kids out of the rear of Thing One. Dropping to the ground, I went to our ad hoc ammo store and started carrying boxes of silver thirty cal over to the Humvee.

"What's going on?" Miller asked, coming down into the funeral home.

"Found some more survivors," I grunted, grabbing two more cans and hauling them over to Johnson, who was stacking them in the bed of the Tahoe.

"I'm Huey," Huey said to Miller.

"I'm Father Miller," he replied, a puzzled look on his face. I could see him going through the same calculations I'd run back on campus.

"Yeah," I replied, hauling two cans of fifty-cal ammo over to Thing Two. Dalma was transferring our gear to it.

Diindiisi came downstairs, loaded for bear.

I looked at her and raised an eyebrow. She laughed.

"No vision. Your radios are still hot," she replied, putting her gear into Thing Two.

"Davis?" I said.

Davis was loading a sprayer into the back of the Tahoe.

"Yes, Father?"

"Father Miller is going to have his hands full here," I replied.

"Padgett can stay behind," he replied.

"You think two people can cover the entire perimeter?" I replied, pausing to drink a bottle of water.

"Well, no," he replied, taking the sprayer back out of the Tahoe. "I just thought..."

"Look, son," ok, I had ten years on him, twenty at most, but this was one of those Father to parishioner moments. "You lost control at a site that would have made most hardened combat veterans spew chunks. There's no shame in it."

"You didn't lose control," he replied, "and neither did Diindiisi."

"Yeah, but I've been doing this for ten years now, after doing the same thing with Uncle Sam's Misguided Children," I replied. "And hard as it sounds, Diindiisi came up in a very hard school before she met Henry Keith. No one expects you to be hardened to this shit right away."

"But..."

"No buts. Unless Dalma or Hiebert want to swap out?" I said.

Dalma gave him the most bloodthirsty grin I'd ever seen on a human, and Hiebert shook his head.

"Right then, you and Padgett backstop Father Miller, and help Ms...."

"Baxter," Stephanie supplied. "But you can call me Stephanie."

"Help Stephanie and the kids get settled in. Make sure the wards are up. Defend the kids," I said, followed by "Damn."

"What's the matter?"

"This will be easier with one vehicle," I replied, starting to move ammo from the Tahoe to Thing Two.

"Quick in and out?" Johnson laughed, dismounting the M240.

"Something like that, yeah," I replied. "You're up top, I'll lead the dismount team."

He climbed in and up into the turret. We loaded in, and Dalma headed for campus.

"How you want to go, boss?" she asked over the radio.

"The back way, if there is one."

"You worried about the damage?"

"Try not to break the Humvee, huh? Uncle Sugar ain't here to replace it if we break them both," I said.

"No problems. Well, we're going to test the suspension on stairs," she said, slaloming around bollards and driving across an open space near Tower Hall. She then turned and took the Humvee down the broad stairs and back into the Quad.

"Keep the motor running," I said as Diindiisi, Hiebert, and I dismounted and walked towards the building.

"Did Stephanie say where their stuff was?" Hiebert asked just before we entered the building.

I stopped dead in my tracks.

"I knew there was something I forgot to ask," I replied, then opened the door.

The corridor was dark and cool. Too damn dark for my liking. All the lights had been broken out, and the only light down the length was from the glass doors at either end.

"Oh, this is wonderful," Hiebert said, hosing down the door and the area in front of us with holy water.

"Yeah. You sure you still want to go to work for QMG when this is over?" I asked, popping open the door to a restroom and giving it a quick once-over.

"Yeah, beats the hell out of loading freight at my age," Hiebert replied with a chuckle. "Besides, dental."

"True dat," I replied, checking the second bathroom. "Hit the stairwell."

He did, picking the one back by the door we'd entered. There was a slow trickle of ectoplasm down the walls.

"That's not good," Diindiisi said, turning on her head lamp.

Ideally, she should have led, since she was carrying what was described in most roll-playing games as an 'area effect' weapon. Problem was, even though she'd been surviving here for over a century, she lacked experience kicking in doors and shooting things up. And for her to survive getting the experience, I had to risk her shooting me in the back with a ten-gauge.

Honestly, I'd done worse. Damn near got my head shot off by an Iraqi sergeant when we were clearing a house in the Anbar one time. At least Diindiisi had enough sense to keep her finger off the damn trigger until there was something she wanted to ventilate in front of her.

Hiebert hosed down the walls. The ectoplasm retreated.

"I hate to say this," I started.

"Yeah, I was just thinking the same thing," he replied. "I should probably conserve the holy water going forward."

"Yeah, it might mean the difference between being eaten by a grue or not," I replied.

"What's a grue?" Diindiisi whispered.

"Imaginary monster that hides in the dark and eats you when you fail to listen to the game's instructions," I replied. "I'll show you at some point, when we get back to the other side."

I ignored the second-floor door – we'd go to three, then work our way back down, checking the rooms as we went, and working from one end of the building to the other.

The third floor was empty. The classrooms had furniture, but there were no signs of habitation. We went down to two, using the stairwell on the far end, swept around and then headed towards the anthropology department. Which is where we ran into trouble.

"You're kidding, right?" Hiebert said, looking at the skeletons filling the hall.

"Nope. Figured it had to be that way," I said. "Anthro department means skeletons, and that's before you realize there's a forensic anthropologist at Texas State, which means more bodies. Bodies mean things for daemons to inhabit, which means more fun for us."

"Man, you've got a weird idea of fun," Hiebert said, starting to step around the corner and hose the skeletons down.

"Hold one," I said, pulling a couple of small disks from a pouch on my armor.

They were about the size of two cans of dip stacked one atop the other with a complex pin and spoon arrangement.

"What're those?" Hiebert asked. Diindiisi was watching our back trail.

I chuckled.

"Ginsberg, our mad armorer, calls them the Holy Hand Grenade of Antioch," I said. "Flash bangs, filled with colloidal silver. You're going to want to cover your eyes, because these fuckers pack a punch."

I pulled the pin on the first flash bang, stepping around the corner to toss it into the milling mass of skeletons, repeating the process with the second before stepping back around the corner, turning my back on the impending chaos. Even around the corner and looking in the wrong direction with my eyes closed, the light was painful. And the noise was loud enough that our earphones almost shorted out, cancelling the blast effects.

We stepped around the corner. Where there had been a milling herd of skeletons, there was now a fog of colloidal silver and bone hanging in the air, shattered glass cases, and a few bones sticking out of the walls in random directions.

"Holy shit," Hiebert whispered.

The only reason I could hear him was that my earphones were working again.

"Yeah, Ginsberg might be mad, but he's on our side," I said, walking towards the rapidly dissipating cloud. "He's also a firm believer in the Church of Superior Firepower, Explosives Sect."

"I can see that," Hiebert said.

There was a crash as a door blasted across the hall, and a daemon followed it, shaking its head and batting at the air.

It was armored in bone.

"WASTE IT!" I shouted.

Hiebert hosed it down, and Diindiisi hammered at it with the Roadblocker. I waited for the other shoe to drop, because there's always another shoe, somewhere.

The building shook as something landed on it. Over Diindiisi's Roadblocker, I heard Johnson open up with the fifty outside.

"It sounds like someone else has joined the dance," Diindiisi said, pausing to reload.

"Yeah," I replied, listening to the sound of whatever was trying to tear the roof off the building.

I ran forward and checked the room where the daemon had been hiding. Sure enough, there were five packs – three small ones in red, blue, and green, and two larger ones. I tossed the two larger ones into the hall, sweeping the three smaller ones up in one hand.

"GO!"

Hiebert and Diindiisi grabbed the two larger packs and started running for the stairs. Which wasn't the easiest thing to do, with the building crumbling around us as whatever was on the roof ate its way in.

Down the stairs, out the door, and dive into the Humvee. I looked back and could see Tiamat's tail sticking up on the roof as she tore into the building.

"GET US THE FUCK OUT OF HERE!" Hiebert shouted at Dalma.

She got rolling, then hung a hard left around the liberal arts building before driving away from campus.

"Where are you going?" Hiebert gasped over the sound of the fifty hammering away in the turret.

"Y'all didn't see it, but there was a horde of shambling things coming up North LBJ from the Square side," Dalma replied.

I don't know where she'd learned to drive, but she was handling the cranky Humvee like it was a Formula 1 car, and it was responding well. She turned onto Sessom and started up the long hill on the outside of campus.

Johnson in the turret ceased fire, kicking me.

"Trouble, Jesse. Tiamat is following us," he said.

"Roger. Dalma, see if we can keep her away from base, huh?" I said, unstrapping from my seat and turning to the cargo area.

I handed Johnson a box of silver fifty caliber ammo.

"You know, I'd give my left nut for a Mark 19 about now," he said, taking it.

"No shit," I replied with a laugh, digging through the cases. I couldn't remember if I'd put what I was looking for in here this time around.

Then I laid hands on the case. I knew it from the leather covering it, unlike the plastic Pelican cases that held most of the gear we'd stolen from the other side. Besides, this one had been in the bottom of one of my 1650 cases. For just such an emergency.

"Dalma, make some distance and find somewhere to pull over, huh?" I said. "Somewhere with clear lanes of fire, if nothing else."

Diindiisi looked at me over the seat between us.

"What are you planning?" Diindiisi asked.

"I've got a little surprise for Tiamat," I replied, patting the case I'd dragged over the seat.

"What, a sword, vorpal weapon, to go snicker snak?" Dalma asked, pulling into a large parking lot near a dorm on West Campus.

"You might say that," I said, stepping out of the Humvee, slinging the case over my shoulder, and walking away.

"What do you want us to do?" Johnson asked, charging the fifty.

"Distract the bitch while I get set up," I replied.

Tiamat was circling, not sure what to make of our actions. Dalma swapped out with Hiebert, pulling a Barrett fifty cal out of the cargo section, while Diindiisi trotted over to where I stood, feeding fat 40mm grenades into a China Lake grenade launcher.

"What is that?" Diindiisi asked.

"Something that technically doesn't exist," I replied. "Pump action grenade launcher. From the new production run in 2009. I don't know where the hell Ginsburg got it, and I'm not going to ask."

I racked the slide and chambered a round, then fed one more into the magazine. Three in the tube, one in the chamber, and the rest in my pants, I thought. There were twelve more of the fat grenades in the foam in the case. I said a quick prayer, blessing the gun and asking God for strength, and then turned to where Tiamat was still hovering.

"Problem is, for this to work, she's got to be on the ground," I said. "Which means bait."

"Which means you," Diindiisi said, giving me a peck on the cheek. "Be careful."

"Oh, I will," I said, grabbing six of the reloads and stuffing them in the cargo pockets on my pants. The other six were flechette rounds. And if I was using them, my ass was grass for the reaping, because I was way too damn close to an ancient dragon shaped goddess of primordial chaos for comfort.

Once I'd done that, I walked to the center of the parking lot. Behind me I could hear Dalma taking pot shots at the dragon, and the SLAP of the big rounds hitting it. Tiamat was still hovering, so the rounds weren't probably doing more than tickling her.

"TIAMAT!" I shouted, flying the fickle finger of fate in her direction. "You're ugly, and your mother dresses you funny!"

Eh, it was a start.

"I wave my private parts at your aunties!" I shouted, giving her a raspberry.

The classics are the best.

Then I remembered something I'd read in a *'Ripley's Believe It Or Not'* book, thumbing my nose at her.

Believe it or not, that last got her attention and she landed with an abrupt THUMP about a hundred yards away. Clout shot for the grenade launcher, but I really wanted her mouth open.

"My mother, mortal? I had no mother! I am the embodiment of primordial chaos!" she rumbled back.

It was a day of firsts – I got to see an ancient chaos goddess look puzzled.

"You confuse and vex me mortal," she rumbled. "My lord husband has asked for your head, and I think I shall give it to him on this day. Your scrabbling friends have my word they may flee our presence."

"Yeah, I think not," I said as Johnson started pounding her with the fifty.

That got her attention.

"Then you first and your friends after!" Tiamat roared, raising her head skyward and dropping her jaw wide.

I raised the Thumper to my shoulder in a smooth, economical motion, and fired, stroked the pump, and fired again. I adjusted the windage, Kentucky style, and fired the two remaining grenades in the gun, flipped it over, and started reloading.

Tiamat actually swallowed the first grenade before it went off. The explosion of the silver-wrapped-high-explosive warhead nearly decapitated her. The other three grenades pounded her head into mush as she fell to earth, although the skull she wore as a hat never shattered.

"NOOOOOOOOOOOOOOOOOOOOOOOOOOOOOOOO OOOOOOOOOOOOOOOOOOOOOOO!!!!!!!!!!!!!!" Abzu screamed from somewhere nearby.

I ran for the Humvee and dove in. Diindiisi had brought the case back and I slipped the Thumper back in, as Dalma jumped back in as well, and Hiebert took us home past the corpse of an ancient goddess. Abzu coalesced in front of the Humvee, and Hiebert ran him down.

"I WILL KILL YOU ALL!" Abzu thundered in our wake.

"Not if I have anything to say about it!" Johnson replied, flipping the bird before opening fire on him.

Abzu disappeared.

"Chickenshit bastard," Johnson muttered as we drove down the hill to the funeral home.

Diindiisi was giving me a look around Johnson's legs.

"Tell me you planned that," she said.

"Depends on what you mean by 'planned'," I replied with a sardonic grin. "If you mean 'I planned to shoot an ancient goddess with grenades in the hope that y'all could get away', then yes, I planned it."

I sipped from my CamelBak, rinsed the gummy texture from my mouth, and spat before drinking again.

"If, on the other hand, you mean 'I planned for her to swallow the first grenade so it would decapitate her', yeah, I'd be lying if I said I planned that. That was nothing but pure-d luck on my part, and stupidity on hers."

"There's days it's better to be lucky," Diindiisi said with a sigh.

"And this was one of those days," I replied.

Chapter Eighteen
Day 27, 26 April 2018

"Well, one of two things is going to happen, according to what I've read," Miller said around a mouthful of toast. "Either we're going to see an increase in activity from smaller minion types – imps, Nephilim, shayitain, and whatnot. Or Abzu's going to try to raise her again, like he did with the thing that attacked y'all at the Benton Mart."

"No way to tell which way he's going to go, is there?" Davis asked.

"Not really," Miller mumbled. "I was surprised he wasted the material reconstructing her the first time. According to the mythology, she never was that faithful to him."

"That doesn't always matter if you're in love," I replied.

That got me an arched eyebrow.

"Oh, come on, Father, how many folks do you know that are still married to cheating individuals?" Dalma asked.

"Not that many, honestly. I don't ...I don't work in the church counseling the penitent," Miller replied.

"Well, there's a lot of people in relationships where one person has been cheating on the other and the first person sticks around for the kids or for other reasons," Dalma said.

"I understand that happens, yes," Miller said, defensively. "I've just never seen it in my ministry."

Dalma looked at me.

"Yeah, sorry hon, I spend most of my time counseling folks who've seen the wrong thing or making sure the things we put down stay down, but it was mentioned in seminary," I said.

"It happens!" she said before storming out of the kitchen.

"That was…interesting," Padgett said.

"I think she's going to have some interesting discussions when we get back to the other side," Hiebert said quietly.

"Oh, probably," I replied.

Louise came dashing into the room. Today she was in an eye-searing lime green shirt and purple shorts.

"Father Jesse, Steph'nie says, come quick, outback!" Louise spouted before dashing back out the door.

I stood and shrugged into my armor. Diindiisi and Hiebert followed suit, while everyone else dropped what they were doing and went looking for arms.

I trotted lightly down the internal stairs, followed by the others.

"Stephanie? What's up?" I asked.

"Over here," she called from near where we'd parked Thing One the day before. It had stopped dripping coolant when we shut it down, and we'd been too damn tired to deal with it when we got back, honestly.

Johnson had the kids well back from the Humvee and was herding them back inside.

There was a writhing lump of bronze stuck in Thing One's grill.

"What the fuck?" Padgett asked, watching as the lump squirmed and tried to break free of the grill.

"Dalma? I think I found the source of the leak on Thing One!" I shouted over my shoulder.

"Up yours, Father!" she called back in a mocking tone from the sniper's nest on the roof.

A face formed on the spike of bronze.

"Yesss," it hissed. "You are the one. Yesss."

"Looks like you made a new friend, Father," Davis said. "Want me to hose it down?"

"Not yet. Let's see if it has anything to say, first," I replied. "I'm the one, what?"

"The one Abzu seeks. He will reward me greatly…"

It stretched to the limit, trying to spike me. Unfortunately for the daemon in the bronze, there was only so much metal, and its thinned-out form wouldn't reach.

"Hose it," I said as the metal started to recoil in upon itself.

Davis and Hiebert hosed the bronze down. It shrieked when the holy water struck it, then exploded into dust.

"Get the pressure washer, and wash all of that down," I said. "Then hose down Thing One. Stephanie, did it touch the kids?"

"I don't think so," she replied. "Huey said that he'd spoken with 'Mr. Snaky' on the brown car, so I came over to look at it. And then sent Louise up to find you."

"Father Miller?" I called.

"Right," he said, pulling out a laminated card from his pocket.

"What's that?" Stephanie asked as Miller went over to where Johnson was entertaining the kids in the garage.

"Probably the Rite of Exorcism, Extreme Short Form," I said.

I looked around the sky – for the first time in days there wasn't a thing to be seen sculling across the grayness. It was, in my eyes, a good thing.

"I…I don't know about that," Stephanie said. "I don't know that their parents would approve of a," her voice dropping to a whisper, "Catholic ceremony being done on the kids."

"It's not like he's baptizing them," I replied. "Their parents Baptists?"

She got a puzzled look on her face, then sighed.

"No, they were Jedi's," Stephanie replied.

Padgett fell against the wall of the building.

"You're fucking kidding me, right?" he finally managed to gasp.

"No. Their parents are members of the Church of the Jedi," Stephanie said. "What? It's a real religion!"

"Yeah," Padgett said. "Well, at least they got the brown robes and all that."

I drew Stephanie aside for a moment. "Were?" was all I asked.

"Well, look, the day things went south, as we were running from the daycare center on campus, I saw their parent's car in the parking lot. It was covered in those smaller creatures," she said, shuddering.

"That doesn't necessarily mean that both parents are dead," I said.

"They were day traders and worked from home when they weren't attending class, and unless one of them was sick, they'd come to get the kids together."

"They might not both have come through, is all I'm saying," I replied.

"We'll see on the other side then, I guess," Stephanie replied, walking back to the main group.

Diindiisi had watched the entire discussion about the Church of the Jedi with fascination, and I could tell she had more questions that she was saving for later. Miller was still laying on hands and chanting with the kids. Johnson was watching just in case one of the kids grew a third head or something.

"Dalma, you got anything?"

"No. Just another boring, beautiful, crappy day here in the Shadow Lands," she replied from the roof.

Miller finally finished, and the kids scampered out of the garage.

"Well?" I asked when he walked out behind them.

"I didn't find anything," he said, waggling a hand side to side. "And it's the Blessing of Children, not the Exorcism, Short Form, you heretic."

"I stand corrected," I said, laughing.

"We'll watch them for the next couple of days, though, just to be sure the daemon didn't plant something," Miller said.

"Have them drink some holy water flavored Kool-Aid or something," Padgett suggested.

"Dude," Davis replied.

"Hey, I wasn't thinking of Jonestown Kool-Aid or something like that," Padgett replied.

"Not how it came across," Davis said.

"Besides, Jonestown was Flavor Aid," I said. "And QMG has a contract to watch the site down there for the Co-operative Republic."

"The what?" Johnson asked.

"The Co-operative Republic of Guyana. Where Jonestown was," I replied.

"Why do they have a contract there?" Diindiisi asked. "And what was Jonestown?"

I sighed and sat down on the pile of ammo.

"Can't explain one without the other. Jonestown was an experimental agricultural station established by a 'church',"

I used finger quotes here to express my opinion of the People's Temple, "called the People's Temple. It was founded in the sixties. There were good people in it, but the leadership was… questionable."

"That's a good, weasel word for it," Miller said.

"Well, Jones got more than a little weird at the end."

"Yeah, there are things in the archive that they found in San Francisco that are under Papal Seal," Miller replied.

"I'm sure. Anyway, Jones set up this experimental agricultural station in Guyana. It's a nation in northern South America," I said.

"Where?" Diindiisi asked.

"Hmm, it used to be British Guyana if that helps," Miller replied.

"Yes, it does," Diindiisi said. "So this Jones person built a, what did you call it, an agricultural station there?"

"Yes, but like most things, there was more to it. While there were a lot of good people in the People's Temple, something dark had latched onto Jim Jones's soul. And there were rumors of strange behavior in San Francisco before the leadership of the People's Temple left there. Mostly abuse, but a lot of times that covers for other things in groups like that."

Diindiisi nodded.

"So, Jones and his followers go to Guyana, and establish a 'perfect socialist government'. And the rumors start up again, and by 1978, there's members of the church who want to get the hell out of Guyana and back to the States. A US Congress Critter goes down there, meets with Jones and the church members, and offers to bring anyone who wants to return to the US home. After some argument, they arranged to get some folks out, only to be ambushed at the airstrip. The Congress Critter was killed, along with five others. Jones called for everyone still in Jonestown to commit suicide, since the Central Intelligence Agency was coming to kill them all," I said. "The goal being to deny the CIA that coup, I guess. Anyway, they forced most of the remaining members of the group to drink cyanide-laced Flavor Aid, killing them."

"How many died?" Diindiisi asked.

"Nine hundred or so, if I remember correctly," I said.

"That would create a site of great power," Diindiisi whispered.

"Oh, it's better than that," I said. "The location Jones picked for the agricultural station? It absolutely sucked for growing crops. But it sits right on the convergence point for three different Ley Line groups."

Miller choked on the coffee he was sipping.

"Yeah, that's supposed to be a big secret, under Papal Seal and all that," I said with a smirk. "Except I answer to a different Archbishop, so, it's not a big secret on our side. QMG got called in by the US Army Captain in charge of returning the bodies in 1978. They did some checking. Found the Ley Lines, and a couple of other things that didn't make it into the 'official' reports, including Jones's grimoire. That's in Dallas, I think, along with a couple of other books."

I held up a hand to forestall Miller's next comment.

"Above my pay grade," I said. "Jones, from the notes I've seen, was attempting to raise something, what no one's sure. His notes are disjointed at best, but he was on enough drugs to make a 1970's rock band weep in jealousy. Problem was the Congress Critter's arrival had forced his hand, and the moon wasn't in the right phase, or the stars weren't in the right spot, or the aliens missed the signal, or something. But nine hundred dead people pack a hell of a punch, like you said Diindiisi, so QMG monitors the site. From time to time, the team down there kills something, sends photos and samples to Headquarters in Dallas, collects a nice check from the Co-operative Republic, and goes back to watching the site."

"Sounds like an interesting place," Dalma said. She'd come down from the roof while I was talking about Jonestown.

"Hon, it's in the middle of a coastal tropical forest. It rains daily. It misses being a jungle by a cat's whisker, and the only place I've ever been in North, Central, or South America, including Marine Corps Recruit Depot San Diego, that's worse is the Darien Gap in Panama, and that place is a wet slice of hell," I said. "On top of that, the number one thing they kill down there are ghouls. And I have a personal issue with ghouls."

"Still, big check," she argued.

I laughed.

"QMG and Group are not the Catholic Church. There's no vow of poverty, and you'll get paid. Or your survivors will," I said, turning and walking upstairs.

Chapter Nineteen
Day 28, 27 April 2018

Once we got Mr. Snaky out of the grill, it turned out that the fix was simple – wrap duct tape around one of the radiator hoses until it quit leaking. It'd hold for emergency use. Thing One was now the dedicated fire support vehicle for the funeral home, and we'd use Thing Two for rollin' through town.

"Plans?" Johnson asked as I finished hooking Thing One's hood in place.

"Eh. Take another down day. Watch the kids, make sure they're not possessed, that kinda thing, why?"

"We're starting to run low on provisions, with four more mouths to feed," he said.

"Provisions? What the hell, man, we on a wagon train headed west?" I asked, laughing.

He mumbled a response.

"I missed that."

"I said 'It sounded better than we're running out of fucking food!' Little jugs with big ears and all that," he replied.

"Right," I said, looking around to make sure Huey, Dewey, and Louise weren't under foot. "That being the case, I appoint you pledge representative to the social committee."

We'd watched *Animal House* after the kids were put to bed.

"Just you and me?" Johnson asked.

"No, get the list and see who wants to go. Although I think we'll limit it to Thing Two and the box truck. And leave the kids behind."

"That's probably a good idea," Johnson said, heading upstairs to see who wanted to ride along and loot the nearest grocery store.

Twenty minutes later, we were teaching Stephanie the fine art of establishing a holy water perimeter at the local Stumpy's Grocery, followed by how to collect the best bits in the shortest time frame. Johnson swept up a basket of toys. No one said anything to him about it – the kids had imprinted on him. If Stephanie was right, that would be a good thing for the future, if there weren't grandparents and whatnot to fight over custody.

We loaded up the box truck and took everything back to the funeral home, offloaded, and had lunch. Once the kids had tromped out to check out the new toys Uncle John had brought them (how does something weighing fifty pounds manage to sound like an entire herd of elephants when running across a floor?) and we were doing dishes, I looked at Stephanie.

"You said yesterday you thought their parents were dead," I said, handing her a plate to dry.

"Yeah," she said.

"Hard as it sounds, we can make sure," I replied.

"Who's going to watch the kids?" she asked.

"Johnson, Miller, and whoever else wants to stay behind," I replied.

"If you think we can do it," she said.

"I'll poll the others, but yeah, we should make sure," I said.

Naturally, everyone wanted to go. I limited it to five – Padgett driving, Diindiisi, Davis, Stephanie, and me – since Johnson was running the day care for now.

We rolled out to the daycare at the child development center, and Stephanie pointed out the car, a puke-green metallic Kia Soul.

"Figures," I said from the turret while the others went about the fine art of automotive burglary.

They hadn't decided how to open the doors yet – the doors were crusted with dried blood and ectoplasm.

"Jesse? There's probably two bodies here," Davis called.

"Right," I said, dismounting and walking over to the car. My Saint Martin medal went cold. It hadn't done that since we'd been in the Shadow Lands, so things were not looking good for our heroes.

"Back away from the car, slowly," I said, "Everyone but Davis get over by the Humvee."

"Father?" Stephanie asked. She was carrying a sprayer as well, but I didn't need the distraction.

I pulled a stole from a pouch on my armor, kissed it, put it on, and tucked it under my armor. Davis stood by my side, impatiently. I reached into the same pouch and pulled out a silver cross and a laminated 3x5 card. Unlike Miller, I have a sense of humor when it comes to my calling, and the top of the card read, Exorcism/Banishment, the Really Short Form.

We all use cards to get the words right, just like cops in real life read a suspect his Miranda Rights from a card, they don't repeat them from memory. The worst-case scenario for a cop getting Miranda wrong is a tossed case. For a priest or combat exorcist, it could mean eternal damnation or worse. I've learned through the years that there are many things worse than eternal damnation.

I turned to Davis.

"This is going to be ugly, you up for it?"

"Yes," he said through clenched teeth.

"Hose the car," I said, raising the cross and starting the Rite of Exorcism.

Like most things, we'd lifted it whole cloth from the big-C Catholic Church. The combat exorcists (don't ask, really) of QMG had paired it down even further – and it was nothing like Max von Sydow repeatedly saying 'The Power of Christ Compels YOU!' to a floating teenager.

Something vile rose from the car. It wasn't necessarily black – black is a color, and it was more of an absence of color, shot through with silver tracery.

"BEGONE, FOUL DAEMON, LORD OF LIES!" I thundered, raising the cross.

The absence of color tried to expand, but the ritual and the holy water kept it in place long enough, and it rose, shrieking into the air, then exploded.

I lowered the cross and tapped Davis to get him to stop pumping the car with holy water.

"What was that?" he asked.

"That was an unformed Lord of Hell," I replied.

Which does not bode well for the kids' parents, I thought. Something in the car moaned. Davis raised his sprayer, and I held out a hand again.

"end… the... pain..." whispered from the car, barely audible over the Humvee in the background.

I quartered around the car before moving up from the rear, UMP raised.

"Please … for … the … love …"

I lost my lunch when I saw what was speaking. The imps had followed the imperative of their ancient Akkadian master, flaying the occupants alive. Abzu liked the classics as well, apparently. The Lord of Hell had been sustaining them for some reason, probably in response to orders from a higher authority – devils don't do anything without proper paperwork, they're weird that way.

"You ok?" Davis asked, starting towards where I stood, trying not to puke on my shoes.

I waved him back, stood and rinsed out my mouth from my CamelBak, and walked to the open window of the car.

"Pleaaase…"

I put three rounds through both skulls to be sure, then walked back to Davis.

"Give me your sprayer," I said, letting the UMP hang by the sling.

"You sure?" he asked.

"Yeah, you don't want to see this, and I need to search the car," I replied.

He handed over the sprayer, no questions asked. He'd refilled the backpack from a five-gallon jerry can of holy water while I was doing the technicolor yawn. I sprayed down the interior, pulled on a pair of nitrile gloves, and went to work tossing the car as professionally as I could, all things considered. I came up with two heavy leather bookbags and a small chest. When I touched the chest, my Saint Martin's medal tried to burn through my skin, it got so cold.

"Oh, that's really bad," I muttered to myself, walking the bags back over to the Humvee.

I dropped the bags and unstrapped the shovel from the Humvee, and pulled a large trash bag from the cargo area.

"Don't touch the bags," I said, walking back to the Soul, where I spread the trash bag and, using the shovel, dropped the box inside. The box squirmed on the shovel before falling into the plastic.

I tied the bag shut and left it where it was. I washed the shovel with holy water and blessed it for good measure, then put it back on the Humvee. Diindiisi handed me an ammo can.

"How'd you know?" I asked.

"You wouldn't take that kind of precautions for an ordinary object," she replied. "And these are steel – close enough to iron that it should have the same effect."

I walked over, grabbed the bag (no freezer burn this time) and flipped it into the can. I used my boot to flip the lid over and then locked it down, never touching the plastic or what lay inside with my bare flesh. It'd ride back tied with 550 cord to the inside of the front push bar. If it'd cross the wards, I'd turn it over to Miller. He was the researcher, after all. My experience with unholy objects ended at how to get them to people who knew what the hell they were doing – and even then, a lot of those folks ended up gibbering mad or worse. Miller would still get it if it wouldn't cross the wards – he'd just have to work on it outside the protected zone.

I told Hiebert to take it easy going back – the original plan had been to check out the car and confirm the kid's parents were gone, and that was shot to hell. Instead, we'd found them being sustained by a Lord of Hell, and an object of unknown power, but sheer malevolence.

There's days I wish I'd stayed away from this line of work. Ignorance would have been bliss, up to a point.

Sure enough, the Humvee stopped traveling when we hit the edge of the zone projected by the holy bird bath. I got out, untied the ammo can and dropped it to the road, then motioned Hiebert forward. The Humvee crossed, no problem.

"Park it and ask Father Miller to come over here, huh?" I said.

Diindiisi got out and stayed on the safe side of the line, and the Humvee rolled to the funeral home and disappeared around back. It took a few minutes for Miller to show up. Someone had said something, because he was carrying a large pair of bar-b-q tongs, wearing his full robes.

"I see you dressed for the occasion," I said.

"Johnson said you'd found something that unnerved you," he replied.

"You could say that," I said, pulling on a new pair of gloves.

I held my hands out and Miller sprinkled them with holy water. I opened the box and drug out the trash bag, setting it down next to the ammo can before opening it and laying it so that the box inside was exposed.

Miller hissed and drew back from the box before starting to chant in rapid Latin.

He did look a bit silly, crossing himself with a set of tongs in his hand.

"Bad?" I finally asked when he slowed down enough to hear me.

"You could say that – it's pure evil. Don't touch it."

"Wasn't planning on touching it," I replied with a grin.

"Where the… scratch that, where did you find *that*?"

"In the back of the Soul belonging to the kid's parents. The… bodies we found were being sustained by something," I replied.

"Sustained?"

"Yeah, or healed as slowly as possible by whatever was there. They'd been flayed by Abzu's minions at some point – more thoroughly than the girl we weren't able to save in the Square," I said. "They looked like giant, meat colored Barbie dolls, honestly."

"That's a weird description," Miller replied.

"Well, how else would you describe someone with their skin missing?"

"Good point. Were the bodies the kid's parents?"

"I rolled them for their IDs and grabbed a couple of bags, but that's it so far. I figured that this," I indicated the box lying in the bag with a toe, "was a bit more important."

"Yeah, you could say that," Miller replied. "What did the thing doing the sustaining look like?"

"The absence of color, shot through with silver tracery," I replied.

"Hmm," Miller said, flipping the box over with the tongs in his hand.

There was a mark on the other side. Miller looked at it, then looked back at me.

"I think I know who it was, but I need to make sure. You good for a few minutes?"

"Yeah, why don't you have someone bring the bags we found in the car over and I'll go through them while you're checking your hard drive," I said, stepping into the safe zone.

I didn't explode, so I took it as a good sign. Diindiisi stood there watching the box.

"Problem?" I asked.

"No. Yes. Oh, I don't know, honestly," she said.

"Well, that's a helpful answer," I said.

"You think that," she pointed at the box, "belongs to a Lord of Hell?"

"Yup," I replied. "The darker shade of dark that was hovering over it, plus the fact that it was either healing or sustaining the bodies, and the fact that it was operating in Abzu's realm are pretty strong indicators that we're dealing with something pretty powerful on the scale of the damned."

"But why a Lord?" she asked.

"And not a minion?" I replied. "Because Abzu'd punt a minion out of here faster than he'd punt us if he could. From some of my reading in my downtime, ancient chaos gods have about as much use for diabolic minions as the Church. it's been here, reconstructing whoever was in that car for the last twenty-odd days. Slowly, probably to enjoy their pain or extract more of their soul from them, but yeah, still helping a favored mortal instrument."

Johnson walked up, carrying a portable workbench, with both bags over his shoulder.

"Father Miller said to bring you this," he said, setting up the table. "And to tell you he's going to be longer than he first thought – he's researching how to dispose of the box."

"Right," I said. "We'll go through the bags then, while we wait. Why don't you head back to the kids, John?"

"You sure?"

"Yeah. Diindiisi and I have some coverage from our gods for this. I'm not sure you do, honestly."

"Understand, man, just be careful, huh?"

"Oh, I'm not planning on going insane," I replied to his back as he trotted towards the funeral home.

The bags sat there on the table. They were leather, but the leather didn't look quite right – it was pale and stiff.

I handed Diindiisi a pair of gloves, and sprinkled holy water everywhere, just to be on the safe side.

"This is human skin," Diindiisi said, touching the first bag. "It was removed by a skilled hand, smoked and then somewhat well-tanned a second time, but it's human."

"I figured it was going to be something like that, and I don't want to know how you know they're human," I replied, sighing. "We'll burn them once we've gone through them."

Inside the bags were the usual ritual tools you'd find – anthame, various powders and unguents, robes marked with cryptic symbols, grimoire of spells, etc. and ad nauseum. Only these weren't the usual crap that had been ordered off the internet or from the local hippie-dippy alternative religion store that you'd usually find near a failed summoning done by bored housewives or college kids with a little knowledge and a 'friend' from the internet.

"Well, crap," I said when we'd finished going through the stuff.

"These are high-quality tools," Diindiisi said. "Whoever these people were, they're high-level practitioners of dark magic."

"Yeah, that makes sense," Miller said, striding over to where we stood. "I was right – the box is associated with Oeillet."

"Ok, what's an Oeillet on its off days?" I asked.

"You never studied, did you – he/she/it is the fallen angel Lucifer put in charge of tempting men to break their vow of poverty. It's opposed by Saint Martin," Miller said.

"Huh. Explains why my medal got all tingly when I found it," I said. "Yeah, the Prince of Greed would be served by mortal instruments who were money-grubbing."

"More importantly, I think I know how to destroy the box and the artifact it contains," Miller said.

"Artifact?" Diindiisi asked.

"Yes. If the box is like the others that have been found, inside there will be a small lump of a porous black substance. It'll look like a roast that spent too long in the oven, according to the reports from the last one they found," Miller said. "Apparently, when Oeillet was cast out of his earthly form, the form combusted, and his cult took the remainder as, well, holy objects."

"Wait, there's more of these things lying about?" I asked.

"So far, the church has found ten or so over the years. This makes eleven definite hunks of Oeillet's form. Most of the time they're kept hidden away in grottoes and whatnot, not in the back of a Korean import," Miller said. "And it's odd that it made it through the transition boundary to the Shadow Lands."

"It would explain why Oeillet was unable to take full form and protect his followers, though. And yeah, it makes me wonder how the parents made their money," I said. "Jedi day traders my ass."

"Probably. But if they were high enough in the hierarchy to have a lump of their daemon, they were probably very old money," Miller said.

"How old?" I asked.

"Old enough that the formation of the family fortune is buried in a legendary past," he replied.

"So, how do we destroy it?" Diindiisi, ever practical, asked.

"Iron or steel container to contain the box," Miller said.

I taped the empty ammo can with a toe to make it rattle.

"Holy water," he said as Hiebert came up with a sprayer filled with the same. "And a whole lot of chanting by yours truly. The ritual takes several hours."

"And you'll have to be covered the entire time, right?" I asked.

"Yes. If we were on the other side, I'd say move it to consecrated ground, but here?"

"Here it won't cross the barrier from the bird bath," I said, sighing theatrically. "Oh well, I didn't have any plans for tonight anyway. Can I at least sit down for the vigil?"

He sighed theatrically, running a hand across his face.

"Yes, you can sit. I'm going to be kneeling, anyway," he said.

"Then there's no time like the present," I said, perching a cheek on the folding workbench.

Hiebert filled the can with water, then left the sprayer behind. Diindiisi went to the funeral home, returning with two folding chairs and a small bag.

"I thought you'd like to eat while you're watching the Father," she said, handing me a sandwich from the bag.

"Thank you," I replied, sitting in one of the chairs. She took the other. It was probably going to be a long watch, after all.

Miller used the tongs to lift the box from the bag and drop it in the ammo can of holy water, where the water began to boil. He dropped to his knees and started chanting. And chanted for the next eight hours by my watch. The water level in the can never dropped, even though it boiled vigorously the entire time.

Many and manifest are the miracles of the Lord.

Chapter Twenty
Day 29, 28 April 2018

I texted Gunny on the other side with the info on the kids' parents. At least with modern technology, we weren't limited to trying to figure out a way to send complex information, knocking on tables, or using the ideomotor effect and Ouija board. Miller talked to the kids after he got up in the morning, with Stephanie looking on. I did all the other tasks – checked the wards, washed the street, pumped holy water down the drains, and so forth. I was just putting the pressure washer back in the garage when Miller found me.

"They're clean," he said. "Spiritually, anyway. Huey was covered in strawberry jam and wanted to hug me."

"Happens," I said. "But no taint?"

"No. Louise said their parents told them they had a great purpose in the future, and they'd introduce them to it. And she said that they watched a lot of Star Wars related stuff."

"Probably as part of their cover as being members of the Holy Jedi Order or some such," I snarked.

"Yeah, possibly," he said, sitting on the step.

"You ok?" I asked.

"Tired is all," he said.

"Take a day, man. I mean, yeah, I want to go toss the parents' house here in town, but that can wait until you're good. You were in extreme chanting mode yesterday, after all."

"Yeah, and that does take it out of a man. It's a job for a younger priest."

I looked at him and laughed.

"Younger priest? You mean one who gets out of the archives more often than every once and a while to go run down the holy wheelbarrow of Saint John the Semi-Devine," I said.

"There might be some truth to that," he admitted. "Is this what you normally do?"

I tossed my head back and snarled.

"This? This is not how things normally go. Normal is rolling up on a bar where two vampires are beating the living crap out of each other in front of witnesses and having to go inside and put them down, and then convince the poor, dazed, drunken college students that it was just a fight, nothing more, nothing less. Normal is realizing that the oozing trail you've been following through a series of dry sewer lines is being left by a lipid golem that's digesting a small dog, three deer, and the two college kids that created it on a lark. Normal is going out in the middle of nowhere and having to bag and tag half a dozen idiots who summoned something using a bootleg copy of the Necronomicon that they thought they could negotiate with. This? This, Father Miller is a walk in the park on a day full of sunshine and happy birds in comparison to having to explain to a widow that her only daughter won't be coming home ever again, but here's a check to tide you over, and I can't tell you what they died of, but it was in the service of their fellow man," I snapped.

"I didn't know," Miller replied.

"Yeah, I figured. You Jesuits can argue law with Satan himself, but field work kicks your ass every damn time," I said, stepping around him and going up stairs to take a shower.

Diindiisi was waiting for me when I stepped into the room we were sharing.

"Hey," I said, swapping out my t-shirt.

She came over and ran a hand along the U-shaped scar on the back of my arm.

"I've been meaning to ask, where did you get this one?" she asked.

"Ghoul bite," I said, tucking in my t-shirt.

You can take the boy out of the Marines, but you can't take the Marine out of the boy.

"Father Miller seems a bit upset," she said simply, sitting on her bed.

"Yeah, I might have shaken his worldview a bit," I replied. "He was feeling a bit rough about yesterday and asked if this is 'Normal' in our line of work."

"He's a good man," she replied.

"He is. And a good friend. But his view of what we do is limited by spending all his time in archives poring over dusty tomes," I said, tying my boot. "And yeah, I know, the Knights of St. Quintus kick in quite a few doors and kill some serious monster ass, especially in parts of the world where no one bats an eye at the neighbor's kid being hauled off by the local non holiday version of Krampus. But he's damn near vain about the fact that he doesn't know how the real world works, for all his study."

"You think he doesn't know that?" she asked.

"I think he struggles with it," I admitted, tying the other boot. "But honestly, I think he is more concerned with getting back to his dusty tomes than he is about the people the things he studies affect."

"Not everyone is, how did you put it the other day, constitutionally suited for kicking in doors and going hand to hand with the forces of evil," she replied.

We'd been talking about things where we were going and how things had been – Diindiisi was interested in the 21st century where she'd be spending the rest of her life, and I was trying to bring her up to speed on different things. And how Group worked.

I sighed. "Yeah, true. But there's being in a supporting role, and there's being a jock strap," I said.

That earned me a look.

"Ok, a jock strap is a..." I started.

"A device for supporting the male genitalia," she replied. "They were actually in use before I fell into the Shadow."

"Ah."

"And no, I don't think that all Father Miller is good for is making sure your prodigious engine and bollocks aren't squashed when you're riding a bicycle," she said before rising and storming out.

"You know, if I'd known I was going to spend the day with my foot in my mouth, I'd have used ketchup flavored soap when I showered," I said to the world at large.

"Mustard works better with pork," Padgett said from the doorway. "And I've read that humans taste like pork, so mustard flavored soap would probably be a better choice."

I rolled my eyes at him, and he grinned back.

"Father Miller says you should meet him on the roof, by the way," he said before turning and walking away.

I stuck a pistol in a retention holster behind my belt at the small of my back and went outside.

Miller was standing on the roof, looking to the nominal north.

"Dave," I said by way of beginning.

"Jesse, you're right," he said. "I've spent too much time behind a desk."

"Well, I might have been a little rough on you," I replied, uncomfortably.

He turned to face me.

"I forgive you my son," he intoned, with a laugh. "Apology accepted. But that's not why I called you out here."

He pointed north.

The sky there wasn't its 'normal' static gray. It was purple-black and ominous.

"Oh."

"Yeah. Want to bet if it's raining on the other side?"

"Not really. It'd be a sucker bet," I said. "We're going to have to plan on another site."

"It's a cave," he replied.

"Traditional, then," I said with a wry grin.

"And that's if the flooding lets them access it," Miller reminded me.

"If it's out of the flood plain, Gunny'll be there waiting when we come to the other side, even if he has to steal an AAV from somewhere," I said.

"What's an AAV?" Miller asked.

"Amphibious Armored Vehicle. Not really a tank, and it floats, for a given value of 'floats'," I replied.

"Ah. It might be fun. But do you remember that geography class we took from Professor Badger?" he asked.

"No."

"Yup. Bevers cave."

"You know, even with climbing all over that damn cave for geography class I always wondered why we went," I said.

"You're not the only one," Miller replied.

"It's going to make getting the 'water from a flowing spring' part a bit hard, though," I said.

He coughed lightly.

"You ok?" I asked.

"Yes. I was just pondering over a quaint and curious bit of forgotten lore while I was castigating myself over what you said," he said. "The Font of Saint Mark the Evangelist counts as a flowing spring."

"I'll be damned," I said.

"Quite probably," Miller replied. "But if you hew to the true faith, God might see fit to forgive your long list of sins and shortcomings."

He was grinning as he said it. Damn Catholics.

"So, we move the font to the ritual site, along with everything else, and then set it up long enough to fill a pot? Then what? Fight the hordes of Abzu while Diindiisi and the folks on the other side coordinate the spell?"

"Something like that, yeah," Miller said.

I stood there, to quote Carroll, in uffish thought about the plan he'd just outlined. Honestly, it sucked. I'd have to recon the cave to see if it were defensible, and then Johnson and I'd have to spend hours rigging defenses before Diindiisi started the ritual. And we'd have to defend the hell out of the place the entire time. Pulling out of here would probably mean we'd lose the funeral home and its chapel as base of operations, so just in case we'd have to take the box truck loaded with non-perishables...

"Well?" Miller asked.

"I... I like this plan!" I said, slapping him on the back. "I'm excited to be part of it, so let's do it."

"How long will it take to work everything out," he said.

"I'm not writing an operations order here, but it's going to take a couple of days," I replied. "We're going to need to load everything possible supplies-wise into the box truck, and then the font itself."

"Probably make things easier if we transport the font whole," he said.

"Yeah, and that's a problem," I said. "It weighs what, a hundred pounds or so fully assembled, without water, right?"

"Something like that, yeah," he replied.

"Why couldn't you have been looking for the fiberglass birdbath of Saint Mark?" I snarked.

"Probably because there's no way a relic of Saint Mark could have gotten mixed into fiberglass," he replied, seriously.

"Yeah, but it would have made logistics so much easier," I replied.

I sighed.

"What now?" he asked.

"Until I go look at the cave and the area where we're going to do the ritual, I won't know how to build something to carry the font down there," I said. "It's no good to set it up with a palanquin for transport if we can't maneuver the carry arms."

"Ah."

"On top of that, we're going to have to hide the recon of Bevers Cave with something else," I said. "So we will be checking out the kid's house."

"I figured," Miller replied. "Should be fun."

"Yeah, if your idea of fun is looking for traps set by Jedi who follow a Lord of Hell," I replied. "Which makes it a three-person job. Unfortunately, if the three of us fail ..."

"Then the others are probably stuck here forever," he intoned.

Chapter Twenty-One
Day 30, 29 April 2018

In the end, we took Thing Two and the Tacticool Tahoe on the recon, and in addition to the measuring devices, I loaded two cameras into the mix – one normal and one that the wizards (no, really, long beards, pipe smoke and pointy hats and all) had 'tweaked' that one with spells or something so that it would show 'strange, unusual phenomenon'. I figured it might show the best spot to set up the ritual.

Diindiisi added a forked stick she'd cut from one of the trees to her bag.

"Old school?" I asked her, climbing into the turret on Thing Two.

"What?" she replied from the front seat.

I waited until the doors were closed and Padgett had brought Thing Two rumbling to life. "The stick? Old school? Dowsing for ritual sites?" I asked.

"No, this armor makes my back itch," she replied. I could hear the smile in her voice.

"Ah."

"If you're nice to me I might let you borrow it," she replied. "Besides, oak isn't the right kind of wood for dowsing – you need willow for water, and lignum vitae for other things."

"Oak won't work?" I asked as we rolled out.

"Oh, it'll work, sort of," she replied. "It's better for things like killing vampires, though. Although, lignum vitae will stop even an ancient vampire cold."

"We tend to use bois d'arc or mesquite around here," I replied. "They're common, and while not as hard as lignum vitae, they're damn near hard as stone."

"Hmm," she replied as we turned and drove towards the address from the IDs we'd recovered from the Soul. "I wonder if being of a local wood makes a difference as well."

"How so?" I asked, watching the trees for, well, things.

She went into lecture mode. "Vampires are tied to the soil where they are created, as you know. If the trees are grown in the same soil, they'd have some of the same influences on the vampire as the soil itself," she replied as we slowed down in front of the address.

"Oh you have got to be fucking kidding me," Padgett said from the driver's seat. "That place went for close to a million bucks the last time it was sold."

It was a two-story, early twentieth-century mansion in a 'revival' style. There was even a historical marker on the gate.

"Oh, wonderful," Father Miller said, standing next to the historical marker. "Former site of the meeting place of the earliest 'Loyal Fraternal Order of Buffalo' in San Marcos."

I was looking at a map we'd printed out. "Want to bet it's also over Bevers cave?" I asked.

The entrance to that horrible 1950's amusement park was less than half a mile away, behind the house we were looking at.

"No, not going to take that bet," Miller said, shrugging into a water sprayer. "Vow of poverty and all that."

Diindiisi was grinning at him, and I grinned at her before turning back to the Tahoe and Thing Two.

Dalma had climbed up behind the fifty in the turret. I said a quick prayer that she would not need it, because if she did, we were hosed.

I opened the metal gate leading to the property. "I'm not sure how long we'll be gone," I said. "Stay safe. Bug out if you need to."

"As if," Dalma snorted from the turret.

"No worries," Hiebert said from where he was perched, half in, half out of the roof of the Tahoe. "We'll wait."

We'd built a good team. Now, if I could convince Father Miller the grass was greener on my side of the fence...

Besides, he could donate his salary as needed, I thought with an inward chuckle.

"Let's go for a walk, shall we?" I asked, leading the others up the walk to the mansion.

Inside was everything you'd expect of an early 20th-century mansion bought by the followers of the Devil of Greed. Hardwood floors, subdued and conservative furnishings that usually cost more than their flashier, uglier counterparts, and antiques.

"Upstairs or down?" Miller asked, stepping through the door.

"Top down usually works best," I replied, taking the stairs two at a time.

We swept the top floor and found nothing. Unless you count a couple of missing paintings.

"That's a very good copy of Vermeer's *The Concert*," Diindiisi said, looking at the painting hanging over the bed in the master bedroom.

I took a photo with the tricked out camera, then looked at the image on the screen.

"I can't be sure here," I said, "but I suspect when they get to the house on the other side, they're going to find that it's not a copy."

"What do you mean?" she asked as we trooped back down to the first floor to start sweeping it.

"The camera not-so-obscura that the pointy hat and pipe smoke brigade issued me shows that the painting is old. Now it could be that the copy was made on an old canvas, but ..."

"Why aren't you sure?" she asked.

"Could also be bullshit on the part of Oeillet," I replied. "But that's for them on the other side to determine."

We swept the ground floor as well, finding nothing.

"This is unusual," I said, as we stood in the kitchen, looking at shelves of food from Whole Paycheck and Jim's Organic and Fair Trade Emporium. Even the stuff in the fridge was 'good for you', based on its labeling.

"What is tofurky?" Diindiisi asked, closing the freezer door.

"A sin against God and nature," Father Miller replied.

"Seriously?"

"It's a meat substitute made from cheese made of bean milk, and flavored to taste like turkey," I said, tapping my chin while I was looking into the backyard.

There was nothing there except the garage, which looked to have an attached workshop or apartment.

"Bean cheese?" Diindiisi asked. "Is meat that rare in the current day?"

"No, it's a lifestyle choice, mostly," I replied. "Some people have chosen to give up meat either for health or ethical reasons."

"Oh, like the followers of Doctor Kellogg's theories," she replied.

"Something like that, yes," I said. "Although these days there are fewer enemas recommended for overall good health."

"Wait, what?" Miller asked.

"Doctor Kellogg ran the Battle Creek Sanitarium, and espoused a healthy, celibate lifestyle, eating mostly grains and yogurt," Diindiisi said. "I met him when he was on a lecture tour. Very strange man."

I followed that bit of historical and medical wisdom with, "Garage."

"Huh?"

"We found nothing in the house, right?" I asked.

"Well, yes, but we haven't stamped all over the ground floor yet," Miller replied.

"Short of bringing in a ground penetrating radar, I don't think we're going to find anything in the house itself. It was too easy for one of the kids to find it. Remember, you said 'grottoes' for the cult followers, right?"

"Yeahhhhh, but I pulled that out of my rectal cavity," he replied.

"I wish we had a map of the cave's orientation," I said, pulling out the map I'd been looking at earlier. "Want to bet it runs east-west?"

He stepped over and lightly slapped me on the back of the head.

"Dummy. Don't you remember class? The entrance chamber is north-south, but the cave turns about thirty feet down to run east-west," he replied.

"No more Gibbs slaps," I said. "And yeah, I'd forgotten. Wasn't there a sealed-off chamber as well?"

"Yes. They said they'd closed it because people were breaking off bits of the flow stone and crystal structure to take home as souvenirs."

"What if instead it was closed because it's a ritual site?" Diindiisi asked.

"That would make sense," I said. "Still doesn't answer the question about getting there from here, though."

"So let's go search the garage," Miller said.

"Right," I said, leading once again.

The locks on the garage doors were an order of magnitude more expensive than the ones on the million-dollar house, including the ones on the door into the garage apartment.

"Interesting," I said, looking at the lock. My Saint Martin's medal was doing its best imitation of spider senses. "There's something in there, based on the way my medal is throbbing."

"I didn't see any keys in the house," Diindiisi said.

"We'll try the key you're carrying, and if that doesn't work there's a sledgehammer and tanker bar in the Humvee," I said.

"The key I'm carrying?" she asked.

I swapped my UMP for her Roadblocker.

"Yeah. Door's wood," I thumped it, to make sure, "even if the frame is steel. The property is on the 'historical' list. Therefore, they can only use materials common when it was built. They snuck the door frame past the committee but couldn't get the door."

I motioned her and Miller around the corner, then keyed my mike. "Going to be a few gunshots, Dalma," I said.

"Roger that. It's boring here, miss you guys," she replied.

"Boring is good," I said before I stepped up and fired three shots into the door, top, center and bottom, at hinge height.

I then brought up a foot and kicked the door on the hinge side. It resisted at first, then, sagging on the lock, finally fell into the room beyond.

"Damn," Miller said, crossing himself.

"I see why that would make a good key," Diindiisi said, swapping guns with me again.

I waited for her to reload. "Yeah, the only thing better for quick access is explosives," I said.

"What kind of explosives?" she asked.

"When we get home, I'll introduce you to the magic that is called composition four," I replied, chuckling. "You can solve many problems through the judicious application of C-4."

She finished reloading the Roadblocker, and we went through the door.

We'd broken into what I'd thought was the chauffeur's space. It may have been such at one time. Now, all the walls and furnishings had been removed, and it had been converted to a ritual space, complete with a summoning circle painted on the floor.

"Don't cross the circle," we all said to each other at once.

"This isn't good," I said after a laugh.

"It's also somewhat interesting," Miller said.

"How so?"

"Most of its in paint, or worse," he said.

The paint was the color of dried blood. I'd be willing to bet whoever had painted it had used white latex and mixed in blood to get just the right color and effect.

"Human?" Diindiisi asked.

Miller had pulled out a test kit and was cautiously sampling the paint/blood.

"Porcine," he said, showing the result on the kit. "Close enough to human to fool most lesser daemons and devils, but kinda insulting to a Lord of Hell. Might be why he was keeping them alive as torture."

"Or they used this as a gateway for lesser beings, to communicate with him," Diindiisi replied.

"I don't really want to think about the reasoning behind that," I said.

Miller had pulled another tool out of his pouch and extended it. He whispered a blessing, anointed it with oil, and drew it across the circle, breaking the power of the circle by interrupting its unity. My medal stopped trying to alternately freeze and thaw a small spot on my chest as soon as he was done.

"Is that a rake retractor?" I asked, watching him wash the device off with water from the pack on his back.

"Huh? Yeah, they started out as rake retractors, then the R&D team got them. They'll expand out to about a foot, and the tips are made of blessed silver, usually from a cross or other object of worship," he said. "I think they're in the catalog of standard tools issued by the Church to investigators."

"I wonder if Ginsberg can get a copy of the catalog," I mused.

"I'll send you the link," Miller replied snarkily.

"Whatever it is, and wherever you get it, it did the job," Diindiisi said, looking at the circle.

"Check the chests, and then we'll go check the bay area where the cars should be," I said.

The chests along the wall held more paraphernalia –
robes, unfilled grimoires, ritual tools, and unguents.

"Seriously?" Diindiisi said, holding up a box marked
'mystic powders'.

"Yeah, there's a trade in that crap," I replied. "Probably
some mummy brown around here somewhere."

"Mummy brown?" Miller asked.

"Yeah, it used to be a pigment, big with the Pre-
Raphaelites, and made from, you guessed it, ground-up
mummies. These days, the stuff you get in the art store is
made from kaolin, quartz, goethite, and hematite. And it's a
good cover for the stuff made from ground mummies that
still gets traffic from 'practitioners of the mystic artz'," I
said.

"Oh dear god," Diindiisi said.

"Yeah, most of them end up buying the oil paint
pigments rather than the real thing, but occasionally you
run across the real deal," I said, closing the chest I'd been
rummaging through.

"There's nothing here that's too damning," Miller said.

"Yeah, let's go check the bays," I said, opening the door
that led out into the garage proper.

Parked in the far bay was a Range Rover.

"Is that an Autobiography?" Miller asked.

"Really? You know Range Rovers?" I replied, walking
over to it.

"Yeah, they're a weakness of mine. I've wanted one for
years," he replied. "And yes, I know greed is a sin, Father."

I tried the door. It was unlocked, so I opened it and
tossed the glove compartment. Inside were the usual mass
of papers. Closing it, I noticed the scroll work on the door
interior door handle.

"Dave, what's an Autobiography sell for?" I asked.

He rocked a hand side to side.

"Hundred forty to a hundred seventy base price, why?"

"And the Holland and Holland model?"

"Two eighty minimum."

"Yeah, these folks follow a devil of greed," I said. "It's a Holland and Holland."

"Their daily driver was a Soul?" he said, stunned.

"Well, would you want three dirt merchants climbing all over bespoke leather and walnut?" I replied.

"Not really," he admitted.

"Dirt merchant?" Diindiisi asked.

"Children. Dirt merchants, as in they move dirt from one location to another, usually at a cost," I replied.

"Oh. If you're done admiring the car," Diindiisi said, "I'm not finding any trap doors over here."

"There's nothing over here," I said.

I looked at the floor.

"What about the floor drain?" Miller asked.

"Well, it is of unusual size," I replied.

Most of the time if there's a floor drain in a garage it's a six-inch pipe. This one was a grill two feet on a side and hinged for easy access.

It wasn't even locked. And sure enough, there was a visible catch at the bottom of the drain, which caused the entire piece to hinge up, showing that the bottom of the drain was fake. Below the drain was a hole, leading into darkness.

At least there was a ladder.

"Oh, that looks like fun," Diindiisi said.

"Y'all wait up here," I said, shedding my LBE and UMP. I snapped a lanyard on my 1911 and then hooked that around a belt loop, and stuffed spare magazines in a cargo pocket.

"Time to play tunnel rat, Father?" Miller asked.

"Yeah. See you in a few," I said.

I descended into darkness. The ladder went down about ten feet, and then I touched the bottom. Feeling around, I found a switch.

"Nothing ventured," I said, flipping it.

Lights came on in a tunnel leading to the west.

"I think this leads to the cave," I shouted up the shaft. "There's a rope in the back pouch of my armor. Send it down."

My armor came down and I unclipped the carabiner hooked through the drag loop. The rope snaked back up, and my UMP came down as well.

"Right, be right back," I said, heading down the tunnel.

It ran for about a hundred yards and ended at a poorly constructed wooden door.

I eased the door open, looking into what had to be the Crystal Palace of Bevers Cave by the light spilling over my shoulders. A short distance away, there was another ritual set up, including the remnants of a fire. Nearby was a stand holding a grimoire, open to Shakespeare's take on 'Ye Grate Spelle'.

It also looked like something had gone wrong. I took photos of everything, then I walked back to the entrance.

"Diindiisi, come down here, huh?" I said.

She came down the shaft and followed me to the cave.

"Oh my," she said, looking over the remains of the ritual.

"Yeah," I said.

"Improper components," was all she said after a few minutes.

"Huh?"

"They've substituted. I don't know what this is," she pointed to the vat that the pot rested in, "but it isn't baboon's blood".

I sniffed.

"Smells like chocolate and lilac," I said.

"And baboon's blood definitely doesn't smell like chocolate, especially when it's been used as a quench," she replied.

"I've been wondering what we're going to use as a substitute," I said.

"Notice it wasn't on the list of things that your Gunny sent through," she replied. "For very good reason. Baboon's blood is a bit of mummery that Henry convinced Shakespeare to add to the spell for confusion's sake."

"Does it not work?" I asked.

"It causes it not to function as advertised, obviously. Ye Grate Spelle opens a rift in time that you can look through, if you're a low-level practitioner. More skilled practitioners with better quality ingredients can open a rift to a specific time and place. Apparently," she said, dusting her hands and picking up the grimoire and notes from the reading stand, "if you use lilac and chocolate in place of baboon's blood, it opens a rift to the Shadow Lands. Which is not what our little band of devil worshipers was hoping for," she said, placing the grimoire in her bag of many things.

"That explains how they got here, but not us," I replied.

"What was it you said the other day? Mysterious are the ways of God," she said, turning and heading back down the tunnel.

"There is that," I replied, following her up the tunnel. "And then there are the days he has a wicked sense of humor. I think it was more the second than the first."

We'd go over the notes later. Right now, I want to get the measurements we need and then take a long, hot shower. Because what we'd found was seriously creeping me out.

We climbed out, sealed the shaft with holy water and wafer, and made our way to the vehicles.

"Find anything?" Dalma asked, climbing down from the turret.

"You could say that," Diindiisi said, putting the papers she'd grabbed in her bag.

"To Bevers Cave Park-o-Rama," I said to Padgett.

We led Dalma head up and out of the Tacticool Tahoe. In the distance, the purple clouds rolled with silver flashes of light, and to the south, ectoplasm rained in a solid wall, about where the San Marcos city limits would have been.

"Let's get this over with," I said, eyeing the 'weather'.

"Yeah, that looks right nasty," Miller said.

Diindiisi stayed up top, and Padgett came down into the cave to help me run the tape. We followed the markers, mostly, until we reached the door to the Crystal Palace, which was held closed with a honking great lock.

"Want me to go get a set of bolt cutters?" he asked.

"Wouldn't do any good," I said. "It's a disk lock. Nowhere to get a hold of the hasp on the lock. We're going to need to bring a small torch for that one."

"You're not going to shoot the hinges like you did at the garage?" he snarked, holding the tape against the door frame.

"Yeah, no. That technique has its uses. But against a steel grate set in a stone wall? I don't know about you, but I'm not in favor of having to pick ricochets out of my body," I said.

"Yeah, that would be bad, not good," Padgett replied.

Something moved in the darkness around us.

"Father?" Padgett asked, dropping a hand to his UMP.

"Go," I said, pushing him towards the entry.

We were halfway out when the lights failed. I snapped on the light on the muzzle of my UMP, and after a moment or so, Padgett did the same.

"*Did you think you'd escape...*" whispered from the darkness.

"Keep moving," I said to Padgett.

He started walking, swinging the light side to side. I followed, backing so I could cover our rear. A rock sailed out of the darkness, hitting Padgett in the middle of the back before I could say anything.

"Ooof" he grunted. He stayed on his feet, however.

"We're almost there," I said, seeing the sign pointing to the 'Deepest Wishing Well in Texas' we'd passed on the way down.

Something slithered up the shaft of the well in the darkness.

"I can see the entrance," Padgett said.

I reached into a pouch and found one of Ginsberg's enhanced flash bangs.

"Run," I said, pulling the pin and tossing it, before turning and running to the entrance.

There was an unholy noise as the flash bang went off, followed by something battering itself against the walls. I threw another one down the entrance for good measure.

"Problems?" Miller asked as Padgett and I stood there panting.

"Yeah," I finally managed to wheeze out. "You could say that. I think there's a grue down there."

"I'm not sure of what it is — but it's a big something down there," Padgett said. "I turned to make sure you were following and saw eyes the size of dinner platters near the ceiling of the cave."

I stood up.

"We'll have to figure out how to get the font down the other way," I said. "Because I'm not facing whatever is hiding in the dark."

"You sure?" Miller asked.

"I've got no clue what it was, other than large and pissed off at life in general and us in particular. At least that's the feeling I got from the negative waves it was broadcasting," I replied.

Padgett started laughing weakly.

"Always with the negative waves, man," he gasped out.

"Hey now, I've had nothing but good thoughts about that cave since we found it!" I said in reply.

Everyone else looked at us like we were mad. I guess, in that minute we were. But it was a good madness, I think you could say — and we were still alive to enjoy the madness.

Which, sure as hell, beat the alternatives.

Chapter Twenty-Two
Day ?, 30 April 2018

We'd had a serious exchange of text messages with the 'real' side. They'd also moved in and taken over the 1950's style Bevers Cave Park-o-Rama, using the ultimate grease – gobs of cash. My employer, QMG, makes money hand over fist doing legitimate security work for the rich and shameless. Then you add in the money made from killing things that go bump in the night, and even after paying exorbitant salaries, the company was well in the accounting black. Renting a garish, well past its expiration date amusement park was easy by comparison.

Of course, it was still raining on the other side. Upside was the cave, on both sides was well out of the floodplain.

"Weird," Miller said, looking at the weather data Gunny had sent from the other side.

"How so?" Davis asked, looking over his shoulder.

"It's essentially a dry land hurricane at this point," Miller said, gesturing to the screen. "And it's feeding itself with the water it dropped."

"Hurricane Harvey did that," Davis replied.

"Yes, but Harvey was on the coast, and while a bit abnormal, it started as a hurricane. Not a thunderstorm that somehow boosted itself to a tropical depression and then a hurricane while on dry land," Miller said.

"Abzu called in a favor?" I asked from where I was lounging on the couch, watching the kids play.

"What?" Miller asked, turning to where I sat.

"Abzu called in a favor," I replied. "Look, you and I work for, ultimately, a polytheistic monotheism that is in charge of every aspect of life, right?"

"If by polytheistic monotheism you mean the Trinity, then yes," Miller said through gritted teeth.

"Most of the other religions don't have a 'one god fits all' approach to things, though, right?"

"Yes."

"So, there's an Akkadian god or goddess of storms. Abzu needs one site flooded to keep us here so he can wear our skins like a suit or something. and goes through his Rolodex and finds the phone number for that deity. They probably haven't spoken in years, and if it's a she, she's had to find work waiting tables to keep things together," I said.

"Or stripping," Dalma said. "What? Pay's decent, and you can go to school. I looked into it once, but too many of the smaller clubs around here are run by biker gangs."

"So yeah, she's waiting tables or stripping, and then she gets a call from Abzu, and he talks about how things were in the old times – back in the good old days when they were more than just afterthoughts in dusty tomes. You know, back when they had power and worshipers and devotions and shit," I continued. "And she knows he's full of fertilizer, but she listens to him. They had good times back then, you know?"

"Hadad," Davis said.

"Who's Hadad?" I asked.

"According to this," he pointed to Miller's computer, "Hadad is the Akkadian storm god. Kinda changes the 'stripper waiting tables in a strip club' narrative you're establishing."

"Fine, so HE bounces in a strip club," I said. "Anyway, he and Abzu meet up, have a couple of drinks, and talk about the good old days. Abzu mentions he needs a favor, and Hadad owes him – reminds him about that debauch they went on with Zeus where Abzu covered for Hadad with his wife, and then finally mentions he needs a little favor. Who knows, Abzu suggests, Hadad might pick up a few worshipers as a result of the storm."

Miller gave me a look that said I was out of my mind.

"Yeah," Davis said. "But you said the older, weaker gods don't like to share power."

"True. Which is why I think it was a blackmail situation," I replied. "Think about the stories you were taught in school about the Greek and Roman gods. You think they were the only ones having dalliances with mortals and producing demi-gods?"

"Good point," Davis replied.

Miller was looking at both of us like we were growing horns.

"Except," Miller started.

"Except what?" I replied.

"Except that would mean that God was letting Hadad stay on Earth," Miller replied.

"And that kills my theory, how?" I replied.

"Oh, now you're going to say you've run across older gods while working for QMG, right?" he replied.

"Nope. But check your archives," I replied. "There's a red-haired, bearded dude running around Scandinavia that pretty much matches the description of the Thunderer from Snorri Sturluson's work."

"That's a coincidence," Miller said.

"Three hundred years of the same guy showing up is a coincidence?" I replied.

"Nanabozho," Diindiisi said, plopping down on the couch next to me.

"Who?" Miller asked.

"Nanabozho. He's a god, and I've spoken with him," Diindiisi said.

Miller threw up his hands.

"Fine, there are other gods," he said, defeated. "But that doesn't necessarily mean that Abzu called in a favor to park a storm over San Marcos, Texas."

"Doesn't mean he didn't either," I replied. "But yeah, he could be exercising power outside his normal zone, because that happens all the time."

"In my experience, it doesn't," Miller replied.

"That's because you work for the god of everything," Diindiisi replied. "Not everyone does."

"True. But," he said, his eyes lighting up, "Abzu was the god of freshwater, right? So he'd have some control over the waters."

"Yes. But not honking great storms," I replied. "He might have talked his wife into it, but she is the goddess of storms. Besides, she's formless, again."

"Ok, you win. I still think it's more coincidence than a favor, though," he said.

"Father Miller, in our line of work, coincidence is a dirty word, right up there with decaffeinated coffee and luck," I said.

"Then what is it?" he replied.

"In this case? Enemy action," I said.

Stephanie came in and she herded the children out to 'their' room.

"So, what are we going to do about 'enemy action'?" Miller asked once they'd left.

"I'm sure the top minds are on it on the other side. Not a whole lot we could do except whack Abzu, and even then that might not work. Depends on what he's got on Hadad," I said.

"So you're saying the storm could be permanent?"

"No. I'm sure Someone will be sent to point out to Hadad, or whoever is causing the storm, that they're trespassing and it might be in their best interest to lay off," I said.

"Dear God, you make the Lord sound like a mafia don," Miller said.

"You don't think religion is a protection racket?" I asked with a sly grin.

"I'm done," Miller said, storming out.

"So," Davis asked after a minute or so, "who would God send to negotiate?"

"Depends on how he wants the negotiations handled," I replied. "If he's playing nice? Hmm, Saint Lawrence O'Toole."

"The actor?" Davis asked.

"That was Peter O'Toole," Padgett said from the doorway.

"Lawrence was the archbishop of Dublin and was canonized after his death," I said. "If God wants to make a point, he'll send the Archangel Michael."

"Why him?" Padgett asked, coming and sitting down.

"Because he leads the heavenly host and has a very no-nonsense attitude. If it's Michael, there will probably be punching involved to get his point across," I said.

"I heard that!" Miller said from the kitchen. "Michael doesn't just break things."

"Then why's he the patron saint of the infantry?" I replied.

"You heathen," Miller said. He was losing a battle with the giggles, and the giggles finally won.

"What?" I asked. I gave him a look that said butter wouldn't melt in my mouth.

"I was just picturing Saint Michael in a pin-striped suit, negotiating," Miller replied.

"Punch. Now that we've started the negotiations, let me explain what's going to happen," I said.

Miller lost it and slid down the wall to the floor, laughing.

"Punch. You will stop making it rain over Texas. Punch."

"Stop," Miller gasped between laughs.

"Kick. Now that we've come to an understanding, how about you come work for us? Kick. There's some places you can make it rain, and the boss is quite accommodating, punch," I said.

Chapter Twenty-Three
Day ?, 1 May 2018

The lord works in mysterious ways. I don't know if he was listening to our conversation (ok, yeah, He knows when the sparrow falls because He is watching, so it's possible), but we got word the next morning that the rain had stopped falling in San Marcos. The river was still up, but whenever we were ready to try the spell, they were ready on the other side.

We got everything together and argued about moving the font.

"We're going to have to do it in pieces," I said.

"But then we won't have immediate access to holy water or running spring water," Miller argued.

"It weighs over a hundred pounds, Padre," Johnson said. "We can hump the pieces and lower them into the hole y'all found in the garage, but ..."

"But there's not enough room to carry it assembled down the tunnel," I said. "And we're not going to be able to go the other way. You know, mysterious monsters living in the dark and all that."

"You're going to take one of the fifties in," Miller pointed out.

"Yeah, and that heavy bitch is going to be in pieces," Johnson replied. "The gun, the tripod, and everything else. It's going to take two of us to get it in place and set up at the door, and that's not counting the sandbags to hold the feet in place on the stone."

Those were normal bags filled with sand. We weren't going to hump fifty pound bags of sand down the hole then into the cave. Some things even Marines won't do.

"Fine. When do we want to do this?" Miller asked.

"Stephanie? How long will it take to get the kids together?" I asked, turning to her.

"Fifteen-twenty minutes. Mostly just making sure that they've got their toys."

I sent a text to the other side.

"Two hours, people. Let's get moving."

Our bug-out bags were packed. It was time. We did one last check of the funeral home, filled every possible container with water from the font, and then loaded into the two Humvees and the Tacticool Tahoe for what I sincerely hoped was the last time on this side, the font in pieces in the back of the Tahoe.

We stopped long enough for Father Miller to reset the wards, then drove to the house. The atmosphere on the way over was light – the storm to the north was gone, and for once, we couldn't see ectoplasm falling anywhere.

Thing One was parked on the street, and Johnson covered us while we offloaded everything but the kids through the garage doors. We didn't go into the attached apartment for obvious reasons. Stephanie entertained the kids while we started dragging equipment down into the cave. I swapped with Johnson in Thing One so he could set up the fifty in the cave. Nothing even came to bother us.

I'll admit, I was getting worried. We'd been unsparing in our use of holy water, and there was a 'snap' in the air when the font was reassembled.

"We've got everything but the kids in place," Miller said, walking out to Thing One.

"Time to go down into the cave, then," I said, dropping from the turret. "Anything moving in the cave?"

"Not that we've seen. Johnson set up a couple of mines, just in case – tossed them through the grate on the door."

"That should work, as long as they're facing the right direction," I replied, waving to Stephanie to bring the kids.

"Time?" she asked, trotting up with the threesome in tow.

"Yes," I said, turning to Huey, Dewy, and Louise. "We're going to climb down a ladder and into a secret cave."

"Is it the secret place?" Louise asked.

"The secret place?" I asked her.

"Yeah, momma said we'd moved here because there was a secret place we'd learn about when we were older," she said, picking her nose in the most adorable way possible.

"Yes, it's the secret place," I said. "And you're going to have to be as quiet as possible at first. Diindiisi is going to do a..."

"Ceremony?" Stephanie supplied.

"Ceremony," I continued. "When she's done, there's going to be a bright light and we can step through it."

"Ok," Louise said, and her brothers nodded.

"They should be able to handle the ladder," Stephanie said.

"It's ok, we'll hook a harness on them just in case," I said.

Miller was looking intently to the west.

"Crap," he said. I turned and followed his gaze.

"Stephanie, get the kids below," I said. "Tell Diindiisi to start now."

"I think Abzu called in another favor," Miller said.

A column of flame shot smoke was coming towards us, destroying homes as it approached.

"You think?" I asked before we both turned and walked into the garage.

Miller blessed the doors as we went through. Stephanie was disappearing down the shaft, and Johnson was waiting to follow.

"Problem?" he asked.

"Yeah, something wicked this way comes," Miller said.

For the first time since we'd arrived in the Shadow Lands, there was a sound of breeze. Something was drawing the air towards it.

"Fire tornado?" Miller asked as we watched Johnson drop down the shaft.

"Could be," I replied. "Or a pissed off fire god."

"Which one is worse?"

"Does it really matter?" I asked as he began to descend.

"No," he replied before his head dropped below the concrete.

The wind was picking up, and I could hear things burning, followed by a shriek of rage.

"Found the God zone, did you?" I shouted as I went down the ladder, navy style – hands and feet on the outer rails and slid down, using my feet to brake.

Miller was waiting and sprayed the entrance with holy water from a sprayer.

I could hear Diindiisi chanting in the cave.

And then, one of the mines went off.

"Go!" Miller shouted at me.

I pushed past Stephanie, the kids, and Davis. Hiebert was in the cave, handing things to Diindiisi as required. Johnson had just plopped down behind the fifty and was racking the charging handle back as I dashed across the cave.

"CONTACT!" he shouted, slamming his thumbs down on the butterfly trigger.

Ma is loud outside. In a cave? Thank God for hearing protection.

The wind was actually flowing through the cave, drawing back towards the tunnel and shaft.

Johnson let up on the trigger. "See anything?" he asked.

"Negative. You?" I replied.

Dalma cracked a second box of ammo and staged it. Padgett was watching their backs.

"Nope. But it was big, ugly and really dark a minute ago. Where'd the wind come from?" he asked.

"Heap big fire outside," I replied. "Drawing air through the tunnels."

There was a pop behind us, everything froze for just a moment, then I heard a familiar voice.

"It's about damn time, Jesse," Gunny Thomas said, stepping through the gateway Diindiisi had opened.

He was pointing out positions for his team members to take. Capdepon went past, toting another M240 at high port, to support Johnson on the fifty, and Takashi and Polk went towards the shaft to help herd the kids out.

"Everything all right?" Thomas asked.

"Oh, you know, just another day in the Shadow Lands with a giant fire daemon trying to burn his way in," I said. "You?"

He grinned.

"Things are still a bit wet on the other side," he replied. "And the bean counters are a bit miffed. Oh, and Goodhart says when he said take a vacation, he didn't mean go to hell."

I watched a team of technicians come through the gate.

"Whiskey Tango Foxtrot, Gunny?" I asked.

"Someone higher up thinks we can get some data if we leave some equipment here," he replied, shaking his head. "Since the portal will stay open for at least an hour I was voluntold to let them do it."

"Gotcha," I said. "We're going to have to hold this location for an hour?"

"No, you, and everyone else, are going through the portal as fast as your legs can carry you," he said. "Mr. Lo and his technicians have about five minutes to get their sensor rigs in place, grab the magic drinking fountain of Saint Anthony the Great, and then we're following you out."

"It's Saint Mark the Evangelist," Miller said, resignedly.

"Padre, I'm a lapsed, left-handed small-c catholic," Jed said. "Be glad I know it belongs to a Saint."

I just grinned, watching Stephanie and Davis herd the kids through the rift opening. Miller took one last look at the font, then followed them through.

"Hiebert, Johnson, Dalma, Padgett, Diindiisi, go!" I shouted.

"I'm not leaving without you," Diindiisi said.

"I'm right behind you, hon," I said, pushing her towards the rift.

She went through. I followed her into the light, with the words 'Cross into the light children' playing in my head. On the other side, things were shockingly normal. The air was feeling, and there were noises in the cave around us. Michelangelo was standing there, taking stock.

"Boss," I said, walking over to the old vampire.

"Jesse. I trust you're well?"

"As well as you can be after spending almost a month in the Shadow," I said.

Diindiisi was holding back, standing by the rift. Michelangelo strode over to where she was standing.

"It has been a long time, Diindiisi," he said.

"It has," she replied before fainting.

A pair of medics swarmed her, and I stood by as they lifted her to a gurney and moved her out of the cave and up to the surface.

"We've got the reports you sent through, but we'll do a full debrief at some point," Michelangelo said.

"Yes sir," I replied.

"Go after her," he said gently. "Henry had to stay in Dallas, and based on the reports you've sent through, you're probably the closest thing she has to family here. It might be a bit confusing for her to wake up being alone and poked and prodded by 'modern' medicine."

I left the cave and went in search of the medics tent.

Chapter Twenty-Four
Day ?, 5 May 2018

They relocated all of us, except Father Miller, who went off with a couple of really rough looking priests from the Order of Saint Peter, to the training center in Dallas via air, and then to the Trauma Center for observation. No one had spent as much time in the Shadow Lands as we had in recent memory – excluding Diindiisi, who was the all-time record holder, as far as we could tell. She'd slept the entire trip from San Marcos to Dallas, so she missed out on her first flight. I was watching her eat breakfast and listening to her lament missing the experience when Henry Keith strode into the room.

"Henry!" she said, dropping her spoon on the tray.

"Diindiisi," he replied, stepping to the edge of the bed.

She raised her arms to him, and I got to see something rare – Henry Keith hugging someone with joy. Usually, he was a very standoffish guy – not that I blame him, after all, when he was born, they thought bad air or bad humors caused disease, after all.

He turned to face me.

"Father Salazar," he said, bringing his heels together and bowing, once. "I see you found our wayward child."

"Just lucky," I replied.

"That's not what my visions said," Diindiisi said, gesturing me over. When I was standing by her, she took my hand.

"Yes," Henry replied. "How are you feeling?"

"Not bad for a hundred and forty-six-year-old," Diindiisi snarked with an impish look. "But the doctors say they need to run more tests. And all their tests seem to involve sticking me with needles and drawing blood. Were I a suspicious woman, I'd think they were using them for magic."

"There is a modern saying," Henry started, "called Clarke's Third Law, I believe. It goes something like this – any sufficiently advanced technology will appear to be magic."

She thought about that for a minute or so, then grinned up at him.

"Fine, so I won't curse the doctors," she replied.

"That is a load off my mind," Henry replied, drawing over a chair and sitting down. "Jesse, if you don't mind, I'd like to speak with Diindiisi alone for a few minutes."

"Sure thing," I said. "I'll go grab a Coke or something."

I wandered down the hall. QMG has a hell of a hospital set up in Dallas, in part because that's where the training center is, and in part because that's where they're headquartered. And there are some things you can't take an injured team member to the local ER for. They'd tried that in the past, and further contamination ensued. So these days, if you were stable enough for transport, and close enough to Big D by air, you came to the aptly named QMG Trauma Center. Not close to Dallas and covered in the slime of a hellhound? QMG's got a trauma center close. Or they've got a deal with a doctor or three who are read in on what's happening.

Nice thing about the Trauma Center is it was designed by people who weren't thinking 'hospital', so there were small dining areas in each wing and on each floor. I walked to the closest one, and had just sat down with a Coke and a not-quite-stale-Danish, when Hiebert and Padgett wandered in.

"Jesse," Hiebert said.

"Jonathan, John," I said, then waited for them to cage drinks and food.

"How long are we going to be cooped up here?" Padgett asked.

"Depends," I replied.

"That's not half cryptic," Hiebert said before taking a bite out of his Danish.

"Look, they're going to run tests. They're going to contact your doctors, if you've got one, and run checks against any records you have from the past. And they're going to make sure that you weren't…well, tainted for lack of a better word, by your experience on the other side,' I said. "That's the downside. The upside is, they'll be paying you for your time, both here and on the other side."

"Yeah, I got a message from my husband," Hiebert said. "He's happy I'm back, but my employer left a message last month that I didn't need to bother to show up for work again."

"Yeah, employers tend to get a bit shirty about disappearing for a month with no explanation," I said.

"And that's part of the problem," Hiebert said. "I can't exactly tell my husband that I've been on the borders of hell for the last month. He'd insist I talk to a shrink."

"Yeah," Padgett said. "I don't have quite the same problem Jonathan does, but it'd be nice if I had someone to talk to about it, besides the QMG shrinks."

"I know the feeling," I said. "What's the official story?"

"They haven't told you?" Padgett and Hiebert both asked.

"No. I work for Group. Most of the time we're not privy to the cover-up stories that get spread about. Most of us don't have lives outside the company, honestly."

For the very reason that not being able to tell your significant other why you'd just spent a month in Outer Mongolia and come back with new scars that suspiciously look like human bite marks, causes strain on relationships. For the record, Mongolian Death Worms aren't all they're chalked up to be, but they are a gigantic pain in the ass.

"You left that out in the recruiting speech," Hiebert said.

"Yup. Mostly because I didn't think about it, honestly," I said. "Talk to the shrinks. They can actually help with a lot of it. They might even be able to give you hints on how to discuss this with your families. Or, if you come to work for QMG, your families will get a briefing on what you do, even if all you end up doing is shifting pallets at the warehouse."

"I hadn't thought about that," Hiebert said.

"Y'all need baristas?" Padgett asked.

"Yeah, but given what I saw, you can qualify for field work – the pay's much better, to begin with. And the teams are always shorthanded."

"I wonder why?" Davis said, coming up and sitting down.

"Yeah, I'm not going to lie to y'all," I started. "It's dangerous work. But you get to sleep at night, well when you can sleep, knowing that you're actually protecting your fellow man from the things that go bump in the night."

"And the pay is a damn sight better than what Uncle Sugar pays for the same thing," Johnson said, pulling up a chair. "How's Miss Diindiisi doin?"

"Not bad. Chafing to get out of bed, honestly," I said. "She's talking to the boss at the moment."

"Met him earlier," Johnson replied. "Kinda reminds me of this Army Colonel I met in the Mog."

"That was probably him," I replied. "He tends to show up in places far foreign to check on monsters that might take more than a regular team to take out. I actually worked with him in Iraq before I came to work for Group."

"You mentioned that before," Hiebert said. "Can you talk about it at all?"

"Short version is what I told you before – my infantry company got tasked with supporting a SEAL team doing a sweep of Saddam's 'Primate Research Facility' – it said so in both English and Arabic on the signs around the place. The only reason there were primates on site was as cover and to feed to the ghouls Saddam was trying to raise and train there."

"Ghouls?" Padgett asked.

"Yeah, ghouls. Arabic myth, one each. Eaters of dead flesh amongst other things, and really nasty bastards. Anyway, Keith led the SEAL team down into the facility to look for evidence of weapons of mass destruction or some other cover story. They were actually there to assess the site and see what kind of progress Saddam's scientists had made towards controlling ghouls," I said, sipping my Coke.

"And?" Johnson asked.

"And what? Ghouls are not controllable, except by a ghoul queen. They won't even listen to a ghoul king – that's the breeding male, by the way. Best we can tell, from the research that Saddam was doing, they're ant analogues, socially, at least – the queen runs the hive via pheromones, and every ghoul has one job – protecting her. We found that out the hard way," I said. "Other than that, as far as anyone can tell, they don't have a language beyond a few grunts. And they're tough as hell to kill."

"How tough?" Davis asked, fascinated.

"Well, I shot one to doll rags with a fifty cal, and the bastard was still coming towards us when the F-18 covering the USAF F-15E strike rolled in and shot him to hell with its Vulcan cannon," I said. "That was one day I was thankful for Marine Tac-Air. That and 2000-pound bunker busters."

"You know, you can speak of none of this outside these walls," Henry said, walking into the dining nook.

"Not that'd do us any good, Colonel," Johnson said.

"True, Sergeant Johnson. And yes," Henry raised a hand to stop Johnson from replying, "that was me in Mogadishu. That mission turned out much better than the one where I met Father Salazar."

"I'd imagine so," Johnson said.

"We were able to drive the daemon that was eating children back into the jungle for a time, then find her lair and destroy it after the raid on Addid's headquarters," Henry said simply.

"I missed all that fun," Johnson said. "Lost three feet of small intestine about a week earlier on a convoy and woke up after everything was done."

"Happens," Henry said. "However, I'd like to speak to all of you about coming to work for QMG. Since the 1890's we've been the sword and shield of mankind when it comes to things that go bump in the night. I'm sure that Father Salazar has told you both the good and the bad of working for Group at this point."

"Yeah," was the response from all of them.

"Well, I won't have to go over that then," he said, pulling up a chair. "I will say that the pay is very competitive, with quarterly bonuses, and full insurance coverage."

I have to admit, Coke burns when you shoot it out of your nose.

Chapter Twenty-Five
Day ?, 06 May 2018

And like that, they released us all from the hospital that evening and set us up in the barracks where they'd stick teams that were coming in for retraining. Well, everybody but Stephanie and the kids – they went into 'special' housing somewhere on the compound where the experts could keep an eye on the kids and make sure they weren't tainted by Oelliet, or any other devil for that matter.

I got hung up doing paperwork – apparently, the computer wasn't happy that it now had multiple weapons with the same serial numbers, and the IT nerds really needed an explanation, now. By the time I arrived at Building Four, transient housing, the argument had been settled. Hiebert, Johnson, Padgett, and Davis all had one block of four, and I was sharing a second with Dalma and Diindiisi.

"Some people," was all Diindiisi would say in explanation.

Dalma, on the other hand, was more forthcoming the next morning.

"They'd put your gear, what there was of it, in another block, one floor up," she said. "Diindiisi wasn't having any of that and discussed it with the guy in charge. He stood his ground. She called his boss, and explained y'alls relationship, and well, here we are."

"Ah," I said wryly. Not that the rooms were any different – they'd all been designed in the 'institutional ugly' style. "Well, I won't be here that long."

"Oh?" Diindiisi said, walking over to where we were sitting.

We were in the smoke pit. Dalma had a vape but was playing with it more than using it. I was getting ready to do the 'Mission Over' ritual that dated back to my time in Iraq. Only difference was over there, it hadn't involved booze, unless we'd just come back from a mission around the time of the Corps Birthday.

Gunny had left me a package in my room, and Dalma had moved it along with my other gear – mostly a seabag full of emergency clothes that I'd stored in Dallas against need.

In the package was a box of cigars and a bottle of Shackleton Whisky. I'll admit to the heresy of liking blended whisky, and the Shackleton was one I hadn't tried yet. There was also a note – *Welcome back, doofus.*

I looked at my watch and sighed, then broke out the whisky and cigars.

"It's a bit early to be drinking, isn't it?" Dalma asked.

"Sun's over the yardarm somewhere," I replied. "Besides, this is a ritual."

"Oh, then that's different," she snarked back.

I passed the box around. Diindiisi picked a cigar, Dalma deferred. I took two. One went on the ashtray, unlit. I handed Diindiisi the cutter, and she snipped the tip, then handed it back. I cut my cigar and set it aside. I poured four shots – the fourth going next to the cigar, handing the other two to Diindiisi and Dalma.

Then I committed my other heresy, lighting my cigar with an ancient Zippo lighter my grandfather had carried across the Pacific during World War II, then held it so Diindiisi could light hers. Once both cigars were going well, and

Dalma had taken a hit from her vape, I raised my whisky to the fourth glass.

"Absent comrades!" I said before downing the shot.

Doing shots of Shakleton was abusing a good blended whisky, but it was ritual.

I topped off the glasses, and we sat there sipping whisky and smoking cigars. Johnson joined us, and didn't even question what we were doing, just picked a cigar and lit it, then took his whisky.

"Here's to us, and those like us," he said. "There's damn few of them left, and most of them are dead."

We drank.

The rest of the team drifted over. Hiebert and Padgett refused cigars, and Davis turned green on his first puff, but soldiered on. We'd almost finished the first bottle when there was a commotion from the building behind us, and Father Miller stormed out.

"Pull up a chair," I said, waving a hand. I was relaxed and feeling good. Yeah, I'd eaten breakfast, but I hadn't thought to bring snacks for the ritual. I could order something though, once we'd hashed it out.

"Where is the font?" Miller asked, coldly.

"How would I know?" I replied.

"Your company rescued us," he hammered back.

"And? You think I hid it in a cargo pocket before I came through the rift?"

"I think you know where they moved it," he replied. "My superiors won't tell me anything!"

"That's because it's still down in San Marcos on the other side, Father," Padre Polk said, gimping over and sitting down.

She filled a glass and took a cigar.

"I'll be glad when they take the cast off my ankle, it itches something fierce," she said, looking at Miller.

Miller was dumbfounded.

"I know a poultice that might help," Diindiisi said before Miller could reply.

"Dave? You might want to close your mouth, you're starting to draw flies," I said with a grin.

"It's still in the Shadow Lands?" Miller finally squeaked out.

"Yeah. When the team tried to move it, it wouldn't budge. So they tried to take it apart and no go," she replied, after taking a deep drag on her cigar and blowing it towards the sky. "I don't know why your people wouldn't tell you, and I'd have told you if you'd have waited the five minutes it took someone to find me."

"I… nothing personal, ma'am, but I don't know you," Miller replied. "And it's the kind of stunt that Jesse here would pull."

"Father Miller, meet Father Polk," I replied with a grin. "Padre, this is Father Miller of the Knights of Saint Quintus."

"Father, it might be the kind of stunt Jesse would pull, but how?" Polk asked.

"How what?"

"How would he do it?"

"Well, he knows your team lead," Miller temporized.

"And I know Jed biblically," Polk replied. "That doesn't mean they had time to plan a damn thing."

"First time I saw Jed was when he stepped through the rift," I replied, sliding a glass at Miller.

He grabbed it and took a huge gulp, then started choking.

"Warn a fellow next time, huh?" he said when he got the coughing under control.

"Uh-huh," I replied. "Look, I can't tell you why your people didn't tell you where the holy Winston Churchill gnome was. And honestly, I could care less, probably, in some weird way. There's other things bothering me."

"Such as?" He replied.

"Such as how many people disappeared," I replied.

"Four hundred and twenty-seven," Padre replied, sipping her whisky.

"Well, that's better than the worst case," Davis said with a sigh.

"And we brought back eleven, and the IDs of another dozen or so," I said. "How are they covering it up?"

"Well, there was a lot of flooding, and a tornado at one point," Polk said. "And for the first time in a long time, the flooding did serious damage. They're blaming a lot of the missing on that."

"Okay," I said. "And how are they explaining us?"

"Y'all got lucky," she replied. "Hid in a cave and were found by the heroic efforts, blah, blah, blah. You should read the commentary you made on the National Guard."

"Oh, I can imagine. Straight boilerplate?"

"Something like that, yeah. Course, it's now one of the worst disasters in Texas history," she said before finishing her glass. "I've got a course to teach. God, I hate being on injured reserve."

Diindiisi rose also.

"If you'd like, I can try a poultice on you when your day is done," she said as they walked off together.

"So, what are you going to do?" Miller asked me.

I reached into my bag and pulled out a second bottle. "I'm going to finish this drink and sit here and contemplate pizza," I said. "Then I'm going to get blind, stinking drunk. Tomorrow I'm going to find out how we're going to find the other folks who are missing on the other side."

"Sounds like a plan," Johnson said. "Long as the pizza doesn't involve ham and pineapple."

"And that, sir, is the great pizza logical debate of our times, isn't it?" I replied.

Chapter Twenty-Six
Day ?, 7 May 2018

Thing about the good stuff is, no matter how good it is, you're still probably going to get a hell of a hangover the next morning. I'd started drinking water later in the day to fight the effects of alcohol poisoning, but my head was feeling the stress in the morning. It probably didn't help that Diindiisi knocked (loudly) then entered my room at oh my God it's early.

"How're you feeling?" she asked, drawing the curtains back.

"Light. Light bright," I mumbled, putting a pillow over my head.

"Yes," she said, maliciously.

Well, it sounded malicious to me in my state.

"Shower first or a bit of the hair of the dog, then a shower?" she asked.

I peeked out from under the pillow. She stared at me with a sly look and had a cup in her hand.

"Knowing you, there's real dog hair in that," I replied, forcing myself to a seated position.

Her sly look got more vulpine, if anything.

"I'd never do that. Well, unless it was a required ingredient. This is coffee," she said, sipping from the cup.

I took it. Sniffed it. Sure enough, coffee. I sipped.

"Not as good as Padgett's coffee, though," I said after a few seconds.

"Nope. But it's coffee," she replied. "Are you going to get up?"

"I'm still on vacation," I replied. "Or stand down. Actually, I'm not sure what my current status is."

"Stand down," came from the door. "You're still officially being debriefed, and the Committee wants to meet with you in an hour."

I looked over. Jed was standing in the door in 'business casual'. Which meant tactical pants and a polo shirt. Since we were officially on the QMG compound, that also meant he was packing – his grandfather's 1911, if I remembered correctly.

"Fine," I sighed. "I've got time for a shower and to fire back something to eat, I guess."

Jed gave me an evil grin. "I think I've got a couple of vomlet MRE's around here somewhere," he said.

"Oh hell no," I replied. "And before you ask, an MRE is a meal, ready to eat, and a vomlet is a vegetarian omelet from the same. Only eating the package would probably be better for your digestive tract."

Diindiisi grinned. "So something like tofurky?"

"Worse. Far worse. Unflavored seitan tastes better."

"Oh, it can't be that bad," Diindiisi said, tossing back the covers.

I was wearing silky shorts to sleep in.

"Yeah, it can be," I said, stumbling into the shower.

I ran it hot and cold for five minutes, then came out and dried off. Diindiisi had laid out a similar outfit to Jed's – tactical pants and a collared shirt with my dog collar beside it. I swapped out the shirt for a T-shirt that read 'I saw the damned Cow in Picadilly!' and a button down shirt for an over shirt. I left the button down hanging open, covering the knife and pistol on my belt.

Diindiisi came in with a tray as I was finishing getting dressed.

"Are you sure about that shirt?" she asked as I started eating – ham and eggs, with a side of hash browns.

"Yeah," I replied. "No official warning until an hour before the meeting? The Committee is playing games. I'm playing games back."

"Not dressing properly is playing games?" she asked.

She was in what I'd been told was a riding skirt – it looked like a skirt until she moved, and then you realized it was split like trousers. I wondered where she'd gotten the skirt along with the white shirt and bolero jacket, but at this point, I wasn't going to ask. Besides, I'd given her access to my accounts, and it wasn't like I was hurting for money.

"In this case, yes. Not giving me a warning about the meeting until an hour before is seriously wrong. Assholish, even, but wrong. By not wearing my dog collar, I'm telling them I know they're playing games, reminding them that I still kill things for a living."

"I don't understand, but if you say that's the message you'll send, then I guess so," she said. "Now eat."

I finished eating with ten minutes to spare, and we caught a bus to the main office, where the Committee met.

The Committee, it was bandied about, represented about five hundred years of monster-killing experience, albeit in some severely damaged packages. There probably wasn't a whole set of limbs on any one member. Henry and Michelangelo were not members of the Committee – they worked for them, but didn't sit on the Committee. The members also set policy, lobbied governments, etc., ad nauseum. It was where someone with a real hard on for killing monsters ended their days. Personally, I was going to retire somewhere I could keep a whole lot of ammo and watch the grass grow when I got too beat up or just too damn old to keep up with the whole thing. But some folks had to continue to contribute, but their talents weren't suited for teaching others how to stay alive in a scrum with zombies.

There's a trick to it – first, make sure you don't have any exposed skin (zombies are dead humans (mostly, but that's another story) and can't bite through decent denim, let alone Kevlar reinforced nylon) and either keep shooting or cutting until either they're dead or you join the shambling horde.

The first surprise was Diindiisi walking through the door into the meeting room with me. I had figured I was the only one summoned to meet with the Committee, but it did explain why she was dressed in a semi-formal manner. And why she'd wanted me to be dressed the same.

"Father Salazar," Julian, the current Committee chair said, "Ms. Diindiisi, if you'd both please be seated, there are some questions we'd like to ask both of you about your experiences in the Shadow Lands."

He just smirked at the shirt.

"I thought I'd pretty much covered everything in my report and filmed debriefing," I said, sitting down.

Diindiisi took the chair next to me.

"Yes, well, there are some questions we'd like answered," Carne, seated to Julian's left, croaked. She'd lost a lung and leg and arm on her right side to a kraken attack twenty years ago.

"Such as?"

"Ms. Diindiisi, how did you know to meet Father Salazar at the B&B in San Marcos?" Martin, seated in one of the end chairs, asked.

"I didn't know specifically to meet him there," Diindiisi replied. "I'd had a vision before I was trapped in the Shadow Lands that I would meet someone. When the setting shifted, I realized I was in the place from my vision."

"And you had no warning that you were going to enter the Shadow Realm, Father?" Martin asked.

"Well, my knee hurt that morning," I said with a laugh.

"What?"

"Yeah, my knee hurt. But since that was normal when the weather got weird, and it looked like it was going to rain that day, I didn't think anything of it."

"I see," Martin said.

"It really was that simple," I said.

"You were at the worst mass disappearance in the history of the United States, and you say it was simple?" Martin asked, somewhat aghast.

"From my point of view, yes, it was simple. I mean, I didn't get up that morning and say 'hmm, I think I'll cast a cabalistic spell that's going to drag me and almost five hundred people into the Shadow Lands ruled by an obscure Akkadian deity," I said.

I was not hung over enough for this shit.

"And if we told you someone did cast a spell?" Hawn, seated between Carne and Martin, asked. You could see the wheels of her chair above the table they were seated at.

I thought for a minute.

"Then I'd guess it was probably the followers of Oeillet that we found there, who were essentially hoist on their own petard."

"What makes you think it was them?" Rowan, the fifth member of the Committee asked.

"They were being preserved by something, and they had a lot of powerful magic equipment with them," I said.

"If I might?" Diindiisi asked.

Julian nodded.

"I went over the grimoires we found with them, both while we were waiting for the right time for the ritual and over the last few days," she started. "They definitely were followers of Oeillet. Mr. Thomas, the leader of the Brute Squad, also gave me access to what they found when you raided their house on this side."

"He shouldn't have done that," Hawn muttered under her breath.

"He mentioned you'd probably react that way," Diindiisi said with a grin. "But since he did, that's neither here nor there. Based on what I read in the grimoires and the... printouts, yes he called them printouts, the cultists were trying to raise Oeillet's form on Earth again, using a variant of 'Ye Grate Spelle' of Mother Shipton's."

"That damn spell," Julian said. "One of these days I'd like to use it to go explain to Shakespeare what he'd unleashed on future generations."

"Wouldn't do any good," Henry Keith said, entering the room. "Bill was pretty damn sure that the changes he made wouldn't allow the spell to function properly. He was right, and wrong at the same time. Shakespeare adding ingredients that sounded exotic just causes the spell to act in unusual ways or fail, sometimes spectacularly."

Henry took a chair on our side of the table, giving the Committee a go to hell smile.

"Sorry I'm late, I had to sign off on purchasing a small, 1950's amusement park in San Marcos," he said. "I didn't find out about this session until just a few minutes ago."

"Yes, well, that's because we didn't want you here, Henry," Martin said. "We wanted to get a field report without your 'explanations'."

He made air quotes.

I hate politics. I'd avoided them as much as possible when I was in the field. We'd been drawn into a fight between the Committee and our oldest member.

Diindiisi stifled a giggle.

"I figured that, so that's why I had a textgram sent to Henry," she said.

The Committee's heads all swiveled to face her.

"Why?" Julian asked.

"Because, for all your experience, Henry still has more. Besides," she reached over and touched Henry's arm, "I know him. You people, I've just met."

I didn't even bother to hide my smile while I poured a glass of water. It was going to be a long session, but oh so worth it.

"So why do you think it failed?" Carne asked.

"Baboon's blood," Henry and Diindiisi said at the same time.

"What?"

"They used 'baboon's blood' that they ordered from the internet," Henry said. "We're back-tracing the source now. But Harry's House of Occult Goods..."

"Seriously? Harry's House of Occult Goods?" Rowan asked.

"Yes, sir, Harry's House of Occult Goods. They mostly deal in magic tricks and things of that nature, but they do have a few spell components. Mostly along the lines of 'ha-ha' funny things, like acrylic ice cubes with flies in them, that kind of thing. They're one of the larger sources of 'mummy brown' oil paint we find around failed spells," he said with a shake of his head.

"Why haven't we shut them down or got the government to do so?" Julian asked.

"Because, honestly, being stupid and dabbling in the Dark Arts isn't illegal, sir. For that matter, being a vampire isn't strictly illegal – immoral, perhaps, you'd have to take that up with the lawyers, but it isn't illegal," Henry said.

"Yet, we hunt them and are paid by the government for it," Martin replied.

"Yes, sir. But you notice we only hunt the vampires that make themselves into a major pain in the ass? The vampire that's got a small herd of human cattle that he or she isn't actively enlarging? That quietly sits in the shadows and manipulates long-term investments? We don't touch those guys. Just the ones that are out there showing off – turning more mortals to the undead, having fights in bars, that kind of thing. We don't have the time or the manpower worldwide to do anything else. And HHOG is like the quiet vampires. Nothing they sell is what it purports to be, and they post huge disclaimers everywhere on their website that it's all fake."

"Which is exactly what we'd expect them to do if they were selling the real thing," Hawn pointed out.

"Yes, ma'am," Henry said with a sigh. "But we'd also expect to, at some point, either find their dark web activities or get the real thing from them. Every transaction we've found so far has been hokum."

"I see. So what was wrong with their baboon's blood?" Hawn asked.

"It was lilac flavored chocolate in this case," Diindiisi said.

"It was what?" Hawn asked with rising inflection.

I pulled out my phone and pulled up the HHOG website. "Chocolate. Seventy percent cocoa dark chocolate, for fondue" I said. "Baboon's blood comes in three flavors, it turns out – lilac, rose, and chamomile."

"Who the hell would eat chamomile chocolate fondue?" Julian asked.

"Looks to be popular," I said. "They're sold out, and it's on backorder. 'The light chamomile scent and flavoring counteracts the caffeine content of the chocolate, leading to a blissful night's sleep'."

"What the hell?"

"Sorry, that's their ad copy on the chamomile flavor, sir. And before you ask, it has the usual 'The FDA has not evaluated claims about this product or its efficacy' disclaimer, so no, we can't sick the FDA on them over the product. It does have about three pages of bullshit about the historical uses of chamomile, mostly in tea, however," I said.

Look, I like tea. But I don't believe that adding the leaves of this plant or that one is going to make my sleep more restful or cure the heartbreak of psoriasis. And I've seen real magic, from both the sending and receiving ends, and it doesn't work the way they say it does in the books or movies. Yes, belief could convince the powers that you really thought that flower flavored chocolate was a reasonable substitute for the blood of a primate. That didn't mean it had the same chemical makeup or the same occult powers. Nine times out of ten it meant the failure of the spell and the death of the casters, which meant sending in a cleanup crew and exorcists, and sending the families sealed caskets filled with bags of sand. We were dealing with the fallout from the tenth time, which was going to be a right pain in the backside to clean up.

"Fucking hippies," Julian muttered. "So, the spell failed. Then why were people dragged across?"

"We think, emphasis on think, that at the same time the Oeillet followers were trying to raise their favorite devil, Abzu opened his realm in order to feed his minions. From what Diindiisi has said, that was a common occurrence, but she can't really say how common," Henry said.

"Why not?" Carne asked, looking at Diindiisi.

"Easiest explanation?" Diindiisi asked. "There's a song Dalma played for me once we got back on this side, by a band called Nine Inch Nails – *Every Day is Exactly the Same*. Are you familiar with it?"

"Not really," Carne said.

"It sums things up nicely – in the Shadow Lands, nothing changes. There is no night or day, just a gray hazy sky," she said. "I wasn't aware exactly how long I'd been there until Jesse told me the year."

"But by your own report, you'd met other people there."

"Yes. But I didn't always ask them what year it was where they'd been. Honestly, the thought of knowing how long I'd survived alone was more than a little bit terrifying," Diindiisi said, looking down at the table.

I reached over and took her hand.

"But in the end," she looked right at Carne, "I got through it. And now I have so many things to learn."

If the smile on her face had been any larger, she'd have disappeared like the Cheshire Cat.

"And we're glad you're back," Julian said.

"Yes," Carne said. "But we need to know, will Abzu try to avenge Tiamat?"

"He's welcome to try," Henry said. "Here, in this realm, his powers won't work the same as they do in his realm. He's blocked by the Font of Saint Mark the Evangelist from getting near the rift in Bevers cave, and lacks followers on this side, as far as we can tell. So, we don't think he can do anything here."

"I see," Carne replied. "And your thoughts, Father Salazar?"

"I don't think he understands how things work on this side, now. The font seems to lock down his ability to continue to find souls to feed his minions, so he might be facing a revolt if he even tries to do anything here," I said.

"And what about the people you were unable to find?" Hawn asked unexpectedly.

"We should be looking for them," I replied. "Yes, it's going to bugger the cover story all to hell if people that have been listed as dead suddenly show up on this side. Especially after funerals and whatnot. I don't think we'll find them, however."

"Then why waste the manpower and money on looking for them?" Martin asked.

"Because not looking for them sends a message to the teams," I replied.

"None of those people are employees," Rowan said dismissively.

"Going after those people is the right thing to do," I retorted.

"Some people would say you're somewhat biased," she said.

"Why? Because I executed my wife after the lich turned her?" I replied.

"That's cold, but yes," Carne said. "It was the resources of QMG that let you put an end to that particular threat, and you were well paid for it."

I laughed at her.

"Ma'am, if you think the only reason the current teams hunt is money, you've been out of the field far to fucking long, and need to step down from the Committee," I replied.

"How dare you!"

"Honesty hurts don't it?" I slammed back. "Yeah, I know you guys pay us a lot of money to go after things that go bump in the night. But the guys who join for the money? What's their turnover rate? Most of them either wash out after one or two encounters, or get eaten, causing more problems for whatever team has to deal with them. In the end, knowing that if you get turned to the Dark Side, eaten by a slavering grue, or just plain lost, that Group is going to keep looking for you until you're found and dealt with properly makes the job easier."

"That's just your opinion," she replied.

"Yes'm it's my opinion. But when's the last time you polled the Teams and asked how they felt about it? Ya'll pushed out the damn lo-jacks without even asking if people wanted them," I said, scratching the scar over my tracking chip.

"That was for your own safety," Martin said.

"Yes sir, and the teams accepted it as such. But I'd be willing to bet dollars to doughnuts it wasn't just my shrink listening to people bitch about Big Brother following us everywhere," I replied.

"There were some complaints," he admitted, grudgingly.

"And I bet you get a lot of them from incoming classes, right? Show the Teams it's more than lip service to searching for them by looking for the people missing in the Shadow Land. We may never find another living soul there, but the Teams will be better for it."

Julian glanced at his phone.

"You've given us a lot to think about," he said. "But we should probably break for lunch at this point. We will call if we want you to return."

I rose and offered Diindiisi my arm, then swept her out of the room.

"Where would you like to eat?" I asked as we walked down the hall towards the door.

"I overheard one of the trainees talking about a Halal Fusion restaurant just outside the main gate," she said, "and wondered what Halal cooking was."

I stopped and looked at her.

"Halal Fusion? So, properly ritually killed meat and what?"

"I don't know. I'm not even sure what fusion means in this context, so I thought we'd give it a try?" she asked.

We did.

I don't know what the current batch of trainees and employees thought of it, but I'd had better food eating off the locals in Iraq. Probably less of a chance of getting poisoned as well. It was moderately horrible, with a side of fermented camel's milk.

Which was probably the best part of the whole meal, honestly.

Chapter Twenty-Seven
Day ?, 8 May 2018

"They're all fine," Madden, HR wonk extraordinaire (it's what his door says, honest) said. "Physically, mentally, and emotionally, we're hiring them all."

"Great," I replied. Not that I'd been concerned about the folks who'd come through it all not being hired. Even if they'd all secretly been diabetics with heart conditions, QMG would have found jobs for them.

I was sitting in Madden's office, going over paperwork covering back pay and whatnot. Hardest thing so far had been adding Diindiisi as my heir and giving her medical power of attorney until we were married – at that point in Texas, she'd have it without me having to sign it over to her. And that had been hard because she didn't have a Social Security number, that joyous bane of modern American life. QMG would get her one – they got them regularly for beings much older than her, and much weirder, some of whom weren't even human, but until she got one, the paperwork wouldn't be quite finished. Not that she wouldn't inherit – QMG had paid out to a kelpie at one point, because someone had designated it to receive their insurance payout. I'd heard the kelpie now ran a lakeside resort in the Ozarks, and wasn't drowning visitors, so it'd worked out in the end.

Diindiisi was attending the QMG door kicker short course, and planning our wedding (a small affair, she swore) with Dalma's help between classes. Dalma, Padgett, Davis, Hiebert and Johnson were all attending the long course –

start with Monster 101, and work up to Explosives, care, feeding, and use thereof, followed by Zen and the art of Machine Gun Maintenance, along with a lot of running, door kicking, and target practice. Hiebert and Johnson were a bit long in the tooth for field work, but they'd be great in supporting roles – and unlike Dave from Jed's Brute Squad (and the Austin IT guy, Other Dave) they weren't wheelchair bound, so they could actually secure a perimeter or run ammo and other supplies in on a clearing operation. One thing was certain, though. Since Diindiisi and I were getting married, Austin was getting another religious support figure. Polk would be back from the injured reserve before Diindiisi was released to the field, but it was the thought that counted.

I looked across the desk at Madden, who was beating a tattoo on his computer.

"How much paperwork is there, Dave?" I said, thumbing through the inch-high stack I hadn't signed. It sat next to the inch-thick stack I'd already initialed and signed.

"Well," he temporized, "that's it for today. Once you get married, you get this stack."

He dropped my hand to God, a three-inch stack of paperwork on the desk, with an evil grin.

"Upside to that stack is you and Diindiisi sign it, and you're both working for QMG. You ought to see the stack that goes to married couples who both don't work for the company. And you ought to sit in on a meeting to explain why the spouse can no longer seriously talk about work."

"Dear God, do y'all collude with the lawyers to write this stuff?" I asked, initialing my way down a page.

The non-disclosure agreements alone were iron-clad. I was surprised they didn't require a drop of blood to seal the pact, honestly.

He grinned and turned, pouring himself a cup of coffee, then pouring me one, and offering me a small tray with sugar, sugar substitute, and cream.

"I wish. Half my workday is spent making sure that all those damn forms, and two or three hundred others like them are updated, scanned and properly filed, both hard and electronic copies – which all have a drop dead retention date, so the other half of my day is spent making sure that the files are current. I'd much rather be out in the field, but," he kicked both legs against his desk, and the carbon fiber pylons in his prosthetics made a hollow 'tock' sound – nothing but the latest, best tech for the survivors who manned the offices.

"Well, I didn't figure you personally were evil," I replied.

"Just the paperwork," we both said together with a laugh. He sipped his coffee.

"I get that a lot," he said finally.

I went back to signing my life away. Unlike Madden, I'd get back in the field, eventually. He was stuck here, listening to the same complaints from field personnel, day in and day out. I kinda felt sorry for him.

Chapter Twenty-Eight
Day ?, 22 June 2018

S ix weeks spun by – Diindiisi graduated, we got married (I was surprised – other than Henry and Michelangelo, the only guests were the survivors we'd rescued in San Marcos and my parents), went on a quick trip to London where Diindiisi gave me an intimate, blow by blow walkthrough of the events surrounding the Ripper Case and the wendigo, and then came home to Austin, where things had once again gone to shit.

What do you expect in a town where the unofficial motto is 'Keep Austin Weird'? Town's a damn monster magnet. There's a nixie colony in Lady Bird Lake. Vampires hang out on Sixth Street, feeding on college students (we track cases of anemia for that reason), a couple of werewolves who are contracted by the city to keep down the deer population, so forth and so on.

And that's just the supernatural weirdos.

But we came back, set up housekeeping (which led to several discussions and one knockdown, drag-out fight over roles in the marriage) and went back to work.

Which, as I said before, was booming. And was why Jed met us at the airport the day we got back from London. I'd been on long flights before – usually flying cattle class in the military, but Diindiisi and I had made the flight Business Class rather than coach – although I'd been tempted to fly to Dubai for a couple of days, just to take advantage of their First Apartment Class. I'm pretty sure an 18-hour flight with a bed would have been worth it.

We'd deliberately dragged things out on the trip – even flying into Houston and spending a day down in the swamp before coming back to Austin. We weren't 'well rested' but we were rested. And I was feeling fairly well until I saw Jed standing there with Dave at his side, waiting for us near the baggage claim.

We hadn't shipped weapons along. Too many arguments to be had with airport authorities in places. Instead, we'd 'borrowed' gear from QMG offices along the way – although in London we'd actually had an escort from the Quintus Society, the parent organization of QMG, as well as a couple of local Agents. There was even a one hundred and fourteen-year-old member of the Quintus Society there to shake Diindiisi's hand – he'd met her once as a child, and remembered the event.

"Jed," I said, waiting for the carousel to start dumping luggage. We'd packed light – well light if we'd been invading a small country.

"Jesse," he replied, shaking my hand.

"What can I do for you?" I asked.

He looked around. The arrival hall was sparsely populated at the moment – mostly folks that had been on the same plane with Diindiisi and I, and most of them were watching the now spinning carousel for their luggage to come rolling down, so they could get home or to meetings.

"Not here."

"Uh-huh. I'm off duty for another," I checked my watch, "twenty-two hours. Go away."

"Nope. This is a friendly heads up. Stewart has already grabbed the car that was waiting, and is taking it to the safe house," he said. "You're riding with us. It'll be more subtle this way."

I gave him a fish-eyed look as the first luggage started through the opening.

"Subtle? Dave's here" I said, shaking Dave's hand. "That means his Keeper is around here somewhere, which probably means the Combat Winnebago."

"Something like that," Dave grinned.

There was a thump, and the first of the four Pelican 1650's we'd travelled with rolled down the ramp. If you're going to travel, take luggage that's guaranteed against everything except bear attack, shark attack, and children under five. The equipment behind the curtains at the airport probably won't be able to destroy it, and it's worth paying the overweight charges, in my opinion.

While I'd been talking, Diindiisi had secured a couple of Red Caps and carts to help with the luggage.

"Look, you know I wouldn't be here if it wasn't important," Jed said. "I told Goodhart I'd pick you up to keep him from calling you early."

Shit.

"Fine!" I said, tossing up my arms. "Did you at least pick up our case at HQ?"

"It's in the Combat Winnebago," Dave replied, hitting the joystick on his chair and wheeling out the door.

Diindiisi looked at me, and I nodded. She trailed Dave, with the Red Cap in tow.

The arrival hall had cleared somewhat.

"Look. What the hell is going on?" I asked.

"Things have gotten weird in the last week, ten days," Jed said as we walked out the door.

As always the fug of incomplete combustion, heat and humidity that is the lower level of the Austin airport was a slap in the face. Jed had brought the entire team –

Capdepon and Crash were loading the cases into the back of another Tacticool Tahoe while Padre and Diindiisi exchanged hugs.

"Austin weird or 'oh shit, oh shit, oh shit we're all going to die after a thousand years of being digested in the sarlacc pit' weird?" I asked, taking the case Dave handed me.

Inside was a 1911 in a waist holster and a couple of spare magazine. I slid it inside my waistband, feeling fully dressed for the first time in weeks.

"Umm, a little from column A, a little from column B," Jed replied. "Seriously, this can wait until we're rolling."

His statement was punctuated by the slamming of the rear doors on the Tahoe.

"Mount up," he said. "Diindiisi, if you don't mind, ride up here, please."

We waited while Dave deployed the lift and raised his chair into the Combat Winnebago. It isn't an actual Winnebago – it started life as a Mack Granite chassis, and then Dave and the engineers at QMG, along with a couple of mad scientists/mechanics got a hold of it. It was a command vehicle in all senses of the word – with it Dave could hack almost any system on the planet, keeping track of multiple data streams while ensuring that whatever team he was working with was in communication – even if they were on the lunar surface. Admittedly, there would be a bit of lag in that case, but it worked.

No, I don't know of a case that took place on the moon. Doesn't mean that the tech wouldn't be useful, eventually. Eventually is what gives me nightmares these days.

Dave rolled his chair forward and locked it in place next to the driver's seat. His Keeper (yes she has a name, no I've never heard it, and she doesn't answer to anything but

Dave's Keeper these days, because of a vow she took) was behind the wheel.

"So, did you have a good trip?" Padre asked as she took a seat and strapped in.

"Right up until we walked into the arrival hall and saw Jed's ugly mug," I replied as we pulled away from the curb. "What's up?"

"What did Jed tell you?" she asked.

"Not a damn thing," I replied.

She gave Diindiisi a look. A look that said 'MEN!' clearly.

"There's been some strange activity here," Padre said.

"Yeah, he covered that," I replied. "Somewhere between a normal Austin day and death by digestion."

"That's part of the problem," Dave said from the front. "It's a feeling, not a certainty. There's been a spike in activity locally, but with the exception of the attack on Obadiah, nothing we can point to specifically. And even the attack on him was, well, strange."

"Something attacked one of the most powerful white voodoo priests in Austin and you've got nothing except it was strange?" I asked, shocked.

"Yes. Because we don't know what attacked him or when," Jed said. "He didn't come into work one day, and when we went to check on him, his body was there, but not his spirit."

"Plane walking?" Diindiisi asked.

"Could be. Or he could have gone wandering with the loas," Padre replied. "Or stroked out, or any of a hundred other things. It is part of a pattern, we think, but we don't know for sure."

"Which is why you're warning us," I said, shaking my head.

"Something like that, yeah," Jed said. "CYA time."

"CYA?" Diindiisi asked.

"Cover your ass," I replied. "Where was Obadiah when he was attacked?"

"That's the only bright spot – he wasn't in a safe house, he was doing research in the stacks at UT, in the special section. When he didn't show up or check in, they pinged his chip, and then Dave checked the records on it."

"He'd been sitting there for about eighteen hours," Dave said. "Admittedly, the chip only shows gross movement, so he could have been moving about in the stacks but…"

"Yeah," I said, scratching my leg. "What was he looking into?"

"General research on the Shadow Lands, since the portal is now in our district," Jed replied. "There's a copy of Diindiisi's book along with a couple of other pieces in the collection there."

"Do we know what he pulled?" Diindiisi asked.

"No. He was found seated in front of an empty desk. There were several amulets of protection on the desk, and he'd put down at least one ward, but if any materials were pulled they were either shelved or taken by persons unknown," Padre replied.

"And no way to tell what he was looking at," I said.

"Why not?" Diindiisi asked.

"The Special Collection at UT isn't catalogued in the normal manner," I said. "It's mostly by luck or scrying that you find anything in the collection."

"Why?"

"They tried putting a list on a computer back in the 70's when computers first became a big thing," Dave said.

"Apparently, some of the titles, when properly organized, can cause issues."

"Issues?" Diindiisi asked.

"Yeah, like summoning things to the stacks, that don't react well to Holy Water and silver," Jed said. "Ask Jesse to get you the report on the incident, it's a hell of a read."

"At least they found a use for the brownies," I replied. "By the way, where are we going?"

"Your change in marital status got you an upgrade in safe houses," Jed replied with a grin. "The old Indian Motor Court out on North Lamar."

"The Indian Motor Court? Those units are tiny!" I said.

"Yeah, but they're set up for two," Jed said with a grin. "It'll be like being back in Iraq for ya."

"No shit? Two people living together in 180 square feet? What fun!" I replied.

"Sounds bigger than a tipi or wigwam," Diindiisi replied.

"Yeah, and it's bigger than the berthing space on anything we floated on in the Corps," Jed said.

"I know," I said. "But I'd just got my space the way I liked it."

"Terminally messy is not good," Padre said. "We even did your laundry. Although we did have to stun a couple of pairs of socks before we were able to wash them."

I sighed. "Look, not my fault it's been months since I was home."

"True."

Chapter Twenty-Nine
Day ?, 23 June 2018

By zero eight hundred the next morning, Diindiisi and I were waiting outside Director Goodhart's office. He'd been at work since zero six hundred but had graciously allowed us a few minutes – seriously. The man was busier than a one legged man at a butt kicking contest.

"Enter," he called before I could knock on the door.

"I hate it when he does that," I said, sotto voce to Diindiisi as I showed her in.

Goodhart was standing behind his desk, grinning like the proverbial Cheshire Cat.

"Jesse," he said, offering me his hand. "When I said take some time off I didn't expect you to come back with a wife."

"Me either, boss. Diindiisi, our boss, Director Goodhart."

They shook hands. I'd asked Diindiisi about her penchant for shaking hands. She'd replied it was a suffragette thing – to make women equal with men. There were parts of this marriage that were going to be interesting to work through.

"Please, be seated," Goodhart said. "Coffee?"

"Tea, if you have it, Director," Diindiisi replied.

"Lipton's ok?"

"Yes," she replied.

We waited on the tea to brew in silence. Finally, when the tea was done, Goodhart and myself working on our second cups of coffee, he broke the silence.

"I'd like the two of you to continue to work with the rookies you rescued," he said.

"What?" I asked, almost choking on coffee.

"Activity in Austin is on the upswing. Dallas, in its infinite wisdom has granted me the six trainees you brought through the rift, along with ten others," he said. "I'd like you to work with them to bring them up to speed on how we do things in the field, and how that differs from the way they were trained."

"Both of us?" Diindiisi asked.

"Yes. Although, from time to time, as needed, I may pull one of you off the team to backstop another team," he said. "You'll get eight total personnel for your team – since two of the folks you shepherded through are a bit over-aged for field work."

"And if I say no?" I asked.

"Honestly? It'll cause issues with bringing them up to speed," he replied. "Stewart's team would get two of them, along with Ted's Interspacial Trauma Services. For obvious reasons, I can't put any of the rookies with the Brute Squad."

"Why is that obvious?" Diindiisi asked.

I coughed. "Because the Brute Squad is the go-to team when things go to hell. If QMG has a problem in Austin or the surrounding area that no one else can solve, you call in the Brute Squad. And they will solve it. Usually with more damage and destruction than you'd ever want, but they will solve it, if I'm being totally honest."

"And because they tear shit up like that, they occasionally get called out to handle special situations elsewhere," Goodhart replied, delicately.

"In other words, they're kinda special, and deal with more heavy duty crap than the average team sees in years," I said. I looked at Diindiisi. "What do you think?"

"About you taking a team lead slot? Your leadership kept everyone alive in the Shadow Lands," she said. "If you're asking if I've had a vision? No. But I think you can do the job."

"Fine," I said. "When do I meet my team?"

Goodhart looked at his watch. "Ten minutes in the briefing room."

"You bastard," I laughed. "What if I'd said no?"

"I'd have had to go with plan B, which isn't pretty."

"Isn't that dying, in great pain?" I asked.

"Yes. Which is why it isn't pretty," he replied. "Do you want to change?"

I looked at what I had on – blue jeans and a Hawaiian shirt to cover the 1911 at the base of my spine. Diindiisi was dressed similarly, although her shirt was a blue herringbone twill. Goodhart, on the other hand, had on a company polo and tactical trousers, not quite bloused over his boots.

"Why?" I asked. I mean I could put on a dog collar, or polo, but I'd tried to avoid dressing in a uniform or its close cognate since I left the Corps. And business casual made my teeth itch.

He sighed.

"It's not like I didn't dress like this on the other side," I said, rising and offering Diindiisi my hand.

"Dear God and his angels help us all," Goodhart said, following us out of the office.

The others were waiting in the briefing room when we got there – dressed in 'work' clothes, per company regulations – black boots, bloused dark blue combat trousers, dark blue jacket with slash pockets over a dark blue t-shirt. Over one pocket was a tape with 'QMG Security' and the other had a name tape in light blue. Two of them had that strack, just out of the military, saw something weird, got hired, look about them. The six that we'd come through the Shadow Lands with? Apparently, they'd taken advice from Johnson – sleeves were up, and jackets were unbuttoned. Pants were bloused for a given value of bloused, anywhere from the ankle to the top of the boot, except for Johnson. Somewhere, he'd found a pair of Navy issue spats, and dyed them blue. He was wearing them to keep his trousers neat, he swore. I swore it was so he could thumb his nose at the Company, but I'm a bit biased.

"Ladies, gentlemen, I'm Director Goodhart," Goodhart said, stepping behind the podium. "As of today, we are standing your team up under the leadership of Father Jesse Salazar. Father."

He gestured to me to take the podium.

"I'd quote Tolkien here, but that speech is a farewell, not a beginning," I said with a grin. "Besides, the Director dropped this idea on me about ten minutes ago."

Johnson laughed, followed by the others.

"Now, I know some of you, rather well," I said, turning to the other two. "Mr. Wilson, and Mr. Hovis, I haven't seen your records, yet, but I will. We'll also take time to get to know each other. I'm hoping we'll have time to do a couple of runs through at the shoot house as a team."

Hovis was a lanky, good old boy looking type, and Wilson was a compact, dark skinned individual with a shaved head.

I looked at Goodhart and he nodded.

"So, let's go get coffee," I said with a grin.

Gear bags were grabbed and loaded into Tahoes – we didn't rate something like the Command Winnebago, yet. Although both Tahoes had enough radio equipment to come across your fillings, on top of everything else. They also got suck ass gas mileage, but I wasn't paying for it. I took Wilson, Hovis, and Stephanie, putting the other five in the second unit.

"Where to?" Johnson asked.

"Over off Metric. There's a coffee shop near the ACC campus there. They put up with us. Hell, it should be programmed in the GPS unit, for that matter," I said.

"Or I could just follow your matte black ass through town," he replied.

"That too," I said, settling behind the wheel and strapping in.

"Have any of you ever driven in Austin?" I asked the back seat.

"I've driven through Austin," Dalma replied. "I-35 five sucks."

"Avoid I-35 like the plague. MOPAC is ok, if you take advantage of the HOV/Express lane. And with this," I tapped the TexTag on the windshield, "You can do just that. Here endeth the first lesson."

I backed out and turned on Anderson Mill to run to 183.

"Hovis, what's your background," I asked.

"Army EOD, sir," he replied.

"First thing, I was a Marine lance corporal. Calling me sir makes my teeth hurt," I said, grinning at him in the mirror.

"Yes si ...Father," he said with a wry grin.

"Force of habit, I know, and the fact that most of the instructors were DI's in their former lives doesn't help," I replied. "How'd you get suckered into working for Group?"

"My unit was clearing an old Soviet ammo dump in Afghanistan. Problem was there was a chimera in the area and he thought it was his property. I used a little high explosives to clear the problem, and my commander put me in touch with some representatives of QMG when he saw the trophy we'd brought back down the mountain," Hovis replied.

"Makes sense. We'll talk about how I joined at some point," I said. "And you, Wilson?"

Wilson actually looked embarrassed when I caught his eye.

"Air Force photojournalist, Father," he finally said.

I couldn't help myself, I started channeling R. Lee Ermy from *Full Metal Jacket.*

"You gotta be shittin' me, Mr. Wilson. You think you're Mickey Spillane? You think you're some kind of a fucking writer?"

Wilson, Hovis, and Dalma broke up laughing.

"Told you guys not to worry, he wasn't a stick in the mud kinda priest," she finally said after a few minutes.

"Seriously, though, how'd you end up here?"

"I was on Diego Garcia for a story, taking photos," Wilson said. "The island got attacked by a… a giant squid. I saved a couple of folks and got a call from a number in the States that turned out to be QMG."

"Yeah, things like that are the normal recruiting strategy for Group," I said. "It's not like they can put an ad in the paper – Did you kill something strange and unusual? Want to kill more things for high dollar? Call QMG today to see about opportunities in the monster-hunting field."

"Probably be easier if they could," Diindiisi said.

"Weapon of choice?" I asked both of them.

"UMP," Wilson replied.

"Shotgun, or high explosives," Hovis said.

"Dalma, I know what you prefer," I said.

"I got a new long gun," was all she said.

"Oh?"

"Yes. .338 Lapua. Apparently, the rounds are cheaper than using .50 BMG. Although I went through a lot of .50 BMG in training," she replied.

I wasn't sure how we'd use a sniper, honestly. I knew that QMG hired them. I knew that other teams used them. Unfortunately, most of my work had been close in, in areas where snipers couldn't see the target.

Oh well, I'd figure it out. That was my job now, after all.

Authors afterward, or where did this one come from?

So, I've kinda been sitting on the base concept for this one (a couple of priests who know each other meeting in San Marcos Texas and everything going to hell on them) for twenty years now. The idea comes from a Vampire the Role Playing game session I was involved with after my first divorce – five of us packed in a car, all playing priest of various denominations (ok two priests, one Catholic, one Episcopalian, a Lutheran, and two Baptists) and drove down to San Marcos to help 'perk up' a failing game on the Texas State Campus. We did that in spades. When that night's session was over, eight or so characters (if I remember correctly, I might have killed brain cells since then) were being either re-written, or new characters generated. That's kinda what happens when you lock vampires in an area with characters who have true faith.

Then, back in April, I was talking with another author on that great time sink, Facebook, and made an offhand crack along the lines of 'what did he think about a story about two vampire hunting priests who meet up on vacation', and, well, Shadow Lands was born.

I'm a pantser when I write – I sit in front of the computer and the Point of View character tells his story to me. Which is how Diindiisi inserted herself here – I knew there would be another powerful religious figure joining our merry crew, but I wasn't aware she'd be joining us from another work in progress. Which has now managed to move itself up in the to be finished que. Most of the crew from San Marcos are named (and hopefully I got some of your characteristics down on the page, guys) for folks I hung out with in the Blue Pearl Coffee shop in my misspent youth – they might be younger than their actual ages in the story, but they're real people. Even the 'One more John and we're running a brothel' jokes dates from then - at one point we had about ten Johns in the group, with various nick names to distinguish them.

I hope y'all enjoyed it and are looking forward to a bit more of Diindiisi's origin story.

L.A. Behm II
Electra, TX

We hope that you enjoyed this title and look forward to many more to come. Please, leave us a review! Reviews matter to all of our authors.

And don't forget to check out the latest edition of *Car Wars*

http://www.sjgames.com/car-wars/

Or the other amazing titles from
Steve Jackson Games

http://www.sjgames.com

...or the latest in the Car Warriors: Autoduel Chronicle fiction series.
https://threeravenspublishing.com/car-warriors-autoduel-chronicles/

IT CAME FROM THE
TRAILER PARK

DECLAN FINN
DECLAN FINN
DECLAN FINN
DECLAN FINN
Demons are Forever
Honor at Stake
Live and Let Bite
Good to the Last Drop
The Dragon Award Nominated Series
FREE on Kindle Unlimited!

AVAILABLE ON
AMAZON
JOINT TASK FORCE
13
HOLDING THE LINE
BETWEEN HEAVEN AND HELL
13

MYSTERY,
MAGIC &
MAYHEM
WITH A TWIST
OF ROMANCE
J.F. POSTHUMUS
ON AMAZON
FIND ME
B.C.N.T.
BIOLOGIC
ENHANCED
NASCENT
TALENT

3R
Three Ravens Publishing
Are you looking for fun, new fiction?
The Written Word Will Never Be The Same…
https://www.threeravenspublishing.com
Veteran Owned and Operated

You can also keep up to date with our latest release announcements on Scifi.radio and get some of the best fandom programing on the planet.

Scifi for your Wifi

And don't forget to check out our other Sponsors and Affiliates

Revolution X is a testament to the power of collaboration, blending four unique styles into a cohesive, revolutionary sound. When these four individuals unite, the result is nothing short of musical Revolution!

https://www.reverbnation.com/revolutionx6

https://www.facebook.com/REVOLUTIONXBAND/

A southern Appalachian jewel for craft beer lovers, Buck Bald Brewing offers something for everyone. With delicious, locally brewed beverages from across the spectrum, Buck Bald Brewing offers craft brews that are consistently amazing.

From the dark and smooth Shesquatch Scottish ale, to the intense hops of Hippibilly IPA, to the puckering sour of the blackberry and cinnamon in Berry My Heart at the Trailer Park, and more than 60+ rotating brews, you'll find what you're looking for and more.

With smiling faces behind the bar ready to help you find your next favorite brew, a constantly rotating selection of delicious craft beverages, toe-tapping tunes always playing, and the biggest games on TV, you can kick your feet up in either Copperhill, Tennessee or Murphy, North Carolina and immerse yourself in the Buck Bald Brewing experience.

So, come out, fill a pint, fill a growler, and fill your mind at your new favorite family-owned craft brewery.

To discover more visit us at <u>buckbaldbrewing.com</u> or follow us on Facebook @buckbaldbrewing and @buckbaldbrewingmurphy.

Vesper Wren's
TRAILER PARK
PIXIE
PUNCH
· A PEACH STRAWBERRY SELTZER ·
BUCK BALD BREWING

BRAXTON
HICKS
MIDNIGHT MOCHA MILK
STOUT
BUCK BALD BREWING

www.ingramcontent.com/pod-product-compliance
Lightning Source LLC
Chambersburg PA
CBHW030922300726
48970CB00001B/284